HAUNTED YULETIDE

EDITED BY JAY AND JULIE BARNSON

Immortal Works LLC
1505 Glenrose Drive
Salt Lake City, Utah 84104
Tel: (385) 202-0116

JULIE'S INTRODUCTION

Halloween has ruined Christmas in America. That's saying a lot, coming from a person who adores Halloween up until the last rotten jack-o'-lantern is thrown out. But the truth is, with Halloween, we get all of our love of things spooky and sinister out of our systems so we are ready to be grateful at Thanksgiving, and then to be filled with the spirit of giving and peace and joy for Christmas. Even Tim Burton's movie, "The Nightmare Before Christmas" demonstrates it. Halloween and Christmas don't mix. They have their own separate doors and combining them seems to be a disaster.

But if you think about it, we celebrate Christmas at the darkest point of the year, when the nights are long and the days are cold. We want to huddle in our homes and brave the cold only when required by the social occasions of the season. Even with the twinkling lights on the Christmas tree, we look outside and know we have a long, bleak winter ahead of us. It is, truthfully, a perfect time for ghost stories.

Over a hundred years ago, people over in England understood that. Ghost stories were a Christmas tradition, and short stories were published specifically for the wintertime. Charles Dickens published his own magazines that featured ghost stories, before and after "The Christmas Carol" was published. The Christmas ghost story tradition continued well into the 20th century, all the way until Halloween traditions drifted over from the United States. October became the time for ghost stories, and the Christmas tradition faded.

There are some of us, however, who never truly want to give up the tales of ghosts after October is done. We look out at the dark, lit up by the Christmas lights on the neighbors' houses, and we still long for a tale to bring us the shivers. To be the perfect contrast to the beauty and spirit of the Christmas season. This collection is here for you.

JAY'S INTRODUCTION

Ah, December. For me, the "holiday season" starts with Thanksgiving here in the U.S., and lasts through New Year's Day. It is a wonderful time for friendship, family, the spirit of giving, remembrance, gratitude, spirituality, reverence, setting new goals, and filling the chilly winter air of the early Winter with a warm glow of optimism to tide us all over through the dark and dreary weeks until Spring.

Do you want to know what else it is a wonderful time for?

Monsters. Ghosts. Vengeful Spirits. Haunts. Oh, and *flamethrowers.* All that good stuff.

I'm delighted to present to you this anthology of stories for the holiday season. All of these stories take place in the wintertime, somewhere in December. All contain a healthy dose of the spooky, supernatural, uncanny, or monstrous. Beyond that, however, the similarities end. We left the submission guidelines broad to attract variety in the stories, and these talented authors did not disappoint! These tales run the spectrum from spine-tingling to broad comedy, from over-the-top action to heart-wrenching family drama. We have stories of the spirit of the New Year, creepy spirits of winter solstice, Christmas, and even one bubbly greeting of "Happy Hanukkah!" The authors themselves range from seasoned veterans whom you have probably seen in many other books and magazines, to fresh voices for whom this anthology is one of their first times in print.

While I feel these tales can be enjoyed at any time (just like that wonderful Christmas movie, *Die Hard*—yes, it's a Christmas movie, and you cannot convince me otherwise), they work particularly well for the holiday season and the cold winter months that follow. I hope you will find them as thrilling–and sometimes as creepy–as we did, in whatever season you are reading this. Happy Hauntings!

DON'T DISTURB THE CAROLLERS

BY LAUREN STOKELD

It was the view of the church from the bedroom window which finally persuaded Ada to rent the cottage. The ridge of the valley loomed protectively behind the church steeple, and elm trees surrounded the whole building like sentinels, so the winter sun could only touch part of the stone. Half in light, half in shadow; betwixt and between. Ada felt an overwhelming desire to set up her easel and fix the church in watercolour.

"So, you'll take it?" The landlady's nasal voice made Ada jump; she hadn't realized how long she'd been staring out the window.

"Yes," Ada replied, wrenching her gaze round to the interior of the room. "I think I'll get along nicely here."

The landlady, Mrs Forrester, nodded with satisfaction. "When do you think you'll be moving in? After Christmas or after New Year?"

"Well, I was rather hoping I could move in sooner than that," Ada said, a little crestfallen. "This week, if possible."

"But what about moving all of your things?"

Ada laughed. "Oh, it's just me, a few suitcases, and an easel. I like being mobile. I find it refreshing. For my art," she added, by way of justification.

This argument had no effect on Mrs Forrester, however, who still looked perturbed. "But so close to Christmas! Won't you be going home to your family?"

Folding her arms and striking a negotiation power pose, Ada said, "I won't be going home until Christmas Eve, which is over a week away." The landlady was still hesitant, and Ada was starting to lose patience. Beautiful though the cottage was, it had clearly been unoccupied for some time. Was this woman really in a position to turn down a tenant? "I'll pay extra for this week. Otherwise, I'll go elsewhere."

Mrs Forrester bit her lip thoughtfully, silently confirming Ada's theory that business had been slow. She presumed that village life didn't always agree with everyone, especially in a place as small as Hesby St Matthew.

"Very well," the landlady said eventually, "you have a deal."

Two days later, Ada arrived as promised with three suitcases and her painting equipment in the back of her car. Mrs Forrester met her as she pulled into the driveway and helped Ada with her bags.

"Blimey, this is big." The squat landlady huffed as she set Ada's easel down in the hallway. "You planning on painting the village?"

"I think so," Ada said, unpacking some groceries in the kitchen. "I'm going to start with the church this week." A small crash sounded behind her in the hall. Ada swung round to see what had happened. "Is everything all right?"

"Oh. Oh, yes. I just knocked the coat stand over. My own fault, how silly of me. The church, you say? How lovely." Mrs Forrester's cheeks glowed bright as she hurriedly stood the wooden frame back up. "Well, er, I'd better let you settle in without me breaking the place."

"Thank you," Ada said, suppressing a laugh.

"Just a few bits of local information and some house rules, if you don't mind? The village has its own little corner shop near the pub if you need any essentials, but otherwise there's a big supermarket in the nearest town. Recycling is collected every other Monday. Oh, and please don't feed the tabby cat that comes by. He belongs to Mr Haglin, and he's on a diet. The cat, that is, not Mr Haglin. Well, I think that's...that's about all." Mrs Forrester pulled the house keys out of her pocket and Ada stretched out her hand to receive them. Mrs Forrester's hand drew hesitantly back, however, and she seemed to be chewing over something she wanted to say.

"Everything all right?" Ada asked.

"Yes, yes," Mrs Forrester replied briskly. "It's just...it's very silly, just a small thing but quite important to me. At night, would you mind just keeping all the windows and curtains closed? This is an old house with old timbering and when the wind gets in at this time of year...well, it isn't safe. For the house, you understand? And, well, it would be freezing for you too. What with the drafts and all that. The heating in an old house is never perfect, and I wouldn't want you to get cold. So best just to keep everything locked up and covered, and you keep yourself tucked up inside." She spoke fast, her justifications tumbling out one after another. The urgency in Mrs Forrester's words seemed ill-matched to the mundanity of the request, and Ada wondered if her landlady was quite right in the head.

"Of course, you don't need to worry." Ada spoke in the appeasing tones reserved for the overwrought, proffering her open hand for the keys once more. Mrs Forrester's face relaxed, and her dry hand pressed the cool metal into Ada's palm.

"Well, in that case, if you have no more questions, I'll leave you to it. Do ring if you need anything, I'm just down the road on the High Street." Mrs Forrester continued her platitudes as Ada ushered her gently out of the house. On the doorstep, she shook Ada's hand and gave her a strange little appraising look, then walked down the little garden path and turned right towards the village centre. Ada closed the door behind her with some relief.

She spent the rest of the morning unpacking and watching the grey sky, hoping against hope that it would snow. The village would look like a perfect Victorian Christmas card once it was robed in white. But, sadly, the sky had cleared by the time she set up her easel in the front garden and looked towards the church up the hill opposite. With the focussed eyes of an artist, Ada assessed the view before her. The pallid light of a December afternoon washed up against the church's western façade and crept around the corner of the building until it was choked by the shadows which oozed out from behind a copse of elm trees. Next, her gaze drifted to the graveyard, which fanned out down the western side of the hill; from her distance, each headstone looked like a small animal peeking out from underground to test the winter air.

She spent the first hour sketching the outlines of the landscape before her, making special efforts on the filigree, arterial branches of the elm trees. Stripped bare of their summer leaves, they looked almost skeletal. Eventually, she felt ready to add colour. Distinguishing the many shades of grey was no mean task and she mixed her palette wrong several times. But on the fourth attempt she was happy with the result and braved putting brush to canvas, starting on the north wall of the church. As she painted, Ada flicked her gaze obsessively from her creation to the original on the hill. Dusk was crawling slowly towards the village and every time she looked back up, the colours seemed to have changed. The shadows of the gravestones elongated eastwards with the setting sun until they looked like people inching purposefully to the church entrance.

Ada looked back at her canvas to touch up a corner of the tower. But, when she glanced back up to the church, her breath caught in her chest. A figure was silhouetted in the window nearest to the church porch. It was almost like one of the gravestone shadows had succeeded in entering the holy building. Suddenly, without being able to explain why, Ada found herself leaning forward, gripping her canvas, her eyes sweeping across the graveyard in search of a headstone that had lost its shadow.

"Hullo, there."

Ada leapt out of her skin and dropped her paintbrush onto the patio with a clatter. She looked over to see a corpulent man with very red cheeks standing on the verge of the road just over the garden hedge. He chuckled at her surprise. "Sorry, lass, didn't mean to startle you."

"No, no, it's all right. I was just...engrossed in my work." She bent down to retrieve her brush.

"You'll be Hannah's new tenant, then," he continued. "I'm Dan Scott, Scotty to my friends. I run the little garage on the High Street." Scotty leant across the small hedge to shake her hand. His palm was rough and greasy. Ada's first impression of him was that he was the personification of a pork pie. Stealthily, she wiped the oil from his hands off her fingers onto a paper towel.

"Ada Nolan, nice to meet you," she said distractedly. Her eyes were being dragged inexorably back to the church. The window was now empty again. Scotty followed her line of sight.

"You all right?"

Ada gave a jittery laugh. "Yes, there was just...there was a shadow in one of the windows." As they watched, the church door opened and someone stepped out. "Presumably their shadow," she admitted, a little abashed.

"Aha, that'll be Reverend Daniels." Scotty waved at the figure and bellowed, "Oi, Reverend! Hullo!" The figure disappeared into the dimness cast by the elms. "Heh. He probably can't hear me from here, anyway. Hey, why don't you come to the pub tonight, meet some more people? Bob does a shut-in till one on the run up to Christmas."

"Perhaps tomorrow," Ada said. "It's my first night here so I want to settle in to the house."

"Fair enough. But make sure you get to bed early: it's a school night," Scotty said, waggling a teacher-like finger at her.

"Right," Ada replied, laughing a little awkwardly. *Nice guy*, she thought as he went whistling down the road. *Odd, but nice.*

At 10 p.m., Ada stood chewing her cheek at her new bedroom window. As per Mrs Forrester's request, she had diligently drawn all the curtains and made sure all the windows were closed in every other room of the house. But she always kept a window ajar when she slept, even in the depths of winter. So, she hesitated.

It was reasonable, of course, for Mrs Forrester to be concerned for the upkeep of her house, but now that it came to it, her instructions seemed...excessive. The window frames weren't so fragile that a small gust would be a danger to them, and as for the cold, well, that wasn't for Mrs Forrester to worry about. Ada felt a sudden flare of fearlessness. She could leave the small top window open and deal with the consequences like an adult.

So, it was with a degree of self-assurance that Ada reached up and pushed the little window open before closing the curtains. Exhausted from moving in, she collapsed straight asleep in bed and never heard the music that slithered in through the open window at midnight.

THE NEXT MORNING, Ada awoke from a curiously disturbed sleep. At breakfast she made a double-dose of coffee. Then, after slight deliberation, she made a third pot. While she ate, she looked out towards the church and decided she would finish her painting this afternoon when the light was right. But first she wanted to have a good look around the village centre and try to meet some people.

Wrapped up in her favourite red scarf, she crunched cheerfully along the frozen verge in the direction of the High Street. The first thing she saw when she walked onto the village green was Scotty dragging a large Christmas tree out the back of a van.

"Ho ho ho!" He called out when he spotted her. "Did you have a nice evening in?"

"I did, thank you."

"Did you sleep well?"

"I thought so," she said. "But I seem quite tired today. How was the pub?"

"Very nice night. You should join us this evening."

Ada smiled. "There's something I want to see on TV tonight. But tomorrow, I will be there for sure. Well, I need some supplies. I can only eat so many microwave meals in one week." She gave Scotty a salute, which he returned, causing him to drop the tree. Chortling, Ada turned away to head to the small corner shop.

The shop was the sort of place you would find in a 1970s sitcom; there was a little of everything all jumbled up on dark shelves. Behind the counter, a young woman in a hideous Christmas jumper was wearily serving an old man who struggled to hold his walking stick while also fumbling for change in his wallet. Ada suppressed a slightly wicked smile and browsed the first aisle. As she rounded the second block of shelves, she found a vicar crouched on the floor, looking dejectedly from an old-fashioned snap-and-kill mousetrap in his left hand to a more humane mechanism in his right.

"You must be Reverend Daniels," Ada exclaimed. The man blinked up at her confusedly.

"I'm sorry, have we…?"

"Oh, sorry," Ada said, wide-eyed. "That must have sounded incredibly creepy. Scotty pointed you out to me while I was painting the church. I'm Ada Nolan. I've just taken Hannah Forrester's cottage."

Reverend Daniels' face cleared. "Ah yes, a pleasure to meet you, a pleasure. And you were painting the church, you say? Yes, very good indeed." His accent was more clipped than Scotty's or Mrs Forrester's, as though he hadn't always lived in Hesby St Matthew.

"It's very beautiful," Ada agreed. "I plan to finish the painting today and maybe visit the real thing tomorrow."

"Yes, please do. That would be most agreeable," Reverend Daniels said, his words slowing as his attention turned back to the two mousetraps. "The church has mice, you know," he explained. "I can't let them stay, of course, they'll chew the altar cloth and ruin the biscuit store, but I do so hate the idea of killing them. They're still God's creatures, innocent creatures indeed. So really, I should buy this humane trap and release them in the woods." He lifted his right hand with the perforated box, as though the scale was tipping in its favour. "But the devil of it is that I am so afraid of rodents, terrified indeed, that I cannot bear the idea of carrying a live one outside. So, I am forced to choose this horror." He now raised the mouse guillotine with his left hand until it was at equal height with his right hand. "But then I am back to my moral plight and my debate perpetuates itself, until Judgement Day perhaps." He looked up at her and through his glasses his eyes twinkled with a gentle humour.

"How's this, then? You buy the humane trap, and I'll come and release the mouse for you." Ada offered. "In exchange for a tour of the church, perhaps?"

"Well now," Reverend Daniels said, his face lighting up. "That's a very good deal, a bargain indeed. I'll take you up on that. Miss Nolan, was it?" He stood, the Happy Mouse House under one arm, and shook her hand warmly. "Welcome indeed to Hesby St Matthew."

Feeling somewhat buoyed, Ada bought some food, had a polite, one-sided conversation with the disinterested girl at the till, and went home to continue with her painting. Soon, she was back outside with her easel and brushes.

Today, the shadows on the church seemed to come alive as clouds shifted overhead. The cold wind which whipped up the trees and blew dead leaves along the road bit at Ada's hands and cheeks. Her teeth chattered. Yet she could not bring herself to stop painting. She found that her creation was coming together faster than she had expected: the church, the elm trees, the fields all conceding to her brushstrokes. The only thing she couldn't reconcile on the canvas was the graveyard. While she had counted at least fifty headstones on the hill, she could only make thirty-two sit nicely in the frame of her painted landscape. No more than that seemed to belong. Eventually she accepted that she couldn't change it, and she let herself sign off the painting as it was.

Before night had truly fallen, Ada had already packed up her equipment and gone back inside. She spent a far more relaxed evening than she had the day before, so when she went to bed she wasn't fully tired. For a while she sat up reading, but after turning out the light she lay awhile in the dark, half-awake, half-asleep, drifting in a heavy silence. But after a blurred time that could have been minutes or hours, the sound of a mournful, beautiful melody crept through the quiet. Although subtle, the notes assailed Ada's senses and ensnared her thoughts like thorns, forbidding sleep. She sat up. Where was the music coming from?

Swinging out of bed, she followed her ears and found herself approaching the window. With each step the song became more distinct. It was *O Come, O Come, Emmanuel.* Once at the curtains, she could feel a light, chill breeze on her skin. It came through from the small window, which she had once again left open, and the melody crept in with the breeze like a mist. Peeling back one of the drapes, Ada looked out at the view. Everything was engulfed in a pure blackness; everything but the church, which stood dead ahead, its windows glowing a fierce gold. The light almost burned.

Like a siren's call, the harmonies and the light drew Ada and, without thinking, she opened the main windows fully and drank in the sound of the holy chords. Although the music was now clearer, it had a warped quality to it, as though the notes were buffeted about on the wind as they came down the hill and arrived in not quite the right configuration. She shivered. Mrs Forrester had been right about the bitter cold.

With sudden resolve, Ada closed the windows, drew the curtains shut and returned to bed. *Why on earth are they rehearsing so late,* she asked herself as the ghost of the song washed over her and followed her into a troubled sleep.

THE FOLLOWING MORNING, Ada drank four coffees at breakfast. She couldn't shake off the sluggish pressure of tiredness and decided to go for a brisk walk to wake herself up.

Wrapped up well for a damp, wintry morning, she stepped out into the garden and deliberated where to go. Her eyes fell immediately on the church. After last night's musical interlude, of which she had only hazy, sleepy memories, she felt even more compelled than before to visit the church in the daylight.

A little path began in the trees opposite her cottage and wound its way up the hill towards the churchyard. She was glad for her Wellington boots as the path was made of ruts and puddles and half-frozen mud. Dappled sunlight bleached patches of ground. Halfway up the hill, partly obscured by the dense trees, Ada could make out the little vicarage. A friendly plume of smoke curled out of the chimney. She smiled. Even though she had only met him once, it seemed very like Reverend Daniels to keep a real fire burning.

She followed the path past the house up to the church entrance. Turning, she looked briefly back down to her cottage. It seemed quite lonely on the road from up here. The graveyard stood before her, looking enticingly peaceful and inviting exploration, but a brisk wind hurried her towards the church. Inside the wooden porch she saw posters with curled-up corners advertising local clubs and charities and also a small donation box. She fished around in her pocket for some change and fed the coins into the slot, hearing the clack as they hit the bottom of the metal case. Then she twisted the ring-handle and entered the nave.

Inside was, to Ada's untrained eye, pretty much identical to every other village church she had ever been in. If she had known what to look for, she might have recognised the Romanesque archway to the chancel or the original fifteenth-century font. Oblivious, Ada walked right past these. She paused instead at a modern stained-glass window depicting a miracle she didn't recognise. The church was almost entirely in monotone shades of grey, but light streamed through this window into a rainbow which dashed against the pale stone wall, brightening the building up. Nothing she had seen so far seemed unique to this church. In fact, it all felt overwhelmingly familiar.

But in the north transept Ada found a patch of stone wall which stood out against the rest of the church. It was blackened and necrotic, like a rotting wound which was trying to spread. Somehow it seemed to be spreading towards her. Suddenly, the silence of the church seemed very full, as though dozens of people were behind her in the pews, breathing, waiting, watching. Ada looked over her shoulder. There was no one there. Tucking her hands into her coat pocket and pulling up her shoulders, she marched out of the building into the weak sunlight outside.

The strange sensation she had felt inside seemed exorcised by the daylight, and instead she took in the view of the village to her left through the trees. The sky had turned the colour of old milk, and Ada wondered if it would finally snow.

She crossed her arms against the chill and stepped away from the church into the graveyard. The headstones had been waiting for her, quiet and patient, while she had shunned them for the church interior. As if by way of apology, Ada started reading their epitaphs attentively. Those closest to the church were from the eighteenth century and as she moved further along, she saw the dates rush forwards: past American Independence, the Battle of Trafalgar, Victoria's accession, the first telephone conversation. Each epitaph was formulaic and matter-of-fact. Mother and sister. Beloved son.

But then... Ada stopped in front of an inscription which stood out among the rest. Connie Evans. 11 January 1843–21 December 1887. Beloved daughter and sister. Mezzo-Soprano.

It was such a curious fact to put onto a headstone that it startled her. She presumed Connie Evans had been a uniquely passionate singer. But the next headstone was the same. Benjamin Thurrow. 19 April 1861–21 December 1887. Son and Tenor. The next one, too, bore the date of death as 21 December 1887 and the deceased's vocal part. And the next one. And the next. Ada found herself scurrying from one grave to another, feeling like she was stuck in some sort of nightmare, being forced to watch a massacre.

As suddenly as the 1887 Christmas deaths had started, they ended. Yet the odd mention of vocal parts persisted. A baritone popped up in 1918 and two sopranos in the twenties. She bent down to pick lichen off a headstone from the forties immortalising Emma Winsley, (Mother, Daughter and Alto). As she crouched at the graveside, a shadow fell over the ground before her. Ada stood up with a start and tripped backwards onto the foot of the shadow's owner.

Reverend Daniels gave a yelp of pain.

"Oh my, I–I'm so sorry!" Ada exclaimed.

"No permanent damage done," Reverend Daniels said, shaking his foot off. "I'll probably forgive you." He looked at Ada with twinkling eyes. "Admiring our headstones?"

"Yes. Strange epitaphs. Most of them from—"

"Eighteen-eighty-seven. Yes... There was a fire that year in the church. Arson, some say. Others think it was just a horrible accident. But the village choir was stuck inside and, well..." He didn't finish the sentence, but Ada understood.

"I saw the blackened stone inside," she said.

"Mm...indeed. They grit-cleaned the rest at the turn of the century, but left the north transept as a memorial."

"And these later epitaphs with the voice parts. Also a memorial to the choir?"

Reverend Daniels coughed and rubbed his bare hands together. "Oh, I think it became a bit of a village tradition after a while. They still do it today if they bury someone here. The last was ten years ago. My wife." He pointed to an elegant headstone a few feet away.

"Oh, I'm so sorry. I didn't know." Ada looked at Reverend Daniels' face, which seemed more lined and weary than she'd noticed before.

He took a deep, affected breath. "The Lord works in mysterious ways. But sometimes I do wish he would give us a heads-up. Well, have a good afternoon. I'll let you know when the mouse takes the bait." The vicar walked away and into the church, his shoulders hunched.

AFTER DINNER THAT EVENING, Ada remembered her promise to go to the pub. As she pulled her boots on, she felt a slight reluctance to go out. She didn't really know anyone. But, she told herself as she wrapped her red scarf around her neck tightly, it would be much easier to become acquainted with the locals once she had become well acquainted with the local brews.

The Lamb was a sagging, white-washed building at the very heart of the village. It stood on the green, opposite the strange little grocer's she had gone into yesterday, and its windows shone like bright eyes across the dark high street. Getting closer, Ada could hear the pub buzzing like a hive with activity and conversation. She stamped the frigid mud from her boots under the church-like porch at the entrance and then opened the door.

After the sharp, singeing cold of the wind outside, the pub air seemed to hit her like a wall. It was warm, sticky, full of the smells of spirits and smoke. Ada looked to her left and saw an ancient, shrivelled old woman sitting on a bench, a pipe in her mouth. A dense cloud of acrid fumes coiled around her. Ada stared for a few seconds. Then the old woman plucked the pipe out of her mouth.

"Close the door, girl," she said with a commanding and cadaverous croak. She sounded exactly the way she looked: like someone who was only still alive because the Grim Reaper was too scared to bother her. Hurriedly, Ada closed the door and moved further inside.

To the left of the bar a large red-and-gold Christmas tree stooped to fit under dark beams, and a dog slept by a roaring fire. Lively conversations surrounded Ada, and she was heartened to see that she recognised some of the faces. The doddery old man from the corner shop was bringing a shaking whiskey glass to his lips at a table where two other men were playing cards. The disinterested teenage cashier from the same shop was now pulling a pint behind the bar, still sporting her tasteless Christmas jumper. From over her shoulder, Ada could clearly make out her landlady's nasal tones cutting through the general drone. It all felt so cosy and familiar. Like every pub in every village in England. The only person obviously missing was the Reverend.

A hand suddenly landed heavily on her left shoulder. "Ada! Good to see you." She turned to see Scotty, the red of his cheeks like hot coals. Ada wondered how long he had been drinking.

"Thought I'd better show my face," she said.

"Good, good. Look, first one's on me, to say 'well done' for braving the cold and making it. What'll it be?"

"Ooh." Ada browsed the taps and bottles on show. "I suppose it'll have to be a pint of whatever's most local."

Soon Ada was sitting on a barstool, a pint of Nectar of the Dogs in her hand, with Scotty, Mrs Forrester, and two other locals whose names she immediately forgot, spread out along the bar on either side of her.

"So what do you think of The Lamb?" Scotty asked.

"Very nice, mostly. I suppose I'm just not used to pubs with smoke in them nowadays." She nodded surreptitiously over to the door where the old woman was still puffing away. "She does know it's illegal, right?"

Scotty gave a hollow laugh. "Oh, she knows all right. But Mrs Dole has been smoking in this pub since before the people who passed the smoking ban were born. Anyway, do you want to be the one to tell her she's not allowed?"

They both looked over at Mrs Dole huddled on her bench. She glared mutinously back at them.

"Not really," Ada admitted.

As the evening went on, Ada's companions bought her a few more pints and introduced her to more people. All of them gave little noises of surprise at her occupation and expressed an interest in seeing her painting of the church. Everyone made her feel very welcome. The beer wasn't bad either.

It could have been such a charming night. If only she hadn't mentioned the music.

"When are you off home for Christmas? Home-home, I mean," Scotty asked Ada during a lull in the conversation.

"Are you suggesting my cottage doesn't feel like a home-home?" Mrs Forrester exclaimed with mock outrage.

Everyone chuckled, spirits buoyed by beer.

"I'm not entirely sure," Ada replied. "In a few days, maybe. I'm determined to see the village in the snow, though, so I don't want to leave too early."

"Ah, we can't make any promises there," Scotty said, wiping a handkerchief over his flushed and shining face.

Ada smiled. "Well, maybe I'll wait until the choir's carol service instead."

The faces of everyone in the conversation fell. Mrs Forrester lowered her wine glass slowly.

"What choir, dear?"

Ada blinked. "The one I heard rehearsing last night."

"We don't have a choir here," Mrs Forrester said.

"I heard music."

"You must be mistaken." Mrs Forrester looked like she wanted to move the conversation on, but Ada was having none of it.

"There were lights on in the church and I heard carols." Her voice rose slightly in defiance, not wanting to be called a liar or a fool. A couple of other people nearby stopped and turned towards them. The girl behind the bar kept wiping an already spotless glass with her mouth slightly open.

"Think about it," Mrs Forrester said with the handling tone of an inquisitor. "You wouldn't be able to hear music from the church down at the cottage, especially not indoors. You must have left a radio on somewhere."

The little world around Ada seemed to shift. Where before there had been bustle, now there was only uncomfortable quiet. Eyes from all around were on her.

Mrs Forrester continued her glacial logic. "As for the lights in the church, maybe the reverend forgot to switch them off. Perhaps it was the moon's reflection."

No, Ada wanted to argue back, *I'm not making this up*. She looked around for an ally. But Scotty was nodding solemnly in agreement with Mrs Forrester. The other two sitting in their group wore stony faces, and further afield in the pub she saw looks of unmistakable mistrust aimed at her. She suddenly felt very alone.

"Yeah, perhaps. That makes sense," Ada said placatingly. The surrounding faces still watched carefully. "Yeah, you're right, that must be it. I've...I've been overtired from moving."

The pub around her seemed to exhale a shared breath.

"That's all right, lass," Scotty said comfortingly. "We all have odd moments. But you're among friends now, so drink up."

Obligingly, Ada put her glass to her lips. Warm conversation grew up in the pub again as though nothing had happened. But something had happened. Was this some sort of village game? A hazing for the new neighbour? Or had she genuinely imagined it? Maybe a radio and a forgotten light-switch weren't so far-fetched.

Maybe she really was overtired.

But now it seemed like there was a glass wall between her and the others. Their friendly chatter and smiling faces reached her hazily, as if through an old window in a church. She finished her pint somewhat faster than she would have normally.

After a while, someone called out, "Hey! It's snowing!"

As people got up to look out at the flurries of white, Ada took her opportunity to leave, muttering farewells and yanking her coat on. She avoided peoples' eyes, trying to escape unnoticed and unhindered. But when she reached the door, a claw-like hand grabbed at her sleeve. She looked down in surprise at the burning eyes of the old woman.

"Don't disturb the carollers," she rasped.

Recoiling, Ada tugged her sleeve away and pushed through the door, out into the wintry night. She spent the walk home wondering what had happened in the pub and barely noted the shroud of snow settling on the village, even though she had hoped for it for the last two days. The brisk air sobered her up, and she thought more clearly about the events of the evening. *Don't disturb the carollers*, the old woman had said. So, she thought there was a choir. Had Mrs Forrester and the others been lying, or did they just not know? Or was Mrs Dole batty, and Ada along with her?

Back at her cottage, Ada could see that the church was dark, empty, asleep. She rubbed her face. This was ridiculous. It didn't even matter. She needed to get inside and get some sleep. She could speak to the reverend about it in the morning; she was sure he would tell her the truth.

At her front door she fumbled for her keys, wishing she had thought to turn the security light on before she went out. Eventually she had the bunch in hand and was trying to feed the key into the lock when she heard it. A single line of melody whispered suddenly from behind her, then opened out into poignant harmony: *O Come, O Come, Emmanuel.*

Haltingly, Ada turned and saw that the church was now smouldering with internal light. Her brow furrowed. So, she hadn't been imagining it. Abruptly she walked down her garden path and across the road, getting closer for a better view. The singing was definitely, undeniably, coming from the church.

A flood of hot anger washed away any semblance of tiredness. She felt a fury towards the villagers who had tried to trick her, but also towards the secret choir who rehearsed at ridiculous hours, who had kept her up at night, and who were the source of this unease. She would go up and prove to herself that she wasn't imagining anything, so no one could convince her tomorrow that she was mad.

Don't disturb the carollers.

She wouldn't need to disturb anyone. Just a peek and a photo and then back home for a well-earned sleep. Fuelled by a defiant curiosity, she marched up the little wooded path, skirting the vicarage. Despite her sudden boldness, she didn't want to be caught sneaking around the churchyard.

Once she had reached the top of the path near the church entrance, the music was indisputable. The light from inside the church flooded the pristine, snowy ground and gave the headstones long, malevolent shadows. Somehow she needed to get a look inside. She spotted an old, half-broken stone coffin standing flush against the north wall underneath a window.

Punching holes in the perfect snow, Ada trotted over and carefully, quietly, clambered up onto the lid. She waited on her hands and knees for a moment to be sure the sarcophagus wouldn't wobble and give way, and then knelt up to peer in through the glass. Her eyes widened. Her breath caught.

The pews were populated by what looked like statues covered in dust sheets. Except that whatever things the cloths covered were swaying with the lilt of the music. Here and there among the white-clad figures were people clothed in ragged suits and dresses which hadn't been in fashion for decades.

The sight was so ludicrous that at first Ada had to suppress a laugh. Was this why the villagers had lied, because they were embarrassed? But then she noticed that a man in a tweed jacket at the back was singing through blue and bloated lips. His entire face was swollen and his hair, his skin, his shirt were slick with water. Each movement he made was grotesque, like a waxwork come unwillingly to life.

He was quite clearly dead.

He wasn't the only one. Just beneath Ada's window stood a woman in more modern dress with beautiful platinum hair falling to her shoulders, except at the back where her skull had been caved in. Ada tasted bile. Then there were the figures in sheets, whose hands protruded from under the folds to grasp at music books. Each one was charred, scorched and skeletal. She watched as the whole choir turned a page, the clothed members with pale, mottled fingers, the veiled singers with blackened bones.

What gathered in this church shouldn't be possible. Yet Ada had never seen anything more real.

In her mind, she heard the reverend saying, *there was a fire, the village choir was stuck inside.* She couldn't move, only sweep her gaze uncontrollably over the singers to their conductor before the altar, standing tall, completely shrouded but for ruined, gesturing arms which escaped the white folds. With horror she heard the nightmare choir incite her to rejoice in the Saviour's birth and in the eternal life he offered, seemingly oblivious to the irony of the lyrics.

She was looking at hell, and it was in heavenly harmony.

Suddenly, the stone beneath her knees shifted. Ada gasped, clutching forwards at the window to steady herself. Her hands hit the glass with a dull thud. As though she had flicked a switch, the singing stopped. All was suddenly, unnaturally still.

Don't disturb the carollers.

What happened when you did?

Ada ran her eyes anxiously over the frozen choir. Every nerve in her body screamed to get away unseen, to move before they did. Carefully, she peeled her hands off the window, lowered them to the frame, minutely shifted her legs ready to jump, all the while vigilantly watching the choir. The ghosts.

For a second, she looked down at her feet. When her eyes returned to the church interior, they met the clouded eyes of the man in the tweed suit. With horror, Ada scanned the choir. They were all looking directly at her. Sheeted faces were angled towards hers, and two unburnt women in forties-style dresses had jagged slit throats which yawned open as they turned their heads to stare glassily at her.

The faces she could see all pulled their bulging, discoloured lips back into smiles. Then they turned away, rose, and silently moved out of the pews. Towards the door! With intuition born of terror, Ada knew they were coming for her.

She almost fell from her perch in her hurry to get away. Slipping and tripping on the snowy ground, she pelted down the hill, ignoring the path and avoiding the church entrance. She didn't look back until she was on the road near her house. The church was dark again, and she had no way of seeing if robed shadows really were leaving the building and following her.

She considered going back to her house, but there she would be all alone and it was so close to the church. No, she needed to be around people. She turned towards the village and ran along the road, keeping her eyes trained on the treeline to her left. The clawed branches covered in snow looked like dry, thin arms reaching out from under death shrouds, trying to grab her. She wasn't used to sprinting and found herself stopping sooner than she would have liked, in the middle of the road, dry-heaving from fear and lack of breath. A car's headlights swept round the corner, forcing her to leap onto the verge she was so afraid of. As the car whipped past her, she spun around on the spot, looking for movement that might betray her pursuers, dead and deadly and determined.

It was from the direction of the village that she heard the voices in the end. How had they got there before her? Suddenly the trees, which seconds before had seemed so foreboding, now offered her protection. As stealthily as possible, she crept in a few trees deep. In the woods, the ground was too wet for snow to settle. She thanked her lucky stars for the lumpy mud which disguised her footprints and muffled her steps. Though would such human clues matter to the dead? She stopped behind a large elm tree, her back to the trunk, and pressed both hands over her face to smother the sound of her ragged breathing.

The footsteps drew nearer along the road and passed her slightly, clearly approaching the path to the church. A scent of smoke slipped through her fingers as the walkers went by. Fire smoke, she thought at first. But no...pipe smoke. Carefully, frowning, she turned to the side and leaned her shoulders against the elm, listening.

"Church is dark. That's a bad sign." It was Mrs Forrester's voice. From her new position, Ada could make out about ten figures grouped a little distance away from her. The old woman's pipe smoke curled upwards as the snow whirled down.

"I knew we shouldn't have trusted her," she heard Scotty say. "We shouldn't have let her leave the pub."

"I warned her. I said not to disturb them," the old woman croaked.

So they had all known. They had all known what horrors were up that hill, and they had rented the cottage to her anyway. Had acted like they were her friends.

"We all tried to keep her safe," Mrs Forrester agreed. "But she's gone and done it now. If she's sensible she'll be a long way from the church. John, Evelyn, Emma, go back to The Lamb and wait for her there." Despite the betrayal she felt, Ada was relieved and grateful that they were at least out looking for her. She was about to step out from behind her tree and announce herself, when Mrs Forrester continued. "There are plenty of knives and the like in there."

Ada froze. What was she hearing?

"Sam, Mrs Dole, Jackson, go to the cottage. She might have thought going home was a good idea. I hope she hasn't driven off." Ada mentally kicked herself for having not thought of that. "Check the car, check the house. You'll have to improvise with what you find in the house if she's there."

"Don't worry," a rough voice said. "I can do it with my bare hands."

"Wear gloves if so," Mrs Forrester stated coolly. Something squeaked, like leather on leather. "The rest of us will look up and down the main road. Except for you, Scotty. Get up to the church. And start digging."

Ada clung to the elm, horrified, as she heard the group split and move off in their different directions. Were they mad? Were their intentions as dark as they sounded? She waited until the sounds of walking had gone. Then, just to be sure, she waited a bit longer. She needed to call the police. But would they believe her? Would anyone?

She looked up and saw smoke. Chimney smoke this time.

Reverend Daniels. Quirky, humane, not quite part of the village. A vicar, a man of God. Sanctuary. She could use his phone, hide there and then get away. Watching for villagers and carollers alike, Ada picked her way through the undergrowth in the worst possible direction, the only possible direction: back towards the church.

She crept round to the back of the vicarage where she saw the reverend making tea in his kitchen. With desperate vigour, Ada rapped on the window. He looked up, surprised, and hurried to unlock the back door.

"Miss Nolan!" he exclaimed. "What's the matter?"

"Please, please, please, you have to help me. The music and the church and then the other villagers. I think they're mad—I think they want to kill me!"

"What? Slow down." He let her in, closed the door, and led her through to the living room. Guiding her into an armchair, he said, "They want to kill you? Who wants to kill you?"

"Everyone," she gasped. "The dead. The living. I need to ring the police, but I don't think they'll believe me."

While she spoke, the reverend rummaged round in a small cupboard and brought out a tumbler and a bottle of amber liquid. He poured her a measure and pressed it into her hands.

"Here, drink this. Tell me everything."

The whiskey raked Ada's throat, but slowly, hesitantly, she recounted her evening, what she had seen and what she had heard. The reverend, sitting in a chair opposite, listened with fingers pressed together before his mouth like a steeple.

"And now I don't know what's worse," she continued. "These things that I saw in the church, or the neighbours I thought I could trust. What in the name of God is going on?"

"Oh, He's not involved." The vicar said, rubbing a hand over his face. "God, that is. No, indeed. Something else is at work here. I'm afraid you've stumbled onto a nasty truth about this village. One I had to learn when I came here."

"What do you mean?" Ada asked, her voice thick with exhaustion.

"Do you remember the choir I told you about? The one that burned in 1887?"

Ada nodded languidly.

"Well, let's just say that they never stopped singing at Christmas. And they don't like to be disturbed. If they are, well...then they go carolling round the houses of the village. Yes, carolling...but not with goodwill to all men. No, indeed." Ada's gaze fixed on the vicar, whose face again seemed despondent and worn. "The village learned the hard way that to stop the carolling, you had to give the choir a new member. The disturber, preferably."

He looked pointedly up at her, and she wanted to ask him again what he meant. But she found that she couldn't get the words out. Her jaw was unresponsive, her hands numb. The glass slipped through her fingers and cracked on the wooden floor. A burning fear rushed through her veins.

"Various people have made the same mistake as you over the years. Villagers at first, but then only strangers. My wife, for example. Not long after we moved here. That is, of course, when the truth was revealed to me. That was when I learned the hard way that sometimes the most difficult choice is the right one." A baleful knock came from the front door. "Ah, that will be the others now."

The vicar stood and went into the hallway, out of sight. Ada struggled desperately against her unwilling body, begging it to get up, to run. But she was now a living statue, and she sat helplessly as Reverend Daniels led Mrs Forrester and the others into the living room. Many of the faces were in shadow, cramped into the hall and the corner of the room. But she could see Scotty, red-faced Scotty, her new friend, standing grimly at the front with a spade over his shoulder. Its blade was caked in fresh mud.

Tears rolled down Ada's cheeks, which she was unable to wipe away.

"I do wish you hadn't gone to the church," Reverend Daniels

said, towering before her. "I am sorry it has to be like this. But it's one life or many. This way is the pragmatic way; it is the *humane* thing to do. Indeed, it is the only thing to do."

Ada wanted to scream but paralysis gagged her. Her now insupportably heavy head sank down onto her chest. She saw Reverend Daniels' shadow come closer, felt his hand cup under her chin, and he tilted her face back up so her imploring eyes met his.

"I know, I know," he said, almost soothingly. "You must have so many questions. But the only one that matters is: are you an alto or a soprano?"

A SOLSTICE SCARE

BY ROBIN CRANNEY

Kenzie fidgeted on the couch, causing her cat, Gibbyns, to adjust his position on her lap. For the last hour, she'd wrestled with reading *Frankenstein*. Not for the first time, she questioned her plan to get a head start on the required reading list for next semester's English course. It was stupid that she even had to take the class. It wasn't like she planned to be an English teacher.

She smothered a yawn. Give her David Eddings or Brandon Sanderson any day. Heck, she'd even take Christopher Paolini. She loved deep fantasy because it didn't attempt to be realistic. Everyone knew elves and trolls and dragons didn't exist. But stuff like *Frankenstein* bugged her because it skirted close enough to real life that stupid people could be convinced of the plot's plausibility. Creatures like Mary Shelley's "wretch" or ghosts or jackalopes were fictitious nonsense, and authors shouldn't try to convince people otherwise.

The sparkling lights on the pre-lit white fir in the corner of the living room snagged her attention. This year, Mom had decorated it with fiber optic puffballs and gold netting. Kenzie wished they'd go back to the traditional decorations they'd used when she was a kid, but Mom liked to be trendy.

Wow. Talk about getting distracted. *Focus, Kenzie!* If she

concentrated, she could get through another few chapters before dinner.

"He's here!" Her mom's sudden shout, followed by the clatter of dishes falling in the sink, brought Kenzie's head up. In the next instant, her mom ran out of the kitchen and toward the front door.

Gibbyns leaped from Kenzie's lap and ran after her, his raccoon-striped tail shooting straight out behind him.

Kenzie sighed. Her brother was back from his senior-class trip to eastern Europe. Two weeks away from home, and the parents were pulling out the red carpet. Kenzie had been at college for four months, but all she'd gotten when she came home was a kiss on the cheek.

The pounding roar of her youngest brother, Tim, racing down the hall provided added encouragement to toss aside her book. Might as well join in the hoopla.

Upon reaching the door, Kenzie peered over her mom's shoulder into the twilit evening. It was a mild winter, just above freezing and no snow. The grass was even a little green. Her dad and Andrew came up the walk, each lugging a suitcase. Andrew was as tall and skinny as he'd been the last time she saw him in August. He kept saying that one day he'd fill out like Captain America.

She snickered. Maybe in his dreams.

Andrew grinned and dropped his suitcase on the front steps. "Hi, Mom."

She hugged him. "Welcome home. We missed you."

"Missed you, too. No wreath this year?" he asked.

Kenzie hadn't noticed the lack of a wreath on the door. Instead, her mom had hung a painted sign with "Let it Snow" in fancy lettering.

"No wreath," Mom said. "Did you have a good trip?"

"The best." He started to move past her, but she grabbed a chunk of his jacket, holding him in place.

"Did you behave yourself?" she asked in that direct, no-nonsense tone of hers.

"Of course! I always do."

Kenzie rolled her eyes. What a liar! Andrew didn't just get into trouble like most boys his age, he led the pack. He was the instigator. The holy of terrors. He was sixteen months younger than her and had the maturity of a toddler. When he was in second grade, he'd cut off her hair while she was sleeping. In sixth grade, he convinced his friends to make Chinese lanterns, which accidentally set the neighbor's shed on fire. In ninth grade he had a crush on a policeman's daughter and egged their house, thinking it would get her attention. It did, and her dad's too. Junior year, he'd actually gotten arrested for breaking into a junkyard to steal parts for a blimp he was trying to make. Yes, a blimp. No fixing up old cars for him; he had to be original.

Kenzie loved him, but it irked her how he could be so stupid all the time. It was a wonder his German teacher had even allowed him to go on the trip with the rest of the class.

"Hey, monkey." Andrew gave Tim a noogie. "How does it feel to be twelve? Sorry I missed it."

Tim jerked his head free. "It's fine. You bring me anything cool?"

"Yeah. Christmas is in three days, isn't it?" Andrew smiled at Kenzie. "I even got Kenzie something."

"Oh, boy," Kenzie muttered. But she smiled. Andrew occasionally surprised her with his sweetness.

"You'll like it. It's spooky." He wiggled his fingers in the air like he was casting a spell.

"Well, get yourself unpacked," Mom said. "Just throw the laundry down the stairs. Dinner's in half an hour."

Andrew picked up his luggage. As he stepped into the hall, Gibbyns puffed up like an electrocuted cotton ball and hissed.

"Woah. Miss me much?" Andrew skirted around the agitated cat. "What's up with him?"

Kenzie shrugged. Gibbyns normally liked Andrew, but perhaps her brother smelled weird from his trip. With the excitement over, she returned to the couch and forced herself to pick up her novel. She struggled for a few minutes, then Tim's happy exclamation rang down the hall, giving her an excuse to snap the book shut again. Andrew must have pulled out the presents.

Gibbyns sat sentinel at the hallway entrance, his attention pinned on the merry sounds. Kenzie scooped him up and headed to Andrew's room. As she reached the door, Gibbyns squirmed in her arms, then yowled angrily and prodded her skin with his claws.

"Ouch!" She dropped him, and he shot back down the hall like she'd tied a stick of dynamite to his tail. "Psycho-cat."

Andrew looked up from where he sat cross-legged on the ground. Mom had cleaned his room while he'd been gone, but Andrew's clothing was already strewn across the floor and his desk littered with papers and knickknacks from the trip. His suitcase was open before him.

"Hey, sis."

Tim, who was sitting with his back to the door, suddenly twisted around. "You'll never believe what he brought me!"

At first, she thought the white object Tim held up was an old stone, then he rotated it, and she saw the empty eye sockets and nasal cavity.

"Gross!" She drew back.

Her brothers burst into laughter. Tim, grinning, jumped up. "It's just a skull. Here. You want to hold it, don't you?" He walked toward her, arms outstretched as if to give her the hideous thing.

She held up her hands to ward him off. "Please tell me that's not real. Ugh! Get away from me!"

Tim only grinned wider.

"Seriously, stop. Jeez, where did you get that?"

"He got it from the bone church." Tim dropped to the floor by the bed, resting his back against it as he held up the skull for further examination. "Isn't it awesome?"

"You took this from a church?" She turned to Andrew, incredulous.

"Relax," Andrew said. "It's not real. I got it from the gift shop. Pretty dope, huh?"

She glanced again at the bone, which Tim was tossing like a ghoulish basketball. "It looks pretty real to me."

"It's supposed to, smarty. The Sedlec Ossuary in Czech. It has, like, fifty thousand bodies buried there. Or was it seventy thousand? I can't remember. There are so many bones, the monks decorated the whole church with them. There's even a bone chandelier."

"That's disgusting." She nodded at his suitcase. "So, what did you get me?"

Andrew's hazel eyes twinkled. "Can't wait till Christmas morning, huh?"

Kenzie shrugged. "You gave Tim his gift."

Andrew shuffled through the belongings. "Here it is. Merry Christmas."

He handed her a cardboard box about six or seven inches long and four inches wide. The box weighed no more than a paperback. The words "Made in Triberg" were stamped on one end above a picture of the German flag.

"Triberg," she said. "As in the Black Forest? Like Hansel and Gretel?"

"The birthplace of horror stories." Andrew grinned sadistically.

"Now I'm not sure I want it." She held it out to him.

"I was just messing with you about it being scary. It's not. Open it and see."

Intrigued, she pulled open one end of the box and looked inside. "It's a...figurine?"

"A smoker."

"A smoker?" She pulled out the painted wooden figure. It was shaped like an old woodcutter, with an ax in one hand and a stack of logs in the other. His mouth was in the shape of an oh, like he was crying for help. She looked closer at the ax. A glistening red smear marred the painted silver blade. "Is that blood?"

"What?" Andrew snatched it from her. "Where?"

"On the ax blade."

He looked closer, his eyebrows drawn together. He shook his head after a minute. "No. Someone just messed up on the paint job. Blood? Seriously?"

Now she felt stupid. Of course it wasn't blood. Why would someone put blood on a toy? "Why do they call it a smoker?"

"Here." Andrew wrenched it into two pieces. "He's hollow, see? Except for this brass plate. You light an incense cone and set it here, then put the top back on, and he smokes it out. I have a box of the cones somewhere. I'll give it to you when I find it."

Kenzie had never burned incense before, and she doubted the scent was anything she'd like. Still, she'd only gotten him a scarf and had spent all of five dollars on it. This assuredly cost more than that.

"That's neat," she finally said. "And thoughtful. Thank you."

He shrugged. "I know how much you like Christmas, and since Germany is basically the stomping ground for all the traditions, I figured you'd like something from there."

"Actually," Kenzie began, a mischievous idea forming, "most Christmas traditions weren't meant to be festive."

"What are you talking about?" Andrew said.

"We studied holiday traditions in my history class last semester." At his look of disbelief, she shrugged. "Even math majors have to take history. Anyway, I learned some interesting things."

"Like what?" Tim asked from the bed.

Kenzie smothered a grin, glad she'd learned something useful in the class. "For instance, in Germany, where this little guy came from, they have Krampus—a half-goat, half-demon who visits homes with Saint Nicholas. St. Nick delivers goodies to good little boys and girls, but Krampus steals the naughty children from their beds, stuffs them into a big sack, and carries them down to hell."

Tim stopped tossing around the skull. "Seriously?"

She nodded. "A lot of Christmas traditions started because people wanted to keep evil spirits at bay. Christmas falls around the winter solstice, which some believed was when the veil between the dead and the living was the thinnest."

Andrew's eyes widened. "You mean they were afraid of seeing ghosts? Awesome."

"Ivy, for instance, was supposed to ward off evil spirits. And the glass ornaments people put on trees? They're based on witch balls."

"What do witches have to do with it?" Tim asked.

Kenzie stared down at the smoker to hide her mischief. "The sparkling, colorful glass was believed to attract witches, and when they got too close, the balls would trap them. That way they couldn't cause any trouble. Our house would actually be a prime location for evil spirits to hang out, because Mom doesn't put up any of the traditional stuff."

Andrew and Tim were both silent, and when she looked up, she saw that their faces had taken on a pallor similar to the skull.

"That's a creepy thought," Andrew finally said.

She shrugged. "There's more, but you get the idea. We've convinced ourselves that the holidays are a merry, joyful time. But the fact is, Christmas is the scariest time of year. Especially on the night of the winter solstice. That's tonight, by the way," she added, just to dig it in a little deeper. "Anyway, thanks for the gift."

She waited until she was in the hall before letting loose her grin. It was so much fun to mess with her brothers.

Tim bounded into the hall. "Kenzie, wait."

She forced a neutral expression and faced him. "Yeah?"

"About that ghost stuff... Does mistletoe keep them away?"

Tim probably didn't deserve a sleepless night as much as Andrew. Maybe she could relent a little. "Yeah, it does. Why?"

He whooshed out a breath. "Just curious. A girl taped some to my locker, and I stuffed it in my backpack. I keep meaning to throw it away, but it's still there." He nodded at the bag near the bed.

She raised her eyebrows. "Someone's got a crush on you, huh?"

"Shut up." His cheeks pinked up.

"If you're worried about ghosts, don't be. Cats have been celebrated as guardians against evil spirits across multiple cultures."

"You mean Gibbyns can keep us safe?" Tim asked.

"So long as he's in the house with us, I suppose." She shrugged. He had to know ghosts didn't exist. He was clearly just caught up in her storytelling.

"Okay. Thanks." He walked back to Andrew's room.

As Kenzie returned to the living room, her mom stepped out of the kitchen wearing her gingerbread-man apron.

"Dinner's almost ready." She tapped a wooden spoon against her palm. "I could use some help with the gravy. What's that?"

Kenzie handed her the smoker.

"Andrew bought this for you?"

"He said he got it in the Black Forest. Brothers Grimm territory."

Mom scanned the figure. "It does look a little scary. I think it's his open mouth. Sweet of Andrew to think of you, though."

"I guess," she mumbled.

Mom passed back the smoker. "Since you're not busy, why don't you help me in the kitchen?"

Cooking was Kenzie's least favorite household task. "Didn't Dad say he was going to help tonight?"

"I sent him to the store for dressing."

Thanks to her big brown eyes and pale complexion, Kenzie had mastered the sad-puppy expression years ago. She summoned it now. "Do I have to? I really need to finish my book for next semester's class. You know I'm no good at English."

"Don't think I don't know what you're doing." Mom wagged the spoon at her. "Fine, I'll get Tim to help. Tim!"

"What, Mom?" Tim hollered from the other end of the house.

As Mom shouted orders, Kenzie sank into her cushy seat on the couch and set the smoker on the side table. The woodcutter seemed to stare straight at her, its mouth forever open in an endless, silent scream.

A shiver rippled up her spine. She didn't believe in ghosts or any of that supernatural rubbish, yet she couldn't stop herself from rotating the figure so she could no longer see its freaky face.

She grabbed her book and forced herself to focus. Henry's body had just been discovered, and the Irish townspeople who found it were pinning the murder on Victor. Sometimes she wondered if Victor's murderous "wretch" was really just Victor's alter-personality.

Another shiver wracked her body, this time from a chill in the air. She glanced at the hearthplace near the Christmas tree. Dad had lit a fire before he picked up Andrew, and the flames had gotten low. But that wouldn't cause this much cold, not when they had central heating.

Pulling a blanket around her, she snuggled deeper into the couch and yelled, "Andrew, did you touch the thermostat?"

"No!" came his answer a second later.

"Sure you didn't," she mumbled, turning the page. Andrew had always run hotter than an unsheared sheep in August, and turning down the heat was his MO.

An ear-splitting, pain-filled scream ripped her from her chapter.

"Oh, my—Tim!" Mom shrieked.

Kenzie threw off the blanket and ran to the kitchen. Andrew hurried up behind her.

She pulled up at the threshold and gasped. The gravy pan was bottom-up. Pools of gravy coated the stovetop like mud puddles and dripped down the side of the oven to dirty the floor.

Tim was curled over the sink, his back heaving with sobs as Mom held his hands under cold water flowing at full capacity.

Andrew squeezed past Kenzie. "What happened?"

"I don't know," Mom said, her face gray. She spotted Kenzie in the doorway. "Grab me a clean dish rag from the drawer, will you?"

Kenzie pulled out a soft green one with candy canes embroidered on the edge and handed it to her. Tim's cries of pain as Mom wrapped his hands curdled her stomach. She bit her lip, watching, waiting to see how bad it was.

Tim's face was pale and wet with tears, his dark eyebrows pulled together over pain-glazed eyes when Mom finished patting him dry and removed the towel. Kenzie stood on tiptoe to see over her mother's shoulder. Blisters coated her brother's hands, red and swollen and awful. Andrew swore under his breath, verbalizing Kenzie's thoughts.

"Oh, honey," Mom moaned. "We need to get you to the hospital."

"I think I hear Dad's car." Kenzie chased the noise to the garage door. She threw the door open just as her dad turned off the engine.

"Dad," she cried when he opened the driver's door. "Tim's hurt bad. Mom says he needs to go to the hospital."

He paused, half-way out. "Tim's hurt?"

"Stephen," Mom said behind Kenzie, "can you take him?"

Kenzie turned. Her mom was guiding Tim by the shoulders. Tim held his mutilated hands palms out, as if he feared touching the slightest surface. She didn't blame him. She pressed back against the doorjamb to let them by. Tim wasn't sobbing audibly, but his chin trembled and fresh tears coursed down his cheeks.

Mom helped him into the passenger seat and buckled him in before closing the door. Dad promised they'd be back soon, then he backed the car out of the garage and drove off into the dark winter night.

"That looked painful," Andrew said in Kenzie's ear, shaking her from her stupor.

"Yeah. Poor Tim."

"I guess that means I get to open his presents tomorrow."

She smacked his arm. "You're such a jerk!"

"Why are you getting mad? Someone's got to do it if he can't use his hands. Jeez, lighten up."

"Whatever." She stabbed the button that closed the garage and retreated back into the house.

Kenzie spent the next twenty minutes helping her mom clean up the kitchen while Andrew supposedly unpacked.

"Looks like a late dinner. We'll have to use gravy packets instead of the real stuff," Mom said with a sigh, rifling through the spice shelf.

Kenzie rinsed out the rag she'd been using to sop up the mess on the floor and glanced at the clock above the oven. 7:26. Very late for dinner. "Are we going to wait for Dad and Tim to return before we eat?"

Mom frowned. "I hate the idea of eating without them. This was supposed to be a special dinner to celebrate everyone being home. I'll text your dad and see what he thinks." She grabbed her phone from the counter and tapped on the screen. A minute later it buzzed with an incoming text. She sighed heavily when she read it. "He says it's a long wait and to go ahead."

No one said much during dinner, and Kenzie knew they were all worried about Tim. The ham was overcooked in all the excitement, but the potatoes Kenzie helped mash were tasty, even with instant gravy. By the time the dishes were done and they gathered in the living room to play games, it was nearly ten and they still hadn't heard back from Dad.

"Tell me more about your trip, Andrew." Mom shuffled the Phase Ten deck on the coffee table. "Kenzie said you went to the Black Forest in Germany."

"Yeah, did she show you her gift?" Andrew said.

"She did. It was—Kenzie, isn't that the figurine over there? It's turned the wrong way."

Kenzie reached over the armrest to rotate the smoker. Its freaky face hadn't changed, and she suppressed a grimace. "Did you see what he got Tim?"

Mom dealt the cards. "No."

"A skull," Kenzie said.

Mom froze.

"I got it from a gift shop," Andrew muttered.

Mom's eyebrows flew up. "Makes me wonder what you got me and your dad."

He smiled. "I guess you'll find out Christmas morning."

Mom grinned, and Kenzie sat back against the couch as they played. After the first game, Mom's phone buzzed.

"Uh oh," Mom said, staring at the text.

Kenzie sat up. "Is it Dad? What did the doctors say?"

"They want to keep Tim there tonight," Mom said.

"Poor kid!" Kenzie shared a worried glance with Andrew. Staying the night in the hospital was bad enough, but during the holiday it had to be torture.

Mom sighed and got to her feet. "I'd better pack him an overnight bag. And for me, too."

"You're going to stay with him?" Kenzie tossed her cards on the table and stood.

"One of us will. Your dad and I will work it out." She paused as she was leaving the room. "I'm sorry this evening isn't going like we'd hoped. I know both of you were so excited to come home."

Kenzie crossed the carpet and gave her a hug. "We're still excited to be home, Mom. And Tim will be back tomorrow. We'll have an awesome day."

"Thanks, sweetheart." Mom kissed Kenzie's cheek.

The decorative wall clock in the living room read ten-thirty by the time Kenzie changed into her pajamas.

"Movie?" Andrew asked from the kitchen. "I'm making hot cocoa."

She shrugged. She'd read enough, and a movie sounded good. "Sure. I'll do the popcorn."

"So, what are we watching?" Andrew asked a few minutes later. "*Scrooged?*"

Kenzie shook her head and shook the pan as kernels erupted like mini grenades. "I can't stand Bill Murray."

"You liked him in *Groundhog Day.*"

"Something else." Something to keep her mind off all the crazy this evening had brought.

Andrew grabbed two mugs from the cupboard. "What about *Die Hard*?"

"What about *It's a Wonderful Life*?" she countered, removing the pan from the stove.

He stuck out his tongue. Kenzie grinned and flipped off the stove. The moment she did, a chill swept over her body.

"Brr." She rubbed her arms, then swung around with narrowed eyes. "Did you turn down the temperature again?"

"Me? No." He looked so innocent she almost believed him. She pressed her lips together to contain her annoyance as she buttered and salted the popcorn, then cleaned up the pan.

"Ready?" Andrew lifted the two cocoa-filled mugs.

"Not yet," she growled. "First I'm going to fix the thermostat."

"But I told you—"

She held up a hand to silence him and stalked out of the kitchen. She'd only taken a few steps down the hall when the doorbell rang. Switching directions, she marched for the front door and opened it to find a distinguished elderly man.

"Oh, hello, Judge Crowthers," she greeted. What was he doing here?

"Kenzie. Good to see you back home." Judge Crowthers nodded, but his face was grim. A gust of brisk, mid-thirties wind swept past him into the house, making her shiver.

"I—Is something the matter?" What did Andrew do now? The last time their retired neighbor knocked on their door with that look, Andrew had been swapping his daily newspapers for tabloids. Judge Crowthers had since switched to electronic news.

"Is your mother or father home?" The judge looked past her into the house.

"No." She glanced behind her. Andrew stood at the edge of the foyer, a large white bowl filled with popcorn in his hands. She gave him a stern, accusing look.

He shrugged and shook his head. Again with the innocence, but she didn't buy it.

She faced the judge. "Tim had to go to the hospital, and they're with him. Is there something we can help you with?"

Judge Crowthers released a heavy sigh. "I don't know how to say this…"

She gripped the door handle, worry clawing her stomach. "What?"

He grimaced and wrung his gloved hands. "We were driving back from a party and noticed a lump beneath your front window. It looked like your cat, but it wasn't moving."

That's when Kenzie noticed his car still running on the curb. Through the passenger side window, she spied Mrs. Crowthers staring back at them.

"Gibbyns? Mom must have let him out earlier." Kenzie reached for her coat.

"I checked to be sure," Judge Crowthers was saying. "It's not pleasant."

Kenzie froze in the process of zipping up. Not pleasant? What did that mean?

"What's going on, Kenzie?" Andrew took his own coat from the hook.

"He says Gibbyns is lying on the ground outside." She stuffed her feet into her boots and pushed past the judge. Behind her, Andrew and the judge were saying something, but her focus was on the dark bundle of fur lying on the grass beneath the curtain-dimmed living room window.

She gave a strangled cry as the bundle took on a familiar form. "Gibbyns!" She fell to her knees before it.

Andrew was there in an instant. "What—Oh no."

Gibbyns' gray-striped body was unmoving, the eyes open and dull. He looked like he'd taken a one-way journey to the local taxidermist.

Tears filled Kenzie's eyes, and she stifled a moan. "What happened to him?"

"Think he got hit by a car?" Andrew said.

"He doesn't appear to have any marks on him, though it's hard to tell with this lighting," the judge said behind them. "Old age, perhaps?"

Kenzie couldn't look away from her sweet kitty's dead body. "He was only four."

"I'm very sorry," the judge said gruffly.

"Poor Gibbyns." Kenzie touched a single finger to the cat's head, just between the ears where he liked being petted the most. His body was still warm, proof he hadn't been dead long, and she retracted immediately.

A tear slipped free, then another, and she wiped her cheeks with her sleeve. "We can't just leave him out here. We have to bury him."

"I'll get a shovel," Andrew said quietly, walking away.

"I can help," the judge offered.

"No." Kenzie stood. "Mrs. Crowthers is waiting. Go home and enjoy your night."

"You sure?"

She sniffled and nodded. "The ground isn't frozen. We can handle it. Thank you for telling us. It would've been even worse to find him tomorrow."

The judge awkwardly patted her shoulder. "I'm sorry."

By the time the judge drove to his house across the street, Andrew had returned with the shovel and a biodegradable bag. They decided on a spot under the big maple.

"This is the worst Christmas break ever," Andrew muttered, stabbing the shovel into the ground and lifting out a thick wedge of soil.

Numbness settled in Kenzie's bones as she stared at the widening hole. Andrew was right; it was the worst. Their brother had been severely burned, their usually festive family dinner spoiled, their parents at the hospital all night. And now, Gibbyns was dead.

"If I didn't know better, I'd think we were cursed," she murmured.

The shovel's rhythmic *schlicking* noise suddenly stopped. "Cursed?" Andrew said. "Like, by witches or spirits or something?"

The way he said it, his voice low and wavering, brought Kenzie's head up. Suspicion licked at the corners of her mind, chasing away the numbness. For him to link her comment with what she'd said earlier meant he thought there could be a reason for a curse. Probably something to do with those gifts he'd brought home.

She folded her arms and glared. "Yes, like winter-solstice, ghosts-visiting-from-the-grave, evil-powers-at-force cursed."

There it was, the tell-tale gleam of guilt in Andrew's eyes, visible in the sallow light cast by the streetlamp. He looked hurriedly away, jabbing again at the ground.

Kenzie's grief morphed into anger. "What did you do, Andrew?" she hissed.

Stab, press, lift. Andrew wouldn't meet her eyes. Beyond him, Gibbyns' flimsy coffin mocked her. The combined pressure of anger and pain demanded an outlet, and Andrew was it. Kenzie grabbed the handle of the shovel, forcing him to stop digging.

"What. Did. You. Do?" she gritted out.

He yanked the shovel away. "Nothing!"

The smoker. It had to be. That thing was too creepy to have been purchased from a store.

"You're lying. Where did you get that figure, Andrew? Did you steal it? Take it from some man's gravesite? Is that why you think we're cursed?"

Andrew shook his head. "No." He renewed his digging efforts.

Kenzie was so sick of him and his pranks. When was he going to grow up?

Unkindness contaminated what was left of her holiday cheer. If he wanted to play games, fine. She could play too.

"You know," she said with mocking sweetness, "all those traditions and rumors about the winter solstice and ghosts roaming the earth didn't form out of thin air. People had reasons for believing what they did. Their beliefs lasted centuries, even millennia. You don't think there's some truth behind them?"

"What?" Andrew gulped. "So you're saying the dead really can come back to haunt us?"

"It's certainly not farfetched, especially if you stole something that belonged to one of them."

His face took on a waxy sheen. "Let's just bury Gibbyns and get back inside."

She glanced down. The hole was big enough, and she relinquished her vendetta. "Fine."

It was awful, but she lowered Gibbyns' limp, bagged body into the hole and covered it. Then, because it felt wrong not to, she said a short prayer over the grave, and they went inside.

They didn't speak while taking off their coats and washing up. The popcorn was stale, the hot cocoa tepid. It was the worst night on record, without a doubt.

Kenzie didn't ask before selecting *The Muppet Christmas Carol*. Andrew had gone to his room, and she needed a laugh to upend this miserable night. She grabbed the remote, sat on the edge of the couch, and pressed the "on" button.

As the TV screen flickered to life, the air in the room suddenly dropped in temperature. Goosebumps raced along her skin, the fine hairs on her arms standing on end. She felt as if someone had shoved her into the fissure of a glacier.

"That's it!" Fury roared through her. Throwing down the remote, which bounced off the ivory carpet with a soft thud, she jumped to her feet and stomped down the hall toward the thermostat. Arms wrapped around herself to maintain what little heat she could, she yelled, "Andrew, so help me, if you—"

"Kenzie!" Andrew's fear-filled scream cut her off. He burst from his room, his face white as a snowman's.

Her fury vanished. "What happened?"

He rushed toward her, pointing behind him with a trembling

arm. "Outside my window."

She'd never seen him like this. He was shaking like a child who'd just seen the boogeyman. "What's wrong? What did you see?"

"I don't know." He swallowed hard, his eyes wild. "I think it was a ghost."

"What?"

"I swear I'm not making it up! It was saying something—I don't know what the words mean—then it faded away."

He seriously thought he saw a ghost outside his window? Impatience frayed the edges of her concern. "What was it saying, Andrew?" she snapped.

"Th—the words sounded weird. Foreign. *'Vrat me tow, vrat me tow,'* over and over again."

"Vrat me tow?" It wasn't Spanish or French, that was for sure. She narrowed her eyes. "You're sure that's what 'it' was saying?"

He nodded, and the movement highlighted a sheen of perspiration on his forehead. He was truly frightened.

Her heart gave a repentant twist. This was her fault. She was the one who'd used winter solstice stories to mess with his head. Maybe it was time to back off.

She put her hand on his shoulder. "It was probably some guy who drank too much and forgot what house was his. We can google what he said, if you want; I'm sure something will come up. But first..."

She patted him as she walked the remaining distance to the thermostat. Funny, she was no longer cold. But that was probably just because of all the excitement.

The temperature read seventy-two degrees, exactly what it was supposed to.

"That's weird," she muttered.

"Then you felt it, too, just now?" Andrew said in an unsettled voice. "The drop in temperature?"

She whipped around.

"I felt it," he said, "just before I saw that—that thing at the window."

She stared at him, unwilling to believe.

"And in the kitchen, before Judge Crowthers knocked," Andrew said, "when you suddenly got cold. Well, I felt it then, too. That was when Gibbyns died."

She shook her head. "I know what you're getting at, but it's not true. The chill and those things that happened—it's a coincidence. Ghosts don't exist. All that stuff I told you about the winter solstice and evil spirits was just to spook you. A little sisterly fun."

He held her gaze. "Then why did you also accuse me of lowering the temperature right before Tim burned his hands?"

Her stomach dropped. She'd forgotten about that chill. The first chill.

"No. No, you're wrong," she said. Yet the logical side of her brain was crumbling beneath the pummeling gavel of bizarre possibility. She clutched at her throat and repeated, "Ghosts don't exist."

Andrew stepped closer, holding her gaze. "Are you sure?"

His simple question shattered her fragile hold on the rational world she'd always believed in. Fueled by instinct, she ran past him, back to the living room.

There it was. That awful wooden figurine. She grabbed it and turned it around. The woodcutter's mouth remained in the same suspended yell of horror as earlier, its ax blade no less red.

With a cry, she threw it into the dwindling fire.

"What are you doing?" Andrew yelped, racing toward the hearth. He reached for the burning figure as if to save it, but jumped back as the fire sputtered its joy at receiving more fuel.

"That cost me fifteen Euros," he whined. "I thought you liked it."

"You mean you actually bought it?" she asked.

"I told you I bought it in the Black Forest. I wasn't lying about that."

"Then..." She put her hands on her hips, staring into the flames as if they could burn away the questions and reveal the answer to tonight's puzzle.

Suddenly, she straightened. "*Vrat me tow.* That's what you heard outside your window."

His face lost the rush of color gained from running after her. "Yes."

As her heart pounded, she pulled out her cellphone and opened the translation app. She clicked on the "detect language" option, then hit the voice recording button.

"*Vrat me tow,*" she said into the receiver.

A swirling circle formed on the screen as the app worked. After a moment, the screen changed. Her breath caught as she checked the results, and her blood congealed.

Language: Czech

Translation: Vrat' mi to: Give it back to me.

"Give it back to me," she whispered. The fake Christmas tree glittered beside her, screaming its absence of ornamental glass balls. A sick, sinking sensation inside had her moaning, "No, no... Andrew, what did you do?"

It was one thing to steal a toy that once belonged to some deranged, long-dead soul, but this was far worse.

"I'm sorry," Andrew groaned. "I didn't mean to. I was at the end of the tour group, and the skulls were everywhere. It was so easy to reach over and grab one."

"Andrew!"

"I realized as soon as we left the bone church that what I did was wrong, but I couldn't just return it, you know? They might have arrested me. I turned eighteen this year. Instead, I pretended I bought it at the gift shop and gave it to Tim."

A chill, colder, damper than any of the others, blew over her skin and settled in her bones. She looked at the clock on the far wall. 11:57. Three minutes until midnight on the winter solstice. Three minutes until the veil would be its thinnest, maybe even nonexistent.

"It's coming for me, isn't it?" Andrew's breath fogged the air. "The skull's owner. I stole it from him and now he's coming for me."

She looked again. 11:58.

"No," she said firmly. "Because ghosts aren't real."

Yet she sprinted from the room, spurred on by an abrupt need to get that skull, that stupid skull, out of the house. Last she'd seen it, it had been on Andrew's bed.

She caught herself on the door to his room. The lights were on, the room still a catastrophe of luggage-shed belongings.

Hurry, hurry.

She flipped over the bedcovers, then dropped to her knees to look underneath.

Nothing.

Arctic air settled over her, tightening her exposed skin, slowing her movements. Her breath was a white cloud. Where was it?

Tim. He'd probably taken the skull to his own room.

She skidded into the hall, to the next room. Tim's room was cleaner than Andrew's.

There. On the desk, under *The Grinch* poster.

The skull.

She reached for it. Took it. The smooth bone was so cold it freeze-burned her fingertips. "Ghosts aren't real," she said willing herself to believe.

"Kenzie!" Andrew screamed.

She jerked around. The lights in the hallway flickered. Then Andrew's hair-raising screech of terror filled the house.

"Andrew!" she cried, fear keeping her rooted.

He didn't answer.

"Andrew?" she choked out. She looked at the alarm clock on Tim's nightstand. 12:00.

"I don't believe in ghosts. I don't believe in ghosts," she whispered.

Whole body trembling, she inched forward. The lights in the hall flickered again as, with a ragged breath, she peered out of Tim's room.

Andrew's arm, pale and unmoving, reached across the carpet at the end of the hall. The rest of his body lay hidden around the corner.

Her knees gave way, and she slipped to the floor. Was he dead?

The lights spasmed in the hallway. On and off, faster and faster.

"*Vrat' mi to. Vrat' mi to.*" The voice, whisper-thin yet black-ice clear, drifted to her ears. *Give it back to me.*

The spirit was still in the house. A house devoid of traditional glass ornaments and holly balls and ivy wreaths. And that spirit wouldn't leave until it got what it came for.

The skull. She still held it.

The events leading to this moment hit her at once: Tim touching the skull then getting his hands burned. The cat, an animal regarded as a guardian against evil spirits, dead. Her brother, the thief, silent—possibly even dead—in the living room.

What would the spirit do when it found her, clutching the skull as if staking ownership?

Driven by desperation, she tried to throw it away, but her fingers froze to the marble-like bone. She whimpered, shook her hands, and prayed for the skull to drop. It wouldn't.

Horror wrapped around her in serpentine coils. She scuttled deeper into the room, frantically shaking her hands.

"I don't believe in ghosts," she whimpered brokenly.

The hallway light turned off—and stayed off. Then Tim's bedroom light flickered above her head.

She scanned the room for something to ward it off. There was nothing. Just Jim Carrey's green face smiling down on her through the sporadic light. Then she spotted Tim's backpack beside the bed, and the green leaves poking out from an open compartment.

Mistletoe.

With a cry, she scrambled for it. But she couldn't grasp it, not with her hands full.

"*Vrat' mi to...*" The voice spoke just behind her.

Moaning and crying, her tears sticking in frozen drops to her cheeks, she knocked the skull against the bed's side rail. She hardly felt the tug of the object finally dropping from her fingertips in her haste to snatch up the mistletoe. Just as her fingers clenched around the dried leaves, the lights went out, plunging her into darkness.

Praying she'd been wrong about those foolish traditions of long ago, she turned and thrust out the plant like a shield.

It—the ghost—floated two steps away. Its body was thin and grotesque, wrapped in gauzy fabric that swirled in the air around it. It had no hair, no eyebrows, no color except that grim, awful gray. Kenzie shrieked as its stringy arms reached out as if to grab her.

Suddenly it hissed and recoiled.

Kenzie looked down at the mistletoe. It was surrounded by a soft yellow glow.

The apparition tried again to reach her, and again it cried in pain and withdrew. *"Vrat' mi to,"* it howled. Ice crystals hovered in the air where its breath touched.

The skull was by Kenzie's knee. Keeping the mistletoe outstretched, she rolled the skull to the ghost. "I'm sorry," she blubbered. "I'm so sorry. Take it."

The ghost bent over and picked up the skull, turning it in its spindly fingers. It looked at Kenzie. *"Děkuji."* Then it vanished, leaving Kenzie behind in a world of pitch black.

The air around her warmed, her skin tingling as blood rushed through her body. Her heaving breaths were the only sound in the room.

She was alive. And it was gone.

Andrew!

Her legs shook so forcefully they barely held her. She stumbled to the wall and felt for the light switch. She flipped it on, and light flooded the room. Her stomach clenched as she turned on the hallway lights next, illuminating Andrew's limp, pallid arm. She bit her lip to keep from crying as she looked around the corner.

His body lay prostrate on the living room rug, but there was no blood. No marks of any kind on him that she could see.

She knelt and pressed her fingers to his throat. His skin was warm! And he had a pulse. The ghost must have scared him so badly he'd fainted.

She shook him. "Wake up, Andrew."

His eyes opened, and he shot up into a sitting position, gasping like a drowning victim. "The ghost! The ghost!" he screamed, his gaze darting around the room.

"Ssh," she said. "It's gone."

"Gone?" he wheezed.

"Gone. And so is the skull."

His breathing slowed, and he faced her. "You saw it? How did you get away?"

Before she could answer, the front door swung open.

"Mom!" Kenzie jumped up and ran to her, throwing her arms around her, relief overwhelming her to tears once more. "You're home."

Mom patted her back. "You're trembling, honey. What's going on?"

"I thought you were staying at the hospital," Kenzie cried into her shoulder.

"Your dad decided to stay. What on earth happened?"

"Mom!" Andrew joined them. "You won't believe it."

Mom pulled back from Kenzie. "You're crying?"

"We saw a ghost, Mom," Andrew said.

Kenzie nodded. "It's true. It was here in the house."

The story came out in a rush, from the sudden chills and "accidents" to the ghost's spine-tingling demands for its missing skull.

Mom looked between them, her eyebrows pulled together in confusion. Then her face cleared and she laughed. "Oh, you two are good. Kenzie, you should have been an actress. Was this prank Andrew's idea? Very funny." She walked past them, chuckling.

"Mom," Kenzie said. "We're serious. There was a ghost here."

Mom smiled over her shoulder as she walked to her room. "Good try, you two. You know there's no such thing as ghosts." She disappeared into the master bedroom, her amused laughter trailing behind her.

Kenzie swiped at her tears and met Andrew's gaze. "She'll never believe us. No one will."

He shook his head. His face was still pale, his eyes shadowed. "But it did happen."

"Yes, it did." Gibbyns' death was proof of it, something Mom would believe when she saw the grave in the morning.

"I—I'm sorry, Kenzie." Andrew's voice trembled. "This was all my fault. If I hadn't been so stupid... If I'd resisted the urge..." He shook his head, and a tear trickled down his cheek. "Guess I learned my lesson."

"Yeah," she said quietly. "Guess so." Hopefully after tonight he would finally grow up. It was about time for a change.

"We should try to sleep," she said.

He swallowed. "Do you think you can?"

Exhaustion suddenly weighed heavily over her. "Yeah. Get the foyer light, will you?"

She started down the hall as he flipped the switch, sending a shadow over them.

"Hey, what's that in your hand?" he asked.

She stopped and looked down, and her exhaustion vanished like fog from a desert. She hadn't realized she was still holding Tim's mistletoe. In the dimmed hallway, the sprig glowed with a golden halo.

Her stomach cramped. They'd gotten rid of one ghost, but the night wasn't over. How many more spirits walked the earth this time of year?

The pre-lit glow of their trendy Christmas tree caught her attention. She pursed her lips, then re-routed herself and strode toward the garage.

"Where are you going?" Andrew called behind her.

"I don't know about you," she said over her shoulder, "but I'm not letting any more ghosts in our house. Not this Christmas."

With quick steps she went to the garage where the old decorations were kept. Traditional glass ornaments, holly balls, and ivy wreaths. Not all change was good. It was time for some things to go back to the way they used to be.

ALL THROUGH THE HOUSE

BY SCOTT TAYLOR

Sean Walker bounced, rocked, wiggled in his chair, causing the two slightly longer legs of the chair to knock with each wiggle. Sean's mother and older three siblings ignored the family's youngest member, but Sean's dad didn't. He smiled, seeing Sean so excited for Christmas—set to arrive in mere hours. Sean, age six, had it bad, real bad.

"Sean," Mom said. "You haven't even touched your chicken nuggets. You need to eat something, or Santa won't come."

Sean instantly stopped.

Dad laughed.

"That's better," Mom said. Sean grabbed a nugget and popped it into his mouth. He chewed quickly. Before swallowing it, he shoved in another. Even at this late hour—especially at this late hour—Sean could not afford to screw things up now. Ever since last Christmas Sean had been good, better than good.

Because this year was different.

This year, Sean had something to prove.

In the past year some of the kids at school said things about Santa Sean didn't like. They said Santa wasn't real, that he didn't exist, and if he did, he'd probably fly right pass Sean's house because Santa didn't give presents to kids like Sean.

This year, Sean would prove those bullies wrong. Santa *did* exist. Sean would show them, then *he'd* be the one to tell them *they* were wrong.

"That's a good boy," Mom said. "Now, gather up your dishes and put them in the sink."

Sean obeyed.

With dinner done, the family moved to various places in the house. Sean's two older brothers, Will, age fourteen, and Troy, age eleven, went to the basement where video games called to them like Princess Peach to Mario and Luigi. Sean's only sister, Katie, age eight, stayed in the kitchen with Mom. Dad sat in the front room and turned on a college football game. Sean trotted in and sat down next to him.

"Dad?"

"Yeah, son?" Dad said without taking his eyes off the game.

"Do you think Santa saw me eat all my nuggets?"

Dad laughed. "Son, I *know* Santa saw you being a good kid at dinner," Dad said finally looking away from the TV. "You are a good kid—Santa knows that, too."

"Whew!" Sean said, relieved. "I'm going to bed."

"So soon? It's only six-thirty."

"The sooner I fall asleep, the sooner Santa can come."

"True that," Dad said. "I only wish your brothers had your attitude."

"Goodnight, Dad."

"Goodnight." Sean left the room. "Oh, give your mother a hug and kiss and thank her for dinner."

"Okay," Sean said from halfway down the hall to the kitchen.

SEAN LOVED EVERYTHING ABOUT CHRISTMAS, everything but one small detail—trying to fall asleep Christmas Eve.

Impossible.

Couldn't be done.

Sean tried everything to fall asleep. He put a pillow over his head. It made his head sweat. He counted sheep. He actually didn't know what that meant, but he'd heard adults say they tried counting sheep when they couldn't sleep. Sean imagined a large field full of sheep, and his mind tried counting them all. He usually lost count around seventy—he wasn't sure if the sheep he counted had already been counted or not.

It really didn't matter. Tonight was different. This year, Sean took precautions. He borrowed his big brother's wind-up alarm clock and set it for 3:30 a.m. Tom Peterson, one of Sean's friends at school, said Santa *always* showed up at 3:40 a.m. Tom knew this because he had tried catching Santa the year before. He checked the room at 3:30 a.m. He fell back to sleep, but only for a few minutes. When Tom checked at 3:45 a.m., he saw presents. He was sure Santa came at 3:40 a.m exactly. This year Sean was going to wake up early and just wait for him to arrive.

Tom said another thing, too, and this thing *had* to be done to guarantee a Santa sighting. He said the one-hundred percent way to get Santa to show up was to write him a letter—addressed directly to Santa himself—and take that letter with you when you go to wait for him. Tom said when a kid does that, it's magic and it *makes* it so kids can see him, and Santa has to give the kid whatever he wants.

Even though Sean was sure he could never fall asleep, he was ready. He had the old alarm clock and the letter. Sean had trouble with the letter. He was just learning how to write, so it wasn't long. He was sure he misspelled some of the words, but it was close and it was addressed to Santa. The only thing Sean wrote down that he wanted was to see Santa, in person, in his house.

At 3:30 a.m. on the dot an alarm rang. Before he went to bed, Sean stowed his brother's alarm clock under his pillow so he'd be the only one who heard it.

AT THE FIRST ring of the clock Sean threw off the covers and sprang from the bed. Now, he just had to sneak past his parents' bedroom door and make it to the front room. That's where Santa would be. That's where he'd catch Santa and prove to those bullies they were stupid.

With the letter in his hand, Sean carefully approached his parents' bedroom door. He heard his father snoring and knew at least *he* was asleep. With his parents asleep, Sean tip-toed into the front room. Streetlamp lights filtered through the room's bay window casting light on the couch, chairs, and Christmas tree, which twinkled with colors. Sean knew exactly where he planned to hide, behind his father's big easy chair in the corner. No way Santa would see him there.

Sean entered the room and on his way to the chair, he looked under the tree...

Presents!

Santa had already been there, and he missed him!

Sean was so mad he almost screamed.

Stupid Tom. What did he know, anyway?

I guess Santa doesn't come at three-forty a.m. after all, Sean thought as his shoulders slumped. His head dropped. He crumpled up the letter and threw it into the fireplace, where coals left from the earlier evening's fire ignited the note. Light from the burning paper momentarily brightened the room, then died out.

Dejected, Sean turned to leave. He'd blown his chance this year, all because he believed Tom. He'd have to wait a whole year before he had another chance—and, he'd have to be good for that whole year, too.

"Where are you going, son?" An eerie voice filled the room.

Sean stopped. The voice was close, but the room was empty. Sean slowly turned around.

He wasn't alone.

From behind the Christmas tree a man emerged. He looked down at Sean.

"Sean Walker...am I right?"

Sean, petrified, could only nod. The man standing before him didn't look like what he thought Santa would look like, although there was a red glow surrounding him. He was tall, thin, with no beard. His cheeks were not rosy, his eyes did not twinkle—in fact, they did just the opposite. They were deep-set and glowed red.

And a smell, like rotting garbage, filled the room. Sean couldn't be sure if it came from the man, but if not, it smelled like something died right in their front room.

"Uh...um," Sean began. His throat suddenly dry and the words he wanted to say crackled and stopped.

"Please," the man said. "Have a seat." A long thin arm with a long thin hand motioned to his father's chair. "After all, you invited me here."

"I did?" Sean's curiosity broke through his parched throat.

"Yes." The skeleton-thin hand floated toward the fireplace. The man snapped his boney fingers. Sean watched the charred remains of the letter transform. White replaced black, and the crumpled mass unfurled until the original letter lay perfectly restored in the fire.

"Your friend, Tom Peterson, was right. My name is on the letter, and here I am."

"You're Santa?" Sean asked, his eyes wide with the realization that he might actually be in the presence of Santa himself.

The man chuckled but didn't answer right away. Instead, he walked to the fireplace and retrieved the letter.

"I'm the one you summoned, and who will grant you a wish," he said and released the letter. Sean watched the paper drift slowly over to him as it fell. It came to rest at his feet. Sean bent down and picked it up. He saw his words written in red crayon looking up at him. He remembered writing them, hoping these few words would bring Santa to him. It must have worked. Sean didn't know what to think. Maybe it really was magic after all, especially seeing a burned piece of paper become unburned.

Sean walked to the chair and stood with the letter in both hands.

"Again, please sit," the man said as he came from behind the tree and sat on the couch opposite Sean's father's chair. Usually, if anyone sat on that couch, the old springs creaked and squeaked.

But not this time.

This time...nothing, no sounds, no creaks, no squeaks.

And the rancid smell grew stronger. It must be Santa, Sean thought. With him so close, Sean assumed the red glow would bring warmth, but a chill hung in the air between them like wearing wet clothes on a cold and windy day.

"So, Santa?" Sean didn't know what to ask, even though he'd spent the last year imagining, planning on what he would say to Santa if ever given the chance. Now, Sean's brain went blank—nothing came.

"You've got to stop believing in fairy tales, Sean. You'll only be disappointed."

Of all the let downs of the night, of Tom's lies about Santa's arrival time, of seeing a man who didn't look/act like Santa, of spending all year being good for *this*...those words from Santa hurt most of all. Fairy tales? No, Sean believed—it didn't matter what Santa said.

He believed.

"Fairytales are all lies," Santa said. "You need to grow up."

Sean threw himself into his father's chair. He hated adults telling him how he should act, what he should think. His brothers did it, too. They picked on him and he took it, never talking back—especially this year when he'd tried so hard to be good so he could meet...this man.

Sean glared at Santa and with a huff, crossed his arms over his chest.

"It doesn't matter," Santa looked at the Christmas tree all ablaze in lights. "There's so much children don't—"

"You're a stupid Santa," Sean spit the words directly at the foul-smelling man.

He looked at Sean. Santa's red eyes growled in intensity and heat.

Sean didn't care. He was mad, mad at himself, mad at Tom, and mad at Santa most of all.

"You interrupted me, child. Don't ever do that again."

Fine, maybe I'll just stop talking, thought Sean.

"Now, Sean. Because you invited me here, I must ask you what you want. To deny me this will be rude. You should not be rude to your guests."

"I want you to go," Sean uncrossed, then crossed his arms. He lay almost horizontal as the back of his head barely reached the back of his father's chair, pinning his chin on his chest. "I want you to leave my house and don't come back."

"I see. And what if I don't want to leave?"

"Then you're the rude one."

Santa laughed, a hard cackle filled the room.

Sean sat up, worried the laugh would wake his father. If so, he'd come in the room and see Santa sitting there, and Father would blame Sean, and Sean would be in trouble.

And trouble meant...

Wait. Sean had been trying to be so good for so long, it was habit. He worried getting in trouble would ruin his chance of meeting Santa next year...

But, that didn't matter now. He'd already met Santa, and to Sean, Santa wasn't anything special. In fact, Sean would be glad if he never saw the man ever again.

Santa stopped laughing, and a terrifying scowl flashed across his face.

"Listen, you little titmouse."

The room grew even colder.

"You've got a *lot* to learn about respecting your elders," Santa said, towering over Sean.

"I should smash you like a roach. I should take your parents and rip off their arms and feed them to sewer rats. Tell me why I shouldn't grab your brothers and your sister and burn their skin until they scream and beg for death."

Sean stared up at Santa knowing he should be scared, but something inside burned, the pain of disappointment, all that hard work of being so good all year long came back to him, a fire inside grew and grew until he sprang from the chair, almost hitting heads with the man.

"No!" Sean screamed. The letter fell to the floor. Sean didn't care if anyone else heard—in fact, he hoped his family would come rushing into the room. "No—you listen to me! I don't care if you *are* Santa. You asked me what I wanted and I want you to go—now! I want you to go up the chimney and get in your sleigh and ride back to the North Pole."

Santa stepped back.

Sean stepped forward.

"I should destroy you," Santa fumed.

"Then why don't you?" Sean took another step forward. Santa retreated again.

An idea came to Sean.

"You don't because you can't." Sean said. "If you could, you would."

Santa stared down at Sean. He formed fists with his skeletal hands. His whole body shook, but he remained rooted in place.

"See?" Sean smiled. "You *can't,* can you? You can't do a thing to me. It's because you said you'd grant me a wish and my wish is for you to leave, and that's why you can't do nothing."

Santa got angrier.

"I said, *go!*"

Santa's red eyes narrowed, his head lowered. It came closer to Sean, who stood his ground. It came nearer and nearer, the stench increasing as it drew close.

"Boo!" Sean said.

Santa jumped.

A cold wind hit as if a miniature tornado exploded in the room.

Santa disappeared.

Sean shielded his eyes as the wind died down. He didn't see Santa leave, but assumed he must have gone up the chimney.

"Good," Sean said. "Stupid Santa. He wasn't even nice or jolly. I can't wait to tell Tom that Santa *is* real and he's also a jerk."

Sean surveyed the room. The awful smell began to fade away, replaced by the delicious aroma of the family Christmas tree and the remains of the previous evening's fire.

Sean returned to his room. He couldn't believe all the racket never woke up his parents. He closed his bedroom door, climbed into his bed, and fell into a deep sleep.

"Hey, sleepyhead," Sean's brother Will said through the door.

"Get up—we're all waiting for you—it's Christmas."

Sean rose from his bed, his covers falling around him. Christmas —it arrived. He tumbled from his bed, the new-day fog still swirling around his head.

He threw on his robe. He remembered his letter and Santa. Had it happened? Was it a dream? Did he really wake up in the middle of the night and sneak into the front room?

No, it couldn't have happened. A big stinky Santa threatening to kill his family, who then disappeared when Sean ordered him to go? That was the strangest thing of all. Adults *never* do what kids tell them to do. No, there's no way all those things happened.

Sean donned his slippers and raced from the room. He ran into the front room and jumped on the couch.

"Easy there, buddy," Dad said.

Sean beamed.

"I thought you'd be the first one up and we'd come in here finding you having opened up all your presents," Dad said.

The thought of Santa standing in the exact spot where his dad stood returned, and Sean's smile disappeared.

"What's wrong?" Mom asked.

"Oh, nothing ," Sean said.

"Glad to hear it. Quick, open this." Mom thrust a medium-sized package into Sean's arms.

Ah, my first present, Sean thought. He ripped the wrapping savagely and flung it high in the air. He tore open the box as if it contained food and he hadn't eaten in days. Sean looked down on an orange sweater jammed into the box. Hopefully, better presents were coming.

"What's this?" Troy said. "Looks like it's a letter to Santa." Sean saw his brother lift up a letter—his letter.

"Can I see it?" Katie asked.

"No, you'd better let me see that," Mom said as she walked over to Troy, sitting in his father's chair.

"Yeah—looks like Sean's writing," Troy said and he held up the letter for his mother to snatch.

"Oh, by the way, Sean, you misspelled, 'Santa.' I'd hate to see *this guy* show up."

ANGEL IN THE ATTIC

BY DONEA LEE WEAVER

From the window seat in my living room, I watched the weather blanket my city in white as a beautiful but melancholy tune from some old memory played in my head.

It had snowed like this the day of my grandmother's funeral—all day, heavy, snowflakes the size of quarters. Of course, that was many years ago. But she'd been on my mind lately. More apt, her old house had been on my mind, and today's blizzard brought thoughts of her and her home closer. I drove by the old place on occasion, when I was in the neighborhood, but this week alone I'd been by it at least three times. So many happy memories were made there. Especially at Christmas. But there were sad memories, too.

"Do you still plan on going to that showing today?" my daughter asked.

"I think I have to," I said, sighing and leaving a temporary blur on the cold window glass. "Something's calling me there." I paused, laughing, and craned my neck to look back at her. "Is that too weird?"

Ashley came up behind me and wrapped her arms around my middle, resting her chin on my shoulder, and gazed out the window, too. "No. Just..." She pointed to my car, covered in inches of snow. "This isn't the kind of weather you drive around in if you don't have to."

"Eh." I tried to brush her sensible words off, but shivered instead. "We'll stop for coffee. My car has all-wheel drive, and we can take back roads. It will be fine." *Right?*

She pushed away from me and sucked in a deep breath. "I'll get my coat."

ASHLEY WAS RIGHT. This definitely wasn't a good day to drive. Traffic from snowy fender-benders and slide-offs made us late for my appointment. My nerves frayed like the ends of a scarf as we pulled up to the house and there wasn't a car in sight.

"Maybe the agent's car is in the garage?" Ashley patted my back as I whimpered.

"Yeah, maybe." I pulled into the driveway and stared at the garage door. When I was a kid, you could barely get a car into that thing. Grandma and Grandpa had it filled with bits and bobbles of their life together and, of course, all my Grandma's Shaklee stuff and a freezer full of pineapple sherbet.

By the time Ashley had been born, the house was no longer in the May family's possession, so she'd never been here. I wondered if it would leave any kind of impression on her. It sure looked smaller to me now than it did when I was a kid. Probably not even two-thousand square feet, which was nothing compared to the monster home we were living in.

We got out of the car and pulled our twin black Columbia coats tighter around us. Ashley pointed to an entrance just left of the garage doors. "Do we go in there?"

We used to...

My earliest and fondest memories were of that basement. My cousins and I would huddle up in the spare bedroom-turned-play room, dressing up in old hats, gloves and aprons my grandma had stashed in the closet. It was the place we created and rehearsed all our Christmas Eve plays—for a time, anyhow. Things changed as we got older.

"No." I shook my head, frowning. "Let's use the main entrance."

With those long legs or hers, she beat me to the top of the two small flights of cement stairs leading to the door. My breath caught at a memory of a picture of my grandma in that exact spot. It was a picture my dad had of his young mother. She'd been older than Ashley's seventeen years of age at the time, but they looked uncannily alike. Ashley had her long dark hair and twilit-blue eyes.

When I made it to the top, we both leaned forward to read a sticky note attached to the screen door: "Be back in a jiff. Text me for a code."

I did as the agent asked, and once I had the code, Ashley punched it in and pushed open the front door.

"How many people did you fit in here? Wow."

My grandparents had seven kids. Seven! And everyone always came with their families on Christmas Eve. How had we all squeezed into these small spaces? I shut my eyes, trying to remember.

"I'm not sure." Defeated by brain fog, I shrugged. Some memories were sharper than others. "But here's what I do remember." I pointed to the left corner of the living room. "They always had a big tree over there. A white one, covered in colorful bulbs and tinsel." Pointing left, I said, "And there was a piano in that corner."

We went into the kitchen. "There used to be a round table in here. I remember sitting here with my sisters, eating protein bars and pot roast and homemade cinnamon rolls. That door leads outside to an awesome patio, and she had a little office through there."

We saw old bedrooms and bathrooms, a TV room where my sisters, cousins, and I used to watch Mr. Rogers. We headed downstairs, which seemed like a carbon copy of the layout on the main floor. I closed my eyes and remembered the pair of Dutch wooden shoes that used to sit on top of another piano in the basement. When Grandma passed away, they were the one thing I wanted of hers. But I had no idea where they were now.

"There's an even smaller house behind this one. My great-grandma lived there for a while when she was alive. And a swing-set and some kind of shed and a HUGE garden. Apple and peach trees..." My eyes misted, and I bit the inside of my lower lip to keep from crying. "I wish you could have known her."

Ashley side-hugged me and rested her head on my shoulder. "Me, too."

I dabbed at the corner of my eyes and laughed. "I wish I could show you the yard. Stupid snow. Why couldn't this place be up for sale in the spring?"

"Is there anything else you want to look at inside?"

The attic.

A chill wracked through me at those words. Had someone whispered them? Were they just in my head? Attic? Hmm. In all the time I'd come here as a kid, I don't remember ever going into an attic? Yet...there was access to one. A square door in the ceiling of the upstairs hallway and...yes. A string to pull something down.

"The attic."

She snorted. "Seriously? Why? That's not creepy or anything. Isn't there a family saying about that?"

I scratched at a phantom itch on my index finger. "I...I don't know why. Just feels like the right move. And we should probably do it before the agent gets back." I headed back up the stairs before Ashley had a chance to say anything else or talk me out of it.

As I stared at the attic entrance in the hall, my thoughts grew quiet. There was no buzzing in my head trying to decide if this was a smart move or the most idiotic thing ever—just a weird calm. Weird for me, because my mind almost never stopped buzzing. I took sure-footed steps until I stood right beneath it. A draft from nowhere blew the pull-string, and it shuddered like a warning. I took a firm grasp of it with my left hand, anyhow, and yanked. Dust sprinkled down from the cracks around the door, but other than a light groan, the ladder came down easily.

Ashley coughed. "You're not really going up there, are you?"

I squinted into the black open space above me, lifting my foot onto the first rung. "I sure am."

When I got to the top, the only part of the wooden floor illuminated by the light below looked aged and rotted. The rest of the room was dark. I used the flashlight on my phone to see if I could find a light source. A single bulb in the middle of the space, with another string, was just above me as I teetered on the top step. I pulled the string and the dim light crackled to life, surprisingly, because the fine layer of gray dust and cobwebs over everything made me think that no one had been up here in a really long time.

My nose crinkled like I was about to sneeze. I put a finger under it and held my breath as I took the first step in, wincing as the boards creaked under my weight.

"What's up there?" Ashley called up to me.

I smirked down at her. "Why don't you come up and see for yourself?"

"Funny." As she walked away from view, I thought I caught her humming a few bars of one of my favorite Christmas songs. Or maybe I was just hearing things. Again.

She didn't need to come up here, though. I scanned the dusty attic, turning in careful circles to avoid crashing through the unstable floorboards to the rooms below. There wasn't anything up here. Nothing of interest, anyhow. A few wooden crates sat in a far corner, but they were empty. An old lamp was shoved against the wall, but it was plain and boring and nothing worth claiming as an antique. Slats from a small vent near the roof-top fluttered open, letting in slivers of white light from the snowy glow outside. The bright beams all seemed to train onto a wood panel on the opposite wall.

Leaning in, I saw that a corner of the wood framing in the attic had pulled away from the symmetry of the others. And I wanted to pull on it. I shrugged the urge off, reminding myself that this was an old house, and it was probably water damage or something. I turned to leave, but my knee buckled, sending me falling back in the direction of that wall. I caught myself, my hand scratching against the splintered wood, and cursed.

"Hey!" Ashley called up. "What was that? Are you okay?"

"Just clumsy. I'm good. Heading back down."

I shook my hand like it would throw off the pain or something, and glared at the wall. As if in response, I heard a small click, and then a panel opened on an unseen hinge, revealing a hidden space behind it. A hidden space with a long black shoe box—black as if the dust of age had never found its way onto it.

The fine hairs on my neck raised. That box had been waiting for me. Somehow, I just knew it. I reached out to grab it, but something stilled my hand. Maybe it wasn't a good idea. Maybe I should just leave... From somewhere outside, I heard the squeal of brakes, and my heart panicked. I gripped the box despite my better judgment and tucked it under my arm before shutting the hiding place. I backed to the attic entrance and quick-stepped my way down the ladder.

Ashley was at the door, still humming a familiar tune.

"What are you doing?" I asked. "And are you humming *What Child Is This?*"

"Humming?" She turned from the door and nodded at me. "I think the agent might be back." Then she looked down at the box and shuddered. "What is that?"

I raced up to her. "Hurry. Shove this in your purse." I whisper-hissed the order.

She slid her index finger over the box, and her nose wrinkled. "No. It's creepy."

The agent was definitely back and surely wearing heels, because I could hear the clickety-clack of them ascending the stairs. "It's not creepy and my purse is too small. C'mon. Hurry!"

She pulled her purse tight against her body and flashed wide eyes at me. "No way. You're gonna have to find room in yours."

"Such a brat, sometimes." I glared at her as I tried to shift my wallet and a pack of gum to fit the box in my tiny purse. It wasn't working. The agent was now at the front door, keys jangling in the lock. I took a deep breath and tucked the box inside my jacket, under my arm. Why did I assume she'd think I was stealing something? For all she'd know, whatever was in the box was something I'd brought with me. Right?

The woman opened the door to find my daughter and I with plastered grins on our faces, bodies pressed together side-by-side and clearly trying to hide something.

She cleared her throat. "Oh, good. You made it in okay."

Ashley kicked my ankle when I didn't respond. "Umm, yeah. Just like I remember it."

The agent gave me a "huh?" look.

"I mean, from the pictures. On the website. It...looks...like...you know...it does in pictures."

Ashley groaned beside me.

The agent folded her arms. "So, did you have any questions then?"

I linked arms with my daughter and drove us forward toward the door. "No. We're good. Thanks for your time. We'll be in touch." We zoomed past the bewildered lady and nearly broke our necks sliding down the icy front steps.

"Smooth," Ashley quipped, when we finally made it into my car.

I craned back to put the box in the back seat and then let out a deep sigh as I turned the key in the ignition. "Like butter."

WE STOOD opposite each other on the '70s-green carpet in our large but hopelessly outdated living room, staring at the box that lay on the floor between us. As confident as I'd been before, in the attic, that this...whatever it was...wanted me to take it—well. Now I was equally confident that opening it would be akin to unlocking Pandora's box.

I pointed at the thing. "You open it."

"Umm, no." Ashley's answer was definitive.

I squinted. "I'll give you five dollars if you open it."

She shook her head. "You could offer twenty and the answer would still be hell nah."

I scowled and cocked my head left to get a different perspective of it. "Too rich for my blood."

"I figured as much." My daughter backed away and dropped into a nearby love seat. "Just do it. Rip the top off like a band-aid. What's the worst thing that could be in there, really?"

I straightened my spine and cracked my knuckles. "Oh, let's see. A dead thing. Oh, crap. What if it's a dead mouse or something?" I mini dry-heaved. "Or like a hand or a finger or something? What if it's an old handkerchief from way back when and it has small pox spores on it or something and when I open the box, I let them out on the wind and start another epidemic?!"

Ashley rolled her eyes and made a noise that sounded like she tried to clear a one-pound loogie from her throat. "Why do you immediately go to death and dead things, drama queen? Maybe it's diamonds or old savings bonds or something."

I tapped a finger to my lips, considering. But no. Something told me there was nothing of monetary value in there.

"Oh, c'mon." Ashley prodded. "You wanted the stupid thing. Just open it! And why are you humming?"

"Humming?" I looked at her and she looked at me and my throat went dry. "Twenty-five dollars?"

"Open it!"

I shook the wiggins off and steeled my resolve. Crouching low, my hand hovered over the box for a second before I put my fingers around it and lifted the top. I tossed the box lid to the side and stood back up, pointing at the thing I'd revealed.

"Oh." My shoulders relaxed, and I felt like an idiot. "It's just an angel. Like a Christmas tree topper or something."

Ashley leaned tall over the arm of the love seat to look at it. She scrunched her nose. "A creepy Christmas tree something. And, look —you have the same hair color."

I scowled at her before bending down again to lift the porcelain-faced angel from the box—blonde doll hair, a thin golden wire of halo, a bright white gossamer dress, and tiny feathered wings. She looked brand new and antiqued at the same time, and she was lovely. Why had I been so anxious? It seemed foolish now, even with the strange promptings that had led me to her.

"She's beautiful. What are you talking about, 'creepy'?"

Ashley scratched her chin. "If she's so perfect and beautiful, why was she hidden away in an attic for who-knows-how-many years? Huh?"

I batted her comment away with my hand. "Psh. She's just a lost treasure. And I'm sticking her on the tree."

"Have fun with that."

"Have fun with that," I mocked. I stomped over to our tree, stretched up on my tiptoes to take down our yellow country star, and replaced it with the angel. "Ah, see? She looks great up there."

I did wonder, however, why grandma and grandpa never had this angel on their tree? Had it been hidden before they moved in the house? And if she didn't belong to them, why had I been so intent on going back there? To find something that didn't even have anything to do with my family? There had to be a reason...

Ashley, of course, was unconcerned about any of this. Without looking at the angel, she brushed past me and headed downstairs to her room. "You do you, Mom. Good night."

I TURNED ALL the lights in the house off, except for the tree lights. Curling up on the love seat nearby, I rested my chin on my fisted hand and stared at the newest addition to my Christmas tree. The colored lights cast disconcerting angles on the angel's face, making her look almost...sinister. More so than how Ashley claimed she naturally looked, anyhow.

Perhaps she was right. Perhaps I never saw this on the tree at Christmas Eve when I was a kid because Grandma hid the little porcelain thing in the attic for a reason. Logic and nostalgia fought inside me, and I knew the battle wouldn't be won by either side tonight. I yawned and looked away from the ornament—my eyes heavy with the desire to sleep. Mike would be home from his work trip Christmas morning. Only two days away. I'd sleep on my thoughts tonight and ask him his opinion of the angel when he got home.

"Don't kill us in our sleep just yet," I mumbled to my tree, snorting as I trudged past it. A small crackle made me jolt, and I spun in time to see the top half of my Christmas lights blink out. A chill wracked through me as my eyes panned up to the angel.

I couldn't tell if the room got colder, or if it was just my blood. I didn't move until I realized I'd stopped breathing and sucked in a breath. I shook my head, glancing down another hall to the front door. "It's nothing," I mumbled to myself. Still, I went the opposite direction of my bedroom to make sure the door was locked.

As I walked back, I stared up at the angel again—much harder to see now the lights were out. "Sorry," I said, shrugging. "Good night."

My brows furrowed, hard. I couldn't get them to relax. My mind seemed alert—so much so, I knew it was going to be hard to sleep. But, even alert, my thoughts were hard to pinpoint. I slipped under my covers, bringing all my sheets and blankets up to my neck. I never slept this way, but I wanted the extra cover tonight.

I closed my eyes and listened to the house. I heard the usual creaks and shudders—nothing out of the ordinary. Still, it seemed like hours until I could relax enough to fall asleep. Even then, nightmares plagued my REM cycle. Thoughts of shadows and small spaces raced through my sleepy mind. A baby cried somewhere unseen, and I suddenly wasn't sure if my dreams were my own. I woke with the urge to pee at one point, but I couldn't get out from under the security of my blankets. I wouldn't.

I squeezed my eyes shut, willing the world to go away completely so I could get even a few moments of good sleep.

"Ouch!" A sharp pain in my left foot made me jolt, and I tossed those blankets I relished aside in a flash. I squinted in the darkness to see something, anything, near my feet. *Did something bite me?* My eyes wouldn't adjust fast enough. I leaned back to grab my phone off my dresser, knocking over deodorant and lotion bottles and scattering cough drops.

I flicked on my flashlight and pointed it around the room. Nothing? I whipped my sheets around to make sure nothing was in them. My left heel throbbed. I leaned in to get a better look and there was nothing there. No bite marks, no inflammation, no color. I panned the light around my room one more time.

I threw my legs over the side of the bed, letting my feet dangle. The flashlight on my phone was still on, but it only spot-lighted small areas in the room and on the floor, where I flashed it. I lit up the light switch on the wall by the door, just a few steps away. Why did I think I'd feel something squirming beneath my feet if I hit the carpet?

My hands clenched and relaxed—clenched again. I twisted my neck to glare at Michael's side of the bed. "You would be out of town right now, wouldn't you?"

I closed my eyes, blew out a breath, and slid off the edge of my bed until my toes crumpled into the carpet, followed by my heels. When the whole of me weighed on my feet, I quick-stepped over to the light switch and flicked it on. My nerves calmed a bit. I cracked the bedroom door open next. Down the hall, I could see the multi-colored glow of Christmas lights on the walls.

I crept down the hall and peeked around the corner to the tree. All the lights were on again, all of them working. And the angel's head seemed to have twisted just enough to be looking directly at me. I rubbed my eyes, hard. Impossible.

"Ash got into my head, that's all." I mumbled. I thought about unplugging the tree lights, but that meant getting close to the tree. "All in my head," I told myself. "It's all in my head."

I was being ridiculous and sorting that out of my personality could wait until morning. Still, I locked the bedroom door before I crawled back into bed.

CHRISTMAS EVE MORNING, we always did the same thing—holiday baking extravaganza! The whole house cycled through the smells of cinnamon, vanilla, peppermints, fresh-baked breads and cookies. I played old Christmas movie soundtracks and we'd open all the blinds and curtains in the house—okay with the sun, but always hoping for snow. Between batches of whatever we were cooking, we'd sip hot chocolate, with candy cane stirrers.

Ashley drank her self-concocted libation slowly as she paced back and forth in front of the tree, staring at our new topper. "The eyes are following me."

"Oh, they are not," I said, with less conviction than I'd hoped to intone. After last night, I had doubts of my own.

The buzzer on the oven went off, and I flinched. I grabbed some hot pads and took out a sheet of snowball cookies. "Hey, you wanna help me roll these in powdered sugar when they cool?"

Ashley still paced, still gave the angel the stink eye. "Who do you think hid it in the attic? Great Grandma?"

I'd thought about that a lot last night. Or, I guess, very early this morning. "I don't know. And you didn't answer my question."

She finally came over to the kitchen island and placed her mug on the counter. "I didn't answer because you know, of course I'm going to help. I always do."

I pursed my lips and went on pooling the ingredients I'd need for our mini cranberry-orange bread loaves.

"Do you think they locked it up because it's haunted?"

I whipped around, knocking some measuring spoons to the floor, and winced at the clatter they made. "Haunted? Why do you think that?"

She narrowed her eyes at me. "Wow. Jumpy much?" When I didn't answer, she shrugged. "I didn't sleep well last night. Kept...I don't know. Hearing things. And I could have sworn something hit me in the foot."

I choked on my spit and lurched forward to turn on the faucet so I could drink some water, quick. Ashley was behind me in a flash, patting my back.

"Are you okay?"

I cleared my throat several times and wiped at my mouth with a paper towel. I turned to face her, shaking my head. "I had the same problem last night."

Her face paled at least one shade whiter.

I glanced over at the angel, no longer seeming angelic to me. "Maybe we should take her down."

The moment the last word left my mouth, my eyesight started to fade.

"Mom?"

The air felt heavy, like gravity was pressing its palms down on me, trying to squish me flat. I stumbled around the kitchen island toward my sectional. "I...I need to sit down."

"Mom!"

I swam in a sea of growing dark, thoughts fuzzy, sounds distant, and any desire to spring to action...gone. I heard my daughter's pleas, more like whispers or echoes in a dream. But when the world finally went black, an ear-piercing scream sliced hard through everything.

My body stiffened. I was like a corpse on the couch. My chest ached while my skin shivered. A pinpoint of light brightened, right at the top of my tree, and my heart dropped into my toes.

"Ashley?" I needed to know where she was.

When the room stayed black, except for the angel on the tree, I rolled off onto the floor and crawled closer to it.

"Mom, I can't see anything."

"Hold on. I'm coming to yo..."

BOOM!

"ASHHHHH-LEYYYYY!" Something nearby crashed but I didn't know what.

New panic seized me until my daughter gripped my hand, and I knew it was my girl, even though the room was still pitch black—

blinding. No amount of waiting would adjust our eyes to this darkness. Something flickered in front of us—silvery white. Something small and, at first, a blur. It fuzzed out and then winked in again—closer this time. Features manifested—young. Oh, so young.

My eyes filled with tears as a baby appeared in a long white gown, its eyes sullen, shadowed by dark circles, like it'd seen too much hard life for a soul so new. But...she, yes, she—she wasn't a new soul. She was an old one.

"What the hell is that?" Ashley's voice quivered, and I squeezed her hand tighter. I didn't know how to answer.

The baby flicked in and out of focus, each time getting closer and closer to us, until she was a mere foot away. Her mouth moved, but the sound was off track and incomprehensible. She floated down, trying to get eye level with me while I was still sprawled on my belly, flat against the floor.

I wanted to close my eyes, clench them shut forever, as her face got closer and closer, but I couldn't. Her lips turned into a snarl right before she screamed like a banshee straight from Hell.

My heart stopped at the same moment the lights came back on, and I immediately pulled on Ashley's hand, which I still held. Her face was whiter than fresh snow. We scrambled to sitting positions and pulled each other into a hug.

"Are you okay?"

"No." She eked out. She pulled away from me then, standing, and pointed at the angel still on the tree top. "Get rid of that thing. Now."

I clambered up to my feet, my joints aching something fierce, but ran to the tree as fast as my legs would carry me. I jumped up and grabbed the angel by one of its wings. I raced to the open back door Ashley held for me and flung the angel into the yard.

"Good riddance!" Ashley screamed.

But as we turned back to the tree, the angel was there again. All the lights on the tree started blinking. She was mocking us.

"Oh, I'm out." Shoeless, but managing to grab a coat, Ashley was through the front door faster than I could think.

"Crap." I sauntered sideways through the room, remembering to at least turn the oven off, and then I had my keys and my purse and we were out of there. The chill outside prickled along my skin and made me realize that my heart was, in fact, still beating. "Now what?"

"Should we call your dad?"

Ashley stared out the car window as we drove to my sister, April's, house. Every so often her arm would shudder, and it worried me.

She shrugged, despondent, and sighed. "He's probably traveling. What could he do? He can't be here to help with anything. Just wait until he gets home. Maybe by then..."

To see her like this broke my heart. I touched her shoulder, quieting the quiver there. "Okay. We'll wait."

When we got to April's house, we sat around her kitchen table and told her what had just happened.

She spit out her Honey-nut Cheerios. "You're kidding, right? C'mon. No way."

Ashley just nodded at her, wide-eyed.

I patted her hand guiltily. I'd brought that monstrosity into our house and subjected her to a horror no one should ever have to go through. I hoped she'd forgive me... "Do you remember anything weird happening at Grandma and Grandpa's house back in the day?"

April shrugged. "I mean, the attic was kind of creepy, but other than that, no."

"Wait. You remember the attic? Did you go into it?"

She shook her head violently. "No. Oh, no, no, no."

"Then how did you know it was creepy?"

She gave me her incredulous "huh" face. "The whispers? Surely you heard them as a kid. Didn't you? I mean, you used to hum that one song every time we were over there during the holidays."

I pinched the bridge of my nose. "No. I don't. What the heck. Did I block it out or something? And humming?" A thought clicked. "What Child Is This?"

Ashley visibly jerked at my response and I wanted to cloak her in bubble-wrap.

"That's the one." April stirred her spoon around her cereal bowl absent-mindedly for a second before looking up at me with a haunted look in her eyes. "As for the whispering, the word 'rest' comes to mind, but that's about it." She leaned back in her chair and sighed. "You know who you should talk to, right? Aunt Sam."

Whatever was happening to us, it needed to be resolved and quick. I pulled out my phone and scrolled through my contacts until I found Samantha May. "Do you mind keeping Ashley here until I get back?"

She nodded. "Of course."

"Oh." I turned back to her after gripping the doorknob. "I guess you probably ought to call our sisters and tell them that tonight's festivities are on hold until further notice."

There was no way I was hosting Christmas Eve dinner at my house tonight.

"Oh, honey." My Aunt Sam pulled me into a bear hug. "It's been too long." She pushed back to get a good look at me and squinted. "Why don't we ever get together?"

My mind blanked, as I didn't have a good reason why I never saw her. Or any of my dad's brothers and sisters. Our happy childhood holidays together had stopped once my grandpa passed away and Grandma had to start renting out the basement. Nobody had thought to pick up the mantle of "host" at the time, and so we started creating different traditions.

I shrugged. "It's sad. We totally need to."

"Agreed."

"Oh," I said, pulling out a bottle of Cran-Grape Martinelli's I'd borrowed from my sister's fridge and handing it to her. "Merry Christmas Eve."

"Ah. Thank you, sweetie." She led me inside and offered me a seat on the couch in her living room. "Do you want something to drink?" She shuffled off to the kitchen before letting me answer and returned with two steaming mugs. "Now, what can I help you with? You said you had some questions about Mom's old house?"

I tilted my head and grinned awkwardly at her, not sure how to start this conversation. "So, was Grandma and Grandpa's house...you know, ever haunted?" The blunt approach always worked.

She choked on the sip of tea she'd just taken. "Hm-hmm," she cleared her throat and set her cup down. "Haunted?" She closed her eyes and groaned as she, I could only assume, rifled through memories. "You know my mom always used to say, 'That's why you never look in an attic!'"

It was a phrase my grandma said often. My dad had said it all the time when we were growing up, before he died. Heck, I said it every now and then. But I always thought it meant something like, "don't get into other people's business" or "don't look for what you don't really want to see." It never occurred to me that she was being literal.

"Something weird happened on the first Christmas we spent in that house. I was only five at the time, so the details are fuzzy. Or non-existent." She rubbed at her temples. "And I'm old now, which certainly doesn't help. Although..." She stood without another word and disappeared into the hallway that led to her bedroom.

I tried to relax back into the comfy chair cushions, but every time I closed my eyes, I saw that devil angel's face sneering down at me. I grabbed my tea off the coffee table, my hand shaking under its slight weight. I steadied it with both hands and took a sip. The warm liquid running down my esophagus did nothing to abate the constant chills running up and down my spine.

I'd always believed in ghosts. At least, I thought I had. I was open to the possibility of them—even thought it'd be cool to see one someday. I was wrong. Now all I wanted was for someone to assure me that there was nothing at all supernatural in this world. That reality was normal, boring, mundane, run-of-the-mill and, above all else, safe.

Aunt Sam shuffled back into the room with a tattered book in her hand. "Mom kept a journal," she explained, holding the cover up to me. She sat back down and started ruffling through the pages until she stopped about a fourth of the way in.

She read, "There have always been whispers in this house, since the moment we moved in. On Christmas Eve, they got worse. It's coming from the attic, that vile, disturbing place. My husband called the bishop over to bless it, and that seems to have done the trick. Although, the children still seem to hear things. And hum... I must be diligent with them. Perhaps it will always be best to leave attics alone to keep their secrets."

She flipped through the following pages, scanning sentences. I leaned forward to get a look, though I couldn't comprehend a word of it upside down. My aunt paused to read a few pages and then started flipping again. When she paused a second time, she looked up at me afterward and shrugged. "The two following Christmases were happy ones, by all accounts. I don't remember anything weird happening. Whatever happened, I guess my dad really did take care of it that first year." My aunt shuddered before closing the journal and shrugged.

No. He didn't. He'd just masked the problem. There was more to this whole thing, but what? "Did he keep any journals, by chance?"

"No." She shook her head. "We asked Mom about it after he died, and she said he told her to just write it all down for the both of them. Why are you asking, anyhow? Did something happen? Did you go back to the house?"

I wasn't about to involve a seventy-five-year-old woman in this kind of mayhem, so I just shook my head and smiled. "Something my sister mentioned to me about memories of Christmas Eves at the grandparents' house when we were kids."

She settled back into the couch and sighed, smiling. "Ah, the good old days."

Yeah. Missed them already.

SEARCHING THE INTERNET WAS FUTILE…NOTHING of interest ever happened at my grandma's old house, apparently. I pieced together a list of other owners that had lived there over the years. Even tried to call a few of them, but numbers were old and disconnected or they just wouldn't answer. Could I blame them? It was a holiday, after all.

"Maybe the neighbors know something?" Ashley suggested.

I tapped my temple with my index finger. "Of course. I'm an idiot."

"I'm just pointing out that you said that. Not me." She snickered then grinned at me and I play-glared at her, secretly happy that she seemed better than she had been this morning.

"But, seriously. It's an old neighborhood. Some of the same families have lived in their same houses for years—just passing it on down the line." I closed my eyes, trying to remember the last name of the neighbor to the south. "I think there's some people across the street that have been there forever, and then maybe one family next door. Yes!" I snapped and Ashley startled. "The O'Briens. Their daughter still lives in the house. I should go talk to her."

"Now?"

I grabbed my keys from a nearby desk. "Unless you want to permanently move into Aunt April's basement? Yes. Now."

I raided my sister's kitchen again, throwing some white-chocolate dipped Oreos on a paper plate and covering it with foil and a red bow. Couldn't show up to the neighbor's house empty handed.

"Hey, Ash," I said, stopping at the top of the stairs before I left. "I know you didn't want to involve Dad yet, but in case he heads home early, maybe you should call him and tell him to come to April's house first?"

"Good idea. And good luck. I hope whoever you're going to see can help." She waved crossed fingers at me and flashed a sad grin.

"I'll be back."

I DETOURED BACK to my house before I tried Grandma's old neighbor. Sitting in my driveway, I watched lights flicker on and off behind tempered glass doors and shaded windows. Why was this happening to us? Why now? My fingernails bit into my palms, and I screamed bloody murder inside my car.

"Why are you doing this to me!?"

Why?! Nostalgia had brought me back to that house. Good memories—*good* ones. This didn't make sense. I'd taken that box, hopeful it was something from my family's past and that by setting it on the top of my tree, I'd be honoring my loved ones who'd passed on. Instead, I'd created a nightmare inside my own home.

I flipped my car into reverse, flying backwards onto the street and bottoming out a little in the gutter. "Son of a..."

It took everything in me not to do fifty in a twenty-five zone as I raced out of my neighborhood and to the city next door. I hated imposing on this family on Christmas Eve. Hated it. But I didn't know what else to do. Letting this problem linger wasn't a good idea. I didn't even know anyone else who could help me—not with a ghost.

And I wasn't about to put anyone else in danger.

I scowled at my grandma's old house as I drove past it and stopped in front of the O'Brien's. Dragging my feet up their front steps, I let out a long breath before I knocked on the door. A striking, tall woman answered, one I recognized from the people who'd come through the line at my dad's funeral the year before.

"Hi," I greeted awkwardly, jutting the plate of cookies forward. "Happy Holidays. And I'm so sorry to bother you."

She smiled at me, taking the cookies and ushering me inside. "I recognize you. One of Jack's daughters, right?"

"Right." I shivered in my coat as I stepped inside, gazing around at the cozy décor in her family room and at her beautiful Christmas tree—free of menacing angels. "I know I'm imposing." I stopped to clear my throat and thumbed in the direction of my grandparent's house. "I stopped by the old house the other day and…"

My throat got dry and my eyes started to water. Everything had been so surreal from the moment I opened that box, and now I was just so desperate to close it all down forever.

Mrs. O'Brien grasped me around the shoulders and helped me toward her couch. "Oh, my dear. Is everything okay?"

What did I say to her? I couldn't even find the words. I plopped down onto her couch, trying hard not to sob like a crazy person. I closed my eyes and tried to focus on the music in the room—a Christmas song—but my mind wouldn't let me. When I finally opened my eyes, I found her sitting opposite me with a curious but affable look on her face.

"I found an angel in the attic," I blurted out.

Her forehead creased. "Next door?"

I nodded.

"I see." She rubbed her hands together for a long minute before looking up at me again. "I'd heard stories when I was a kid. I mean, I grew up with your dad and his siblings when they lived in that house. Nothing bad ever really happened. Still…"

"The angel," I whispered. "It's at my house."

Her chest heaved inward as she was visibly terrified for me. "The rumors said that the man and woman who first lived in that house… Well, he wasn't a nice man. The woman got pregnant, but around the time she should have given birth…she didn't. They told everyone it was a fluke, that it never really happened." She paused to gaze out the window, even though the curtains were drawn. "That winter, everyone said that the Mrs. could be seen carrying a porcelain-faced angel in her arms, swaddled like a baby. She wandered up and down the street, even in a snowstorm, carrying that thing around with her and sobbing. And then after Christmas, she died suddenly and her husband disappeared. The house was vacant for about a year after that."

"Oh my gosh, that's awful. But..." I pulled my phone out of my purse. "I searched all over the internet for info on that place. Why wasn't something like that in the archives or the papers?"

Mrs. O'Brien looked at the ceiling and shook her head. "Oh, people back then didn't report stories like that. Besides, I think the neighbors were just happy to get rid of them. They said they could finally rest."

Rest.

The Christmas song in the room came into sharp focus then.

What Child Is This
Who Came to Rest
On Mary's Lap
Is Sleeping...

"Do you know the woman's name?"
She tapped her lip. "Mary Angeles. Huh."
"What?"
"She even had 'angel' in her name."

I THANKED Mrs. O'Brien profusely before I left. A sense of calm came over me as I started my car and sat there, letting the engine warm up. I searched the internet again, this time for the mother's name, and smiled as something relevant finally popped up. According to Find a Grave, a woman with that name was buried in the Ogden City Cemetery. The dates sounded about right, too—she died in 1922 at the age of twenty-three. So sad.

I drove home in a haze—my phone silenced and the radio off.

The hum of the road and passing traffic lulled me into a quiet determination to take care of the problem tonight. It didn't matter how long it took, or how the hours passed, or if it'd be Christmas morning before I was done.

I parked in my driveway, got out, and walked slowly to my front door. There was a blue sticky note tacked up to it with my husband's handwriting scrawled across it: *My key didn't work in the lock? Headed to your sister's house, per our daughter. Call me. Why is your phone off?*

I pulled it down, crumpling it in my left hand and reaching for the doorknob with my right—but the door squeaked open slowly on its own.

Lights still flickered, which was preferable to the blinding blackness, but it still unnerved me. I dragged in a shaky breath before stepping inside. I took a few steps down the hall and heard the front door click closed behind me. The unmistakable turn of the dead-bolt made my blood turn cold. I wasn't one to do a lot of praying, but I pleaded silently with God.

The angel lorded over me at the top of our tree.

"We need to talk," I said.

Its head twisted sharply to face me—the black-painted expression twisted into something I wouldn't want my worst enemy to see. A silvery figure flickered near the bottom of the tree and I decided, yes, I was insane.

As I got closer to the tree, it became harder to walk. Something pushed back. I reached out to touch the tree, but a zing of electricity coursed through my fingers, up my arm, and into my spine when I brushed against a branch.

I jolted back and crumpled to the floor. The room started going pitch again. "No, please!" I pleaded. "I want to help you."

The temperature in the room dropped and my teeth chattered, hard. I couldn't get them to stop. Panic ruled the room, and my body functions started to shut down the blacker the room got. My lungs burned...

"I know where your mom is!" I choked out with the very last of my breath.

In a blink, the room was normal again. My memory of normal, anyhow. I gasped for air, clutching my chest and coughing. When I looked up, the ghostly image of a baby floated in front of me—though the anger from her face had melted away into...expectancy.

"I can take you to her," I said. Her eyes narrowed, distrusting, so I offered her my hand. "I promise."

She reached out her tiny fingers until they brushed against mine, like ice on ice. The ghostly infant disappeared. The moment she drew away, the angel fell from the tree, shattering as it hit the floor, and the room was engulfed in a blinding white light. I gasped. Scattered in the porcelain shards were the delicate bones of a newborn baby.

Horrified and heartbroken, I cried for this poor child. Had her father done this to her? How long had she been entombed in her porcelain prison? It didn't matter. Not now. I knew what I had to do. Fear turned to resolve. I retrieved the black box she'd been hidden in for too many years. I pulled the fragments toward me and gently placed the fragile bones among the angel pieces inside the little box. *Rest little one.* I replaced the lid and tied it closed with a beautiful Christmas ribbon.

I drove to the cemetery in the middle of the night—the sky dark and clear and speckled with stars. No trespassing there after dusk, but I didn't care. My task was too important. I parked across the street in the neighborhood to the south and walked into the cemetery.

Mary's grave, surprisingly, wasn't hard to find. I used the flashlight on my phone to highlight it once I'd found it, just to make sure, and noticed that the time was just two minutes past midnight.

I laid the box in front of her headstone. Snowflakes poured from the sky, just over us and nowhere else, collecting on the box like frozen tears. "Merry Christmas."

I hummed their song and as I did, an icy blue light etched

something on the headstone below Mary's name—"Loving mother to Noelle Angeles."

Whom Angels Greet with Anthem's Sweet...

The verse rang out along with the joyous laughter of a mother and daughter reunited. I stepped back as the whole thing glowed that icy blue and the box and all its contents absorbed into the ground.

I'D TAKEN my family back home sometime around two a.m., and we managed to get a few hours of sleep. We woke up later Christmas morning and stumbled into the family room to gather around the tree, bleary-eyed and still in our PJs.

"Presents or pancakes first?" my husband asked us.

"Pancakes," Ashley and I said in unison.

"I'm not going to have to make extra for creepy angels, am I?"

I threw a couch pillow at him. "Funny."

As Mike stumbled off into the kitchen to start breakfast, Ashley pulled me down next to her on the love seat. "Noelle apologized and wanted me to tell you, 'thanks'," she whispered to me.

"She did?"

"Yeah."

I pulled her closer, and she rested her head on my shoulder. "How did...?"

"In a dream. She thought she should explain—you know. Daughter to daughter."

"Makes sense. But, explain what?"

Ashley pulled the handle on the side of the loveseat so the footrest would pop out. She tapped her fuzzy-slippered feet together and yawned. "She's been trying to get the attention of someone with an emotional connection to that house so they would find her and help her."

"She could have just asked."

"No one ever listened, apparently."

Something about unintelligible whispers flitted through my mind.

"She figured terror would do the trick."

I snorted. "Well, she was right about that."

"Anyhow, she's at rest now. Finally. And she's thankful."

Good. I hugged my daughter tighter, thankful myself that I had her in my life. Christmas brought miracles in all shapes and forms and experiences and all I could be was happy that this encounter ended in a good way. Even if it did involve a ghost.

"Merry Christmas, babe."

"Merry Christmas, Mom."

GHOST TRAIN

BY JOHN M. OLSEN

Snow flurries built up on the road, promising a good storm just in time for a white Christmas. The headlights of Jerry's four-wheel-drive pickup lit up the road and coaxed sparkles from the blowing snow. He had chains in the back if it got too bad, but it would slow him down a lot if it came to that. He'd be home long before the full storm settled in to dump its load on the countryside, he was sure.

The smell of his burger and fries lingered in the truck cab as he glanced in the rear-view mirror at the truck bed. The old bed cover protected the wrapped boxes from his emergency shopping trip, keeping everything dry and safe. This Christmas would be great. He could already envision JJ and Molly stampeding down the stairs in the morning to feast their eyes upon what had appeared overnight under the tree. The local stores had sold out of JJ's special request, a starship model from the latest movie. Jerry had been blessed to find it within driving distance on Christmas Eve. Shannon had sent him on his way with a long kiss and a warning to drive safely before fixing dinner for the kids.

The deserted two-lane road snaked its way through the hills and backwoods of Kentucky just north of the Tennessee border. Falling snow turned the scene into a nighttime wonderland of white, while all the sane people sat wrapped in blankets in their warm homes. According to the map on his phone, the unfamiliar route would get him home more than an hour sooner than taking the big highway that took the long way around the hills, running much farther to the north.

Uncaring radio static took turns with the sound of a mournful steel guitar and lyrics about lost love.

Jerry checked his watch, an old wind-up he inherited from his father. Eleven PM. Picking up the last-minute presents had been the easy part. He'd spent an hour hunting down an open gas station before finally getting on his way home.

Headlights shone in the distance from the right side of the road, but off the shoulder. He slowed, but the lights didn't move. He muttered to himself. "Probably got bald tires and a death wish, being out here tonight." He slowed and pulled over to park with his lights shining on the car. Inside, two people huddled together with wide eyes.

"Hah. Nailed it in one." Jerry got out and walked up to the driver window and motioned for him to roll it down.

The driver hit a button to lower his window and reached a timid hand out as if reluctant to make contact.

Always one to show good Southern manners, Jerry grabbed the driver's hand and shook it, feeling the warmth of the embrace. The man twitched, but then let out a breath. "Been stuck here for a while. Any chance you can give us a tug out of the ditch?"

Jerry wanted to spend the night with his wife and kids, but his father always taught him to help others when he could. You never knew when fate would turn around and you would be the one needing help. "Let me put my chains on and get a tow rope. We'll have you out in no time."

The woman in the passenger seat sat in silence and stared, huddled in a puffy parka. Spinning out in the dark on a deserted road was never fun. She was likely still in shock from the accident. The driver got out and helped Jerry set things up, then climbed back into his car to steer when it came time to pull.

Soon, the car was back on the blacktop, now dusted with a light layer of powdery snow. "Be careful now. You going far?"

"Going back the way we came. We'll try again in the morning when the sun is up. Not safe out here."

Jerry put away his chains and towrope. With a shrug, he shook the snow from his coat and climbed back into his truck. Good deed done for the night, he resumed his trip, singing along with the radio when he could recognize the bits of song. The bends and dips in the road kept him alert.

Coming around a bend, a shape appeared to the side of the road, partially obscured by the falling snow. Closer, it resolved into a young woman. Jerry eased his foot onto the brakes to avoid sliding as he came to a stop just past the woman. It was a night for the record books. Didn't these people have places to be on Christmas Eve?

He rolled down his passenger window and called out as the woman approached. "Need help getting somewhere?" Even up close, he couldn't tell her exact age in the dark. Maybe eighteen. Maybe early twenties. Not who he expected on the side of a road out in the hills so far from any town.

Her hair hung straight in wet tangles, and she wore a heavy wrap of some sort over a coat. The misery of her situation was almost thick enough to scoop up like the gathering snow. "I can make it on my own."

Great. A martyr. Jerry got out, walked around to the passenger side of his truck and opened the door. "Really? There's nothing nearby, and you'll freeze out here. Hop in and I'll get you somewhere dry and warm for the night."

She eyed him for a moment, relief clear on her face, and then slid into the seat. Frosty air swirled past, giving him gooseflesh on his arms and neck as he shivered.

He shut the passenger door and made his way back around to climb in and get underway. The truck was an old tank held together with bailing wire and hope, but at least the engine and heater were in great shape. He dialed up the temperature another notch to make up for having lost all the warm air through the open doors.

"I'm Jerry. What's your name?"

"Crystal, after my grandmother."

"Lots of family tradition like that 'round here. Nice to meet you, Crystal. Got family nearby?"

"Yeah, I've got a wonderful family near here." She held her hands near the air vent, which suddenly seemed to blow nothing but cold air.

Jake turned the heater up to high.

Crystal spread her fingers in the blowing air and smiled.

The truck cab remained cold. If not for her response, he would think the heater had gone out. Something to check after Christmas. Right. He still had important things to do *before* Christmas morning once he got home.

"So, are you headed home for the holidays, Crystal?"

She turned to look out the window. "Yes."

Finding her to be not much of a conversationalist, he probed a little deeper. "I'm headed home with the last-minute toys for the kids. I love the excitement, the music, decorating the tree, nativities. All of it. We sang all the usual hymns in church on Sunday. At home, we have a dozen different nativities set up, including one for the kids made of Playmobil people so they can't break it. Do you have any Christmas traditions?"

"No, I don't do anything at all for Christmas."

Not wanting to press what seemed like a delicate area, Jerry changed subjects. "How did you end up on the side of the road clear out here? Someone had to have dropped you off." There was no way she'd walked there from the nearest town in such nasty weather.

"The others wanted to take me all the way to the train station for its midnight stop."

She let the implications hang in the air rather than fill in details. At least he seemed to be getting somewhere. Someone had brought her part way to where she needed to go. Had it been the people in the stranded car? "A train, you say? How far are you going?"

When she didn't answer immediately, Jerry shut his mouth to keep from filling the silence with his own rambling.

Finally, she said, "I don't know exactly how far it is. I might not recognize the turn in this snow." She clenched her jaw and turned to watch the view out the side window.

"Too bad we've been cursed with this awful weather, isn't it?"

She turned to face Jerry, her wet hair swinging with the movement. "I'm not cursed. That's all just folk tales." Her intense gaze bored into him when he glanced to look her in the eye.

Jerry wasn't sure what to make of her. She seemed spacy, but she spoke clearly and had a strange intensity about her. Her answers were confusing. Maybe she was a drug addict crashing after a high. Some people ran through rough patches. He'd learned to not be too critical of others, lest others judge him unfairly in return. His father had insisted on him attending church every week growing up, and the sermons had given him a solid moral core despite his occasional backsliding into sin.

At some point, the radio had gone from intermittent music to straight static. Jerry turned it down so he could still tell if the signal returned. To the side of the road stood a sign with distances to several destinations. "Anything look familiar?"

She pointed at the sign. "It'll be fine if you get me to the Blue Creek station after midnight. I don't want to inconvenience you."

Jerry wondered at her mental state, probably impaired by drugs. First, she didn't seem to remember things very well. Then there was her apathy about being late, mixed with her confusing intensity. Was it important to make her train at midnight, or not? Snow had stuck to the road sign, but one entry starting with 'Blue' was ten miles off the highway to the north at the next intersection. He couldn't read the full name, but it said something about a historic site. It was the only thing that fit, and it was close.

The trouble with taking a new route was that he didn't know all the towns and tourist traps along this highway like he did the ones near home.

"I can get you there. So, the train stops in Blue Creek? At midnight?"

"Yes, it stops at midnight." At least he'd gotten her to confirm that bit of information.

He pulled onto a rural road, barely better than a dirt track, but the truck was a trooper and carried them through two inches of accumulated snow without major complaint. The flakes had gathered strength. "Sign said ten miles. That's about a half hour at this speed. Looks like I can get you there before midnight. Isn't that an odd time for a train?"

Wondering if she thought he always babbled like that, he stopped talking to see if she would join in and say something. Anything.

"It's a special stop. It's all arranged."

Finally, she spoke more than just one short sentence again. Granted, it was two short sentences, and it sounded like a guilt trip to get him there on time, but it was conversation. Despite the feeling that he made some headway reaching her with conversation, they dropped into silence for several minutes.

Up to this point, she had only answered his direct questions. He tried again. "Should be close, now. Do you see the town yet, Crystal?"

"I can see it up ahead," she said, pointing off a bit to the left. Again, her eyes bored into him when he glanced her way, like she wanted to tell him more.

It took another two hills before Jerry made out the shadowy forms of buildings in the distance. There was no way she could have seen the town when he asked her about it. He checked his wristwatch, then wanting to verify it was accurate, pulled out his phone. The screen was dead, and he'd forgotten his charging cord. "Fifteen minutes to spare, looks like. Mind if I look at your train ticket?"

Jerry reached a hand out, palm up. The truck hit a bump, and his hand brushed where hers had rested on the seat between them moments before. With a rush of frigid air, the temperature dropped in the truck's cab. The faint static on the radio turned into an unpleasant squawk, and he saw a flash of what looked like a blizzard outside. Pulling his hand back and looking forward, the snow returned to its heavy flurries carried by a light breeze.

Her glare was the only answer she gave.

Jerry pulled into a town square surrounded by dark buildings, as if the power were out to the tiny village. Across the far side of the square rested the train station with an office out front and tracks running behind. He breathed a sigh of relief that things seemed to be going according to plan. Soon he would drop her off and be back on his way, leaving Crazy Town and Addict Girl behind him.

"Want me to drive straight to the station and park in front?"

Crystal grimaced. "No, not yet."

"Fine. We can wait here for a bit and watch for the train. Looks like the snow is forming drifts over there, anyway." It would be nothing for the truck to plow through the gathering snow, but he didn't want Crystal to think him rude.

He pulled to a stop across the square where they sat in silence. The homes on his side of the square seemed run down. The limited light of his headlights gave them the look of partially collapsed old derelicts. Still no lights shone anywhere in the rest of the town as snowflakes swirled and twinkled in his headlights. Crystal leaned forward, staring intently at the station.

Noting the lack of lights, Jerry said, "The train station looks closed. Have you got your ticket ready?"

"Yes, of course." Looking to the side, she tapped her chin with a closed hand. Her ticket, maybe?

Rather than argue with Crystal and her weird responses, he opened his door and stepped into the snow. "Would you like me to walk over there with you to make sure you're on the train before I head home?" He walked around the truck and opened her door to let her step down to the snow.

"I can do this on my own." She waved a hand toward the station. "I want you to go."

"Don't be silly. After coming this far, it would be ungentlemanly of me to leave you on your own. Just think what would happen if the train doesn't show."

She smiled as they walked to the station, skirted around the dark building, and out to the large platform behind with him leading the way. Rather than stopping on the platform, she stepped off the platform and led him a few steps out into the snow beyond.

Under the snow, Jerry saw the long straight lumps of the railroad tracks. Looking back toward his truck, he saw his boot tracks in the snow.

Crystal reached out her hand to him in a quick lurch, and he instinctively reached to make sure she didn't fall in the snow.

Cold whipped across his exposed hands and face. Visions of a blizzard flashed before his eyes, and two vague forms stood not too far away beside the train station in what looked like flickering red lantern light.

Words formed in the whipping air, seeming to arise out of the noise of the wind itself. "The train won't make it in this storm."

Another voice joined the first. "Of course, it will. As soon as I see it, I'll set out the lantern so it knows to stop."

Jerry clapped his hands together to rub them for warmth, and the storm returned to gentle flakes on a light breeze. The forms near the station house faded to ordinary shadows. His numb fingers showed early signs of frostbite, a surprise in weather that was barely below freezing. Had he even touched her hand? He didn't recall feeling anything but the cold when he'd reached out to prevent her fall.

She stood beside him with a hand still stretched out toward him. Around her, the snow gathered in a pristine sheet. No footprints. Looking back toward the square, he saw only his own prints in the snow.

He glanced at his watch, then back to her. Three minutes to midnight. Over the whole time with her, he'd never touched her, and she'd let him open the truck door every time for her. She wasn't drug-addled, she was dead. A ghost.

He considered his next question with care. There were too many things he didn't know. Where had the voices come from? Who was she? Why was he really here? Finally, he settled on what he hoped would give him the most information. "Who are they?" Jerry waved toward the shadows near the train station where the forms had appeared.

"They're nobody. They're not important."

Of all the places he could be on Christmas Eve, talking in circles with a ghost in the middle of a growing snowstorm was not part of the plan. He shivered, and not entirely from the cold as gooseflesh rose once again all up and down his arms, also reaching up to prickle at his neck. Whatever she could do to him, she had probably already done. Getting him here. Was that a good thing or a bad thing? When his hand met her insubstantial form, he'd felt a blast of cold and had seen visions of a blizzard. He was still alive and leaving footprints, and she had done nothing to hurt him aside from the intense cold. Maybe he would still make it home tonight. Talking with her had worked, at least somewhat. "Is this like a train to the afterlife? Can't you just go toward the light or something?"

"I was ready for the light, but chose to stay of my own free will. Now it's time for me to *go on the train*." She drew out the last words in a pleading wail as if trying to share something beyond the words, and failing.

The faint sound of a three-pitched horn sounded in the distance from the far side of a hill. The ghost train was coming.

Crystal reached out her arms to enfold him as she stared toward the train office rather than the approaching train. No, not toward the office. Toward the shimmering forms.

As her insubstantial arms reached around to embrace him, the storm grew and spat sleet in a strong wind. The forms near the station became clearer than before as cold seeped into his bones. His movements and thoughts grew sluggish. There was something he was supposed to do. Something to see. Somewhere he had to be. He looked down at the train tracks accumulating snow beneath his feet as his mind numbed.

From near the station, he heard a distant voice cutting through his fading awareness and desire to rest. "There it is. We'd better get the lantern out. They'll never see us in this storm without it."

The smaller shadow reached for a pole with a lantern on the end and stepped toward the tracks, but slipped on the edge of the platform. The pole fell and the lantern hit the snow. The red light vanished with the sound of breaking glass.

Like crinkling paper, the voices reached through his mental haze as the forms gained clarity in the increasing phantom storm. "You did that on purpose."

"Did not!" The form shook its head as long hair whipped in the storm. A girl.

The other, wearing an overcoat and a bowler hat, pointed a finger. "Liar! You always lie. That's why we're sending you away."

Jerry wondered sluggishly at their comments as his will to move, or even reply, faded. The cold spread from his arms to his chest. He shivered as his eyelids drooped, and thoughts of sleep strove to take control. He forced his eyes open only to find her eyes locked on him.

A train horn blared its call across the night. Its bright headlight glinted off the snow as the train appeared from the trees at the edge of the abandoned town. The ghost train thrust the snow to either side in a billowing cloud as it approached.

Something important lurked in the back of his tired thoughts. Something about family. Somewhere to be. Then something about tracks in the snow. Too many thoughts at once. The urgency of his thoughts rose, pulling him from the grasp of slumber. His fingers twitched, and his arms followed suit with a shiver. He realized Crystal had never touched him. Could never touch him. She wasn't holding him at all. She was nothing but a wraith in the night, granting him the ability to see other ghostly forms searching for a lantern in the snow. He could move if he wanted to. Did he want to?

The voices had said something about a liar. Had she lied to him?

What if everything she said was a lie? The urgency in the back of his mind grew, and his head rose from his chest again where it had rested for an instant. The train approached, its horn screeching in a solid wailing cry.

It was the horn of the ghost train. Or a lie. Had she said a single thing to him that was true? The effort to think back to what she had said was too much. True or false, the words spun in a muddled mess inside his head.

The male form searched through the snow, and stood, triumphantly holding a pole with a darkened lantern on its end. The female form with wispy hair embraced him, wrapping her arms around him and the pole he held. The male form struggled to free himself while keeping hold of the pole and its darkened lantern, but the companion of the male figure held him in a tight embrace just as Crystal held Jerry farther down the tracks.

Pooling all his will, Jerry twitched once more, then with a supreme effort he lurched away from Crystal to stumble off the far side of the tracks away from the station platform. He tripped over a rail buried in the snow and fell to his hands and knees on the sloped ground beyond the tracks. Moments later, the train raced by, blasting him with wind, snow, and flecks of ice that stung his face and hands.

The steel wheels of the train click-clacked as ore cars from West Virginia coal country rushed past. Jerry sat up as the end of the train flashed by, then receded into the distance. The smell of the diesel engines lingered even after the train vanished around its next turn.

The stringy-haired girl still stood on the now-cleared tracks, arms stretched out toward him.

Jerry didn't know whether his anger or his fear would win as his words tumbled out. "Crystal. Whoever you are. That wasn't a ghost train, it was real. I tried to help you, and you tried to kill me. Have you been lying to me?"

Crystal folded her arms and raised her head, indignation glowing in her expression. "I never lie. I was a perfect saint when I was alive." Her form became less substantial with each word.

Was it more lies? Was she trying to tell him something, or had she only wanted to kill him like the other ghostly girl had killed both her companion and herself? Was that other image an echo from Crystal's past? If he asked the right questions, he might find the truth. But what was more important; the truth, or finding a way to send the ghost to its next step in the afterlife?

His Good Samaritan nature won out. Lowering his voice to a whisper, he said, "Is there a way I can free you from this curse?" Jerry tilted his head toward where the other images had stood on the tracks.

"Yes, Jerry. Come back next Christmas Eve and I'll show you." She raised her head in a cackling laugh and faded into the swirling snow, now falling in earnest. In moments, no sign of her remained.

From farther down the tracks, a wisp of wind carried one last word that faded into the storm. "Liar!"

The night went still and dark as it only could during a snowstorm at midnight. Jerry stumbled back to his truck, swearing to himself to never drive that stretch of highway again.

A Bloody Merry Christmas

by Mark Minson

Germaine Crabtree stared into the flames flickering in the fireplace. Despite the efficiency of the furnace, he still liked a good fire on stormy nights. Born in the south, pretty mountains and a prettier face brought him north after college. Eleven years had barely dimmed his accent and only increased his love of the scenery. The snow fell wonderfully thick beyond his windows. It blocked out the neighbor's gaudy, blaring Christmas display across the street which, despite the one hundred yards between their houses, illuminated his living room on clear nights. Thank goodness for snow. Only two more days and Christmas would be over. Another week and the horrid lights would go back into storage until next Thanksgiving. Germaine had stopped bothering with a tree or decorations when he realized nobody else saw them. Not worth the effort.

The wood crackled, and the heat pushed past Germaine to the edges of the living room. Since it doubled as his office, it had to be the largest room in the house but still felt crowded with just his recliner, desk, and end table. No need for space when you lived by yourself. He loved the coziness of his home and the years spent telecommuting helped him control his interactions with people. There had been no need for contact with the outside during the holidays since that unfortunate one seven years ago with her.

He let himself slouch further down in his reclining wingback chair. The salesman at the custom furniture store had raised his eyebrows as he looked down his nose when Germaine ordered it. Like he was desecrating the wingback by wanting it to recline. Let the snob be judgmental. Germaine loved it.

Germaine's husky, Grant, *ruffed* and then sprang up. The dog's ears laid back against his head for a moment before he jumped at the window looking into the backyard, barking like a feral beast.

"Grant! Knock it off! Get over here. Nothin's out there during this storm."

The dog continued to bark like he was possessed.

"Stupid dog," Germaine muttered. "Grant! Come! Now!"

Grant paused. His body remained tense, ears flattened, and eyes fixed on the window as he took two steps back. Then he lunged forward and continued barking. What had gotten into that dog? He'd never disobeyed the second command. Even when he had cornered that squirrel last fall, he'd obeyed the command to "Come."

"Grant!" Germaine yelled, hauling himself from his chair. "Shut up, you dumb mutt!" Germaine didn't even glance out the window as he pulled the curtains closed. He hated closing the curtains on the winter outside. But if that would calm Grant down then so be it. He'd open them again in the morning.

Grant backed away from the window again, still growling.

A shiver ran down Germaine's spine. He wiped his suddenly clammy hands on his shirt. Germaine crossed the room, fishing his keys from his pocket. He unlocked the top drawer of his wooden work desk. He pulled out the handgun he had bought to protect Grant as a puppy from the coyotes that came around when they'd first moved here. He had only had to use it twice before his property was surrounded by other homes that kept them away.

Germaine shook his head as he returned to the window. The dumb dog was getting to him. It had been years since he'd even seen a coyote. The harsh winter might have driven a carnivore down into the valley far enough to reach his house, but it would need to travel across acres of land owned by farmers with perfectly edible animals. He had bought the six acres for privacy. Grant had cleared out any prey animals in the first few years.

"Look, Grant. Nothin's out there." Germaine pulled the curtain back. Staring up at him through the window was a wide-eyed child.

Germaine shrieked like a little girl. He pulled the trigger as he stumbled backward, wood splinters bouncing off his bare foot. He hit his chair and fell to the floor. Germaine lay there panting and shaking. His left side hurt from hitting the hardwood. He dropped the gun. He'd almost shot his own foot. How would he have explained that at the hospital? What good would he be to help the child if the bullet had hit him? The girl in a nightgown. Out in a snowstorm. Germaine jumped up. Ouch. He stumbled on wobbly legs to the window.

He couldn't see the girl anywhere through the falling snow. Grant sat calmly on the floor. "Stupid dog." Germaine rushed to the back door. He smashed his feet into his boots. Grabbing his coat from the hook on the wall, he unlocked the deadbolt. Pushing his right arm into the sleeve, Germaine stepped out onto the back porch. The night and the snow hid everything. He stepped off the porch and the motion-detecting light flicked on, illuminating the frozen scene. The cold bit his hands and face.

"Little girl! Little girl!" He zipped up his coat. The snow coated his hair. It landed on his eyelashes, forcing him to blink and put a hand above his eyes to see better. "Little girl!" He stomped through the two feet of snow toward the back window. "Little girl!" No answer.

Visibility didn't extend to the edge of the light. He saw no one. She probably ran away after hearing the gun go off. Good grief. Scared and alone out in this cold. And him being so jumpy. Dang dog. Germaine growled at himself. He looked for a trail so he could track the girl down. Nothing. She had stood right there! But the snow lay in a pristine sheet like unbroken frosting on a cake. He shivered again, attributing it to the cold, before stomping back to the house. If she wasn't going to stick around, he couldn't do anything for her.

He shut and locked the door, hung up his coat, and turned around. The girl stood in the hallway before him.

"Aaah!" he screamed, falling back against the door. It took a moment for him to breathe again. He may have peed a little. Living alone must be affecting him more than he thought. "What on earth were you doing outside in this weather?" he demanded.

Her wide-eyed stare never left his face. "Why?"

"That's not an answer. Why is what I'm askin' you. You could die of hypothermia out in a storm like that with only a nightgown on!"

Her sad, penetrating gaze sent a shiver up his spine. "Why?" she asked again.

He looked closely at her. Her brown curly hair reminded him of Dierdra. He generally only thought of Dierdra at Christmas, but until tonight, he'd avoided thinking of her at all this year. "Why what?" he practically shouted. He took a deep breath. "Look, come in by the fire and get warm. You can dry off, and I'll call your parents to come get you."

He stepped closer to her. Her hair and clothes were dry. Mostly. Something wet dripped down the side of her head. He flicked on the light. Good lord! Blood! "You stay right there. I'll get a washcloth. Maybe sit down!" He rushed past her and turned into the kitchen. How did she get to his house with that kind of injury? He ripped the towel off the stove handle and ran back to the hall. The girl was gone.

The back door was still locked. He rushed to his front door. The deadbolt was locked from the inside. Germaine's heart beat like a runaway train. "Grant!" Nothing. Where was that dog? The living room was empty save for the gun on the floor. Germaine quickly returned it to the desk. He didn't want to shoot himself for real, and movies told him it wouldn't do any good against whatever that little girl was. He should just get rid of the thing based on his apparent incompetence with it. No Grant in the living room. He rushed back to the kitchen. Nothing. The silence in the house pounded against his ears.

Germaine crept down the hall toward the guest bedroom, turning on lights as he went. The doorknob was cold to his sweaty palm. With a deep, stuttered breath, he flung open the door and flipped on the light. Just an empty room. He left the light on. Light scared ghosts and demons, right?

He checked the bathroom, laundry, and finally his bedroom. All empty. Where was Grant? Did the girl take him to be sacrificed? As he turned to leave his bedroom, he heard a soft whimper. He got down on his knees and looked under the bed. Grant lay pressed up against the wall.

"Oh, sure. The big protector when you think the evil can't get in the house, but as soon as she comes inside you turn into a chicken. Come on out. She's gone. The devil girl, or whatever she is, is gone. Come on out."

"Why?"

Germaine jumped, spinning onto his bed. The girl stood in the doorway to his room. "Dang it, girl! I don't know the answer! Leave me and my dog alone! Are you a demon? A ghost from some cemetery? Is this an ancient burial ground?" He had nothing to use as a viable weapon. Not that anything solid would work on a ghost. But she didn't have any transparency to her. Maybe his gun would work? He shook his head. He couldn't shoot a person, dead or not. The thought sickened him.

Her nightgown had the latest animated princess on it. Under the brighter lights of his bedroom, he could see it was definitely blood running down the side of her head. Her large green eyes stayed fixed on him.

"Why did you leave?"

"I don't know what you're talking about! I didn't leave anything or anyone. Especially not you. Who are you?"

"I'm..." she paused. Her face changed expression for the first time. Her gaze dropped to the floor, her eyes blinking furiously as if she struggled to remember. "I'm Merry."

The light in the room flickered like someone flipped the breaker switch off and on. It stopped. The doorway was empty again. Germaine pulled the blankets up over his legs, not removing his boots. He kept his eyes on the doorway. Eventually, Grant crawled out from underneath and joined him on the bed, curled against the wall and headboard.

Sleep found Germaine at some point because he jerked awake at the sun reflecting off the snow outside. He shivered. His neck hurt from the odd angle it had ended up in. The ghost had to be a hallucination. Too many hours spent staring at a fire. Maybe residual stress from the major project his work had shipped last week? But why would that all manifest in a dead little girl? Had he seen a horror flick recently?

He dragged himself out of bed, changed clothes, and slumped into the front room, turning off lights along the way. Grant followed closely. Germaine cranked up the thermostat. The fire had burned out. In the kitchen he made some tea and poured breakfast for Grant.

The girl had asked, *Why did you leave?* Who did she think she was talking to? He'd never left anyone. Well, not recently. And not with malice. Fear. He'd left Dierdra because of overwhelming fear. Afraid of not living up to her image of him. Afraid of screwing it up. He hadn't planned on it being on the eve of their wedding day. But it was. Just over seven years ago. The Christmas wedding that wasn't.

Even the thought of food made his stomach issue a warning. With no other chores to distract him, he went to the desk in his front room where he worked remotely. He moved his cell phone off his laptop and onto the desk. No conference calls for a couple more days. That little girl had died recently based on her nightgown. Maybe if he figured out who she was and what happened to her, she'd leave him alone. That's how it worked in the movies, right? Germaine searched for stories of deaths in the local area and closest big city. He included and excluded the name "Mary." He pored through heartrending stories that choked him up a little, but nothing seemed to match. Nothing that recent.

At three o'clock, he pushed back from his laptop and rubbed his eyes. Now, his stomach protested at its emptiness. He shuffled to the kitchen, Grant still on his heels. "You probably need to go out." Germaine walked to the back door and unlocked it. The afternoon sun nearly blinded him. "Out you go." He waved his hand towards the cold.

Grant didn't move. He just looked up at Germaine with his ears back, then sat with his tail between his legs. The tough husky was not handling this well.

"Fine," Germaine grumbled, pulling on his coat. "Let's go." He stepped outside and Grant followed. He shut the door. Not that it had seemed to matter last night, or maybe it had. Did ghosts have to be invited in the house? Did leaving the door open count? What did Hollywood really know about ghosts anyway? "Go do your business." He waved Grant onward. It took a few more minutes of uncertainty, but finally his faithful companion ventured into the snow.

Germaine stood on the back porch watching Grant jump through the deep powder. In the daylight, he could easily see only his tracks leading to the back window. Probably a hallucination. "Grant! Come on!"

His dog bounded back to him and into the house. Germaine shut the door and dried Grant with a stack of towels. Man, that dog could get wet. Grant licked his face a couple of times. Germaine tossed the wet towels to the other side of the hall. He'd throw them in the dryer later.

He grabbed some leftover pizza from the fridge and went back to the front room. Grant didn't follow him. Maybe the dog had worked out his fear by playing in the snow. Germaine seated himself at his computer again.

"Why?"

"Holy!" Germaine jumped, flinging his pizza. "Stop doing that!" he huffed at the girl as he spun on his chair. She stood several feet behind him. "Can't you appear in front of me for once?" It was one thing for a coworker to walk up behind you in an office where you knew people were around. But when you live alone, it was just rude.

He rubbed the bridge of his nose. "I'm trying to find the answer and figure out what happened to you, ok? Just let me work. Or give me more information! Geez, Mary is such a common name. Do you even know your last name?" He'd never been great with kids and couldn't tell if she was four or eight. Whatever sleep he'd managed last night wasn't enough, and her presence wore on his nerves.

Her face scrunched up again in concentration.

Germaine dropped his head into his hands and rubbed his face.

He heard the clack of his keyboard. He looked back and watched "Merry Stabler" type into the search box. A waking nightmare. Awesome. The "enter" key pressed, starting the search.

Germaine turned back to the room. No more Merry. Crap. Now she could sneak up on him again. He sighed and started to scroll through the results listed on his screen.

"*Mother Injured; Child Killed by Husband*" read one headline dated just five days ago. He clicked on it. The story carried a common theme from the earlier ones he'd read. Abusive spouse finally goes too far. But this time the daughter died. Mom was seriously hurt, and the husband had been arrested. Timothy Stabler was booked into the county jail on murder and attempted murder charges. The deceased was identified as Merry Stabler.

Germaine's heart wrenched, so he stopped reading. The picture accompanying the story was the dead little girl. Well, now he knew. When she came back, he'd be able to tell her and then she could leave him alone. The police had the bad guy. He noticed the city in the article. That was an eight-hour drive from here. Why did she come way out here? The city was where he'd lived before buying this house, though. Maybe she'd lived in his old apartment. Some weird supernatural connection to former tenants must have led her to him.

He rubbed his eyes. What a day. He browsed for results of last night's basketball game. Then he allowed the internet to distract him from the last twenty-four hours.

He finally powered down his laptop and closed it. His watch said eight o'clock. His stomach growled. His pizza! He got up and found one piece on the arm of his chair. The other had landed cheese-down on the floor in front of the hearth. Ugh. He threw them both in the fireplace.

After a dinner of chicken breast and corn, Germaine set about cleaning. He put the towels in the dryer and loaded his bed sheets, dirty from his boots, into the washer. He tried to keep busy and looked for the girl around every corner. He finished re-making his bed at ten but still no appearance. He changed into pajamas.

With a sigh he lit the fire and settled down in his chair to watch his pizza burn. Grant settled down next to the chair and Germaine put a hand on the dog's back. "I wish she'd show, buddy. I'd like this to all be over with." She should come tonight. Charles Dickens said ghosts visit on Christmas Eve. Although if another two showed up after she left, he was going to check himself into a mental institution.

Slowly, the flames dancing across the logs and the faintest hint of roasted pepperoni wafted through the room. Germaine's head slid against one of the wings on his chair.

"Why did you leave?"

"What?" Germaine jerked awake. "Can't you warn a guy? Like make a noise or knock something over?" The fire smoldered and Grant, as usual, was gone. Why did animals get a warning? The girl stood in front of the fireplace.

"Ok, Merry. You were killed by your father. Your mom is hurt but should recover. Your dad is in jail and probably will be for life so you can move on, go towards the light or walk through the pearly gates. Whatever it is you do. Please leave me alone now."

Merry's stare didn't leave him. The glow from his neighbor's display lit one side of her body but the light didn't reflect in her eyes, giving her a far scarier appearance than he'd seen before.

"My father isn't in jail."

"Yes, he is!" Germaine protested, standing. "I can pull up the article so you can read it for yourself." He marched over to his computer. He lifted the screen. "You can read, can't you?"

No answer, so he looked back and Merry had vanished. Thank goodness.

He went to his bedroom. Grant lay on his bed against the wall. "Thanks a lot, tough guy," Germaine said. He climbed into bed. A good night's sleep found him quickly.

"Why did you leave?"

Germaine groaned, pulling his blankets over his head. "Why are you here?" Silence. Couldn't she answer his questions? He rolled onto his back, blinking at the sun blasting through his window.

The girl stood at the foot of his bed. Grant had disappeared again.

"I told you all the details. I'm not playing detective. The cops did that. Why don't you leave? Please! Go on to the other side. Leave me alone!"

Germaine's phone rang from the front room. He sighed. Who would be calling him on Christmas morning? His mom never called until dinner time. A dinner he was never invited to. He rolled out of bed and left the room giving Merry the stink-eye. He better not be stuck with this phenomenon for the rest of his life.

The phone rang again. He picked it up, his brain barely registering the world outside of the horror story his life had become.

"Mommy's calling."

Germaine jumped slightly. The girl stood next to him. He put the phone to his chest. "Stop that!" he hissed. "Hello?" he asked into the phone.

"Hello? Are you there?" the voice on the phone asked.

He glared at Merry as he answered, "Yes, I'm here."

"Germaine Crabtree?" the hoarse voice on the other end asked.

"This is him."

"Germ, it's Dierdra."

After all these years? "Hey, Dierdra. What can I do for you?"

"I have to tell you something."

Anything she could say right now would pale in comparison to what he'd been experiencing. "Go ahead."

A long pause followed. "Well, when you left, I was pregnant. I had a little girl."

"That's great, D. Wait. What?" His mind suddenly engaged. A girl! He had a daughter. He turned away from the ghostly gaze of Merry to face the fireplace. "Why didn't you tell me earlier? Why tell me now?"

Sobbing came across the line. "Because she's dead, Germ. She's dead."

Ice crept into Germaine's veins.

"How?" was all he could muster.

Another long pause filled with crying. "I married a man four years ago named Tim. He started treating me badly, and if I complained he took it out on her." Long pause. "He beat me up when I tried to leave him and killed her."

Germaine whirled around. Merry had vanished but a photograph lay on his closed laptop. He picked it up to find Dierdra's curly brown hair and his green eyes staring back at him. "What was her name?" he whispered.

"I named her Merry. Merry Christmas."

Several minutes later, Germaine hung up the phone and let it fall onto the desk. He sat down, resting his head in his hands. Tears dripped onto the desk.

The silence of the room on Christmas morning bombarded him. No toys, no torn wrapping paper or happy giggling. No loving wife to watch it with. Nothing. So afraid of what life might bring that he missed out on what it did. So many years alone when he shouldn't have been. Regret tore him apart like a pack of wolves. Time passed through memories that never happened.

"Why?"

He didn't jump and couldn't turn around. Couldn't face her. "Because I didn't know."

"What didn't you know?" she asked softly.

He tried to speak several times, and when he finally managed words they were broken and forced past the sob waiting in his throat. "I didn't know how wonderful my life would be. Didn't know about you. Didn't know anything."

"Goodbye, Daddy."

He turned to find the room empty. "Merry Christmas, Merry," he whispered.

Silent Night

by Allan Evans

This had to be what it was like being in a snow globe. Big and fluffy, the flakes were mesmerizing as they swirled around the car. Hannah glanced over at Liam, who seemed equally absorbed by the blizzard. He'd been quiet for most of the ride, which was unusual for him. He always had something to say.

"Earth to Liam, you are totally lost in thought," Hannah said with another glance in his direction.

Hannah paused for the briefest of moments. One thing she'd learned about Liam was he had a passive aggressive side, in that he avoided confrontation and anything even remotely negative. She knew she might have heard only half the story about Liam's family, but given how much she liked what she'd learned so far, she was willing to take the chance. "Are you nervous for me to meet your family?" she asked.

"No, not at all. I can't wait for them to meet my new fiancé."

"Wait, you had an old fiancé?"

"Yes, but she broke it off because she thought I was using her for her social security checks."

Hannah giggled, loving their banter. "That must have been traumatic for you."

Liam nodded. "It was. And I'd just gotten used to having dinner at four-thirty."

"If you prefer, we can start having earlier dinners too. It can be the first of our new traditions."

Hannah had never had a family to celebrate holidays with, and it's all she'd wished and hoped for. Growing up as an only child with two feuding parents didn't exactly make for lasting memories of the good kind.

Hannah was over the moon excited to start traditions with her fiancé. But, even more so to join Liam's family as they celebrated Christmas. He'd often spoken of his family and their traditions at the holidays, and Hannah thought they sounded picturesque, like something out of a Norman Rockwell painting.

Although this was their second Christmas together, this was the first one where she was invited to share the holiday with his family.

Liam described the family farm as a place where everyone got together for cook-outs and holidays. It was a busy and loud place, full of laughter and joy. Hannah never tired of hearing Liam's stories about the old farmhouse and his family Christmas traditions. Christmas Eve was a fabulous dinner that was a dress up occasion. Boys in dress slacks and holiday sweaters, girls in frilly dresses and ribbons in their hair. After dinner, the family adjourned to the living room and sat around the crackling fire, singing carols, playing games, and sharing stories.

After opening presents on Christmas morning, the family gathered in the kitchen to make Christmas cookies. The kids baked and decorated sugar cookies, while the adults made fancier treats using recipes that were handed down through the generations. After that, everyone bundled up and rode in the carriage, pulled by a pair of the farm's largest horses, to deliver cookies and Christmas spirit to the neighboring farms.

It sounded magnificent to Hannah.

"Here we are," Liam said as he slowed down. At the corner of the fence, *Brody Farm* was carved into a slab of wood, the sign marking the family farm's entrance. The road was a curvy gravel path leading to a large farmhouse next to a massive barn and several smaller surrounding buildings. The sun was just setting as the glow radiated through the barren branches of an old oak tree.

"It's beautiful," Hannah said, a measure of awe in her tone. Being a city girl, the country was a new and exciting experience.

The house was lit up, both inside and out. The porch was decorated with evergreen garland, traditional red velvet bows, old-fashioned Christmas lights, vintage skates and a sled. And the largest wreath Hannah had ever seen hung on the front door.

As they approached the house, Liam looked around. "Where is he? Gus is usually the official farm greeter."

"Gus?"

"Our golden retriever. Gus is always excited for company to arrive."

But no dog or people greeted them until they stepped onto the porch, carrying their overnight bags. The front door opened to a smiling woman with styled white hair.

"Mom," Liam said as he dropped his bag and wrapped his arms around her. The woman gave Hannah an appraising look over her son's shoulder. Any trepidation she had about being accepted vanished with the woman's smile. It was warm and genuine, the kind of smile that all the best Hallmark holiday movies featured.

"I'm Joanna," she said as she stepped over to Hannah. "We're all excited to meet you, Hannah. Liam has been raving about you for the longest time."

She gave Hannah a hug before turning to the open door and calling, "Liam is here. And he brought a girl." She drew out the last word pretty much like a big sister teasing her younger brother and winked at Hannah.

The man that came around the corner was tall, thin, and had a full head of gray hair. He had kind, friendly eyes and a ruddy complexion that spoke of many years in the elements. With a passing glance toward Hannah, he turned to Liam.

"Welcome home, son." This had to be Liam's father, Conor Brody.

A twenty something woman joined him and judging by their resemblance, it was Liam's sister, Grace. "Hi," she said with a smile.

"I'd like you to meet Hannah," Liam said.

"Young lady," Mr. Brody said with a nod.

"It's a pleasure to meet you," she began, but Mr. Brody had already turned away.

If Liam had noticed, he didn't say anything.

"It's nice to meet you, Hannah." Grace shook her hand. She shivered and ducked back inside the house.

"Hey, Mom, where's Gus?" Liam asked. "He's always the first to say hello."

Her face clouded. "Gus was really old, Liam. He…"

Liam nodded, his eyes dropping to the bags. "We should get out of this cold."

Hannah followed her fiancé inside.

THE DINNER WAS FESTIVE, fun, and a whirlwind. Liam's mother, Joanna, served baked ham with sides of scalloped potatoes, crushed pineapple, brandy-glazed carrots, and warm dinner rolls. Hannah sat next to Liam and across from his sister, Grace and her husband, Rick. Besides Liam's parents, his Aunt Catherine was also at the table.

"We're so excited you're joining the family, Hannah," Catherine said raising her wine glass. A little sloshed over the side, but no one said anything. "It's about time Liam settled down. And our family can use some fresh blood, truth be told."

Grace cleared her throat. "Speaking of family additions…" Her beaming smile more than finished her sentence.

"Oh my gosh," Joanna said with the joy of a twelve-year-old

unwrapping an unexpected surprise on Christmas morning. "That's amazing."

Rick put his arm around his wife and lifted up his glass. "Here's to our Christmas miracle."

"Joy to the world," Conor said as his kind eyes crinkled and he held up his own glass. And from there, a number of smaller, but by no means quieter conversations broke out around the table.

Hannah leaned into Liam. "I love how loud your family is. It makes it so much fun."

Liam nodded and said in an uncharacteristically solemn tone, "Well, you'll find we're not always loud." He turned to join in a conversation with his sister and her husband. Hannah studied him, wondering what he'd meant. It almost felt like a warning.

"Oooh, I just love your fireplace," Hannah said as they moved into the living room after dinner. With the sounds of Sleigh Ride by Leroy Anderson in the background, Hannah took in the room. The massive rock hearth was a focal point in an already stunning room. It was picture perfect. Rustic wood floors that looked freshly polished, a vaulted ceiling that soared overhead, and windows that were so exquisite it tugged at Hannah's heart. The woodwork didn't just say it was built by a talented craftsman, it positively shouted it all the way to the exposed beams in the rafters.

Hannah sat next to Liam on the couch, while Liam's sister Grace grabbed the other couch. His parents took the twin recliners across from the fireplace.

"Real people live here? This place looks like an advertisement for HGTV," Hannah asked Liam in hushed tones.

"Yes, real people live here. Generations of the Brody family have made this their home. I grew up here as did my father and his father," Liam said. "My great grandfather, Patrick, moved in here with my great grandmother, Anne. And they started popping out kids shortly afterwards."

"They moved in here? So, your family wasn't the original owners?" Hannah asked.

"No, there was someone that had the house first," Liam said. "My great-grandfather got it from him." As Liam was talking, he reached over and tugged at a loose thread on Hannah's sweater.

"Liam," his mother called out sharply. "You could unravel everything by pulling on a loose thread. Be careful, young man."

Liam pulled his hand away. A look flashed between mother and son, but it quickly passed. Hannah thought it best to change the subject. "Well, I couldn't imagine a better place to spend Christmas Eve. Liam's told me about your holiday traditions."

"I'm sure Liam hasn't told you about *all* our family traditions," Catherine said offhandedly. "Otherwise, you wouldn't have come."

Hannah started to laugh but found there was a weight in the air. "Well, my parents were divorced, so the holidays weren't always what I hoped they would be. But, your traditions can be my traditions too."

A towering spruce tree stood in the corner near the window. Twinkling lights and handmade ornaments decorated the Christmas tree. Sashes of silver and gold wrapped around the evergreen, and a glittering gold star topped it all off. Presents of all sizes and shapes lay underneath. It was the most perfect tree Hannah had ever seen.

"I see you like the tree," Grace said. "Dad always goes out into the forest the day after Thanksgiving every year and cuts down the most majestic tree he can find."

Liam laughed. "One year when I went with Dad to cut the tree, it crashed down and a dazed squirrel lurched out and went after Dad. It was the strangest thing."

"You must have taken its home," Hannah said.

There was another look exchanged around the group. Hannah decided she'd ask Liam what was going on when they were alone later.

Singing along with "Jingle Bell Rock," Liam's aunt Catherine came into the room carrying a large serving tray. "Who wants Christmas cocoa?" she asked. "Get it while it's hot."

"You have to have some," Liam said. "Catherine uses an old family recipe, and it's the best you'll ever have. Guaranteed."

"Well, I'm sold. How could I refuse after that sales pitch?" Hannah said.

Catherine beamed as Hannah took a mug. As she glanced up, she saw all eyes were on her as she took a sip. She didn't keep them waiting for her verdict.

"Mmmm, I love it." With a creamy rich chocolate taste and a hint of mint, the cocoa was more than good. It was literally the best hot cocoa she'd ever had.

Just as Nat King Cole started singing about chestnuts roasting on an open fire, the grandfather clock behind Hannah started chiming. She'd heard the steady ticking of the vintage clock, but the chiming was loud enough to startle her and she spilled a little of her cocoa. She turned to look at the beautiful clock. The hands marked the time as eight p.m. The room was quiet, other than the loud chimes that counted up to eight.

Hannah turned back and noticed that everyone looked uneasy. Their eyes didn't meet hers but darted between one another. Liam's aunt had wrapped her arms around herself as if a bitter wind had blown in. Liam's father reached across and put his hand over his wife's hand. Given the haunted look in his eyes, Hannah knew the gesture was more about comfort than about affection. If Joanna noticed, she didn't let on.

That's when she realized Mr. Nat King Cole was no longer singing The Christmas Song, and no other carol was going to follow.

She looked at Liam, but he wouldn't meet her eyes.

There was an odd stillness in the room. The grandfather clock ticked one last time, then stopped. She stared at it. Why had it stopped ticking?

It wasn't only the clock that was acting abnormally, the

temperature in the room felt unusually frigid. Hannah thought she should be able to see her breath. Yet, the fire still burned in the fireplace.

Hannah shivered and set down her cup of Christmas cocoa. When she looked up, all eyes were on her again. Only this time it wasn't out of curiosity. No, something else was there.

Her hand trembled as she reached for Liam's hand. His eyes were wide, his nostrils flared, and his lips thin. It was obvious he was scared. But so was the entire Brody family.

An oppressive silence enveloped the room, smothering all sound. Hannah realized that when she set down her cup of cocoa, the china hadn't made a sound. But that wasn't all. There was no rustle of clothing, no sound of the air the furnace pushed out through the vents, or crackle of fire from the nearby hearth. All was quiet, but calm was another thing all together.

It was as if sleep paralysis had set in, and everyone was now frozen in place, unable to move or speak. Eyes darted frantically and mouths moved in silent horror. This was a waking nightmare.

Hannah felt the urge—no the need—to flee this terrifying silence, but no movement came of it. She was fixed in place, just like the others.

Just when she thought things couldn't get worse, they did.

She hadn't seen the man enter the room, he was just there. A large man, he wore clothing from days long gone: knee-length pants over stockings, a coat with long tails in back and a short front, collar turned up, and a ruffled cravat worn at the neck. He had on a top-hat and carried a walking stick.

Was this a holiday dress up thing? No, the fact that Hannah could see through him made it clear what was in front of her. It had to be a ghost.

No one acknowledged her incredulous look. Everyone but one sat still and watched the ghostly man. Liam's father looked away, staring down at his wringing hands.

Without a sound, the man glided over to Liam's father and glared down at him. There was something contemptuous in the disdainful way the ghost sneered at the senior family member. Worry crossed Hannah's mind when the ghostly man hefted his walking stick. An ugly, carved silver knob adorned the end of the stick, and she suspected he planned on using it on the head of Liam's father.

With the walking stick raised, the ghostly man paused just before he swung it down. Something had caught his eye. With dawning horror, Hannah realized that something was her.

Without taking his eyes off her, he lowered the walking stick and moved toward her. There was something eerie about the way he silently glided. She whimpered in fear but no sound escaped. All was silent.

The ghost leaned in close, their faces inches apart as he stared into her wide eyes. The stench of mold stung Hannah's eyes. She sat rigid as she endured his gaze. His pupils were tight little dots and the whites of his eyes were bloodshot. He sniffed her, making a face that suggested a particularly bad odor had entered the room. He stood and moved away.

After leaving Hannah, the ghostly man from an era gone by made his way to Catherine. She stared at him with wide eyes while her chin trembled. He lifted his walking stick and touched her shoulder with it, looking eerily similar to the queen knighting a loyal subject. Lifting it over her head, he paused, but ultimately turned away.

Liam's mother was next in the strange encounter. The man held his stick out with the silver tip a mere inch away from her eye. She stared at him unflinchingly until he turned away abruptly.

He headed toward Liam. Hannah squeezed his hand, fearing what might happen to her fiancé. This ghost seemed to have no love for the Brody family. The spirit lifted his walking stick and swung it around so the ugly silver handle rested on Liam's cheek. The moment was frozen as neither moved for the longest time. The only sign of Liam's fear was how hard he squeezed Hannah's hand. The ghost ripped the stick from Liam's cheek and turned on Grace and her husband.

Looking more defiant than scared, Grace stared up at the ghostly man. The ghost paused and looked at her hands resting on her belly. After an uncomfortably long moment, he turned away.

With determination in his eyes, he strode across the room, lifting his walking stick. Hannah's breath caught in her throat when the ghostly man stopped again at Liam's father. As if stepping up to bat, the man held the silver handle over his shoulder with both hands gripping the other end.

Hannah tried to shout. Nothing came out.

The man looked down with that same look of contempt as before. He tensed, ready to swing.

Hannah struggled to move, summoning her willpower to fight against what held her in place.

But her muscles did nothing.

If Liam's father knew his life was in danger, he didn't let on. He continued looking down at his hands.

Did Conor Brody know he was the focal point of the ghost's wrath? If he did, he acted like a sheep comfortably waiting for the impending slaughter. Or maybe more of a sacrificial lamb.

Hannah looked to Liam for help. He had to stop this.

But he didn't.

With the assured motion of a designated hitter, the man swung his walking stick.

Time slowed as the stick arced through the air. It swung in a downward strike at Liam's father. There wasn't even the slightest chance it would miss Conor Brody's head. This would be a killing blow.

But it wasn't.

The stick sliced through his head like it wasn't there. The handle continued its journey as it crashed into a crystal water pitcher. A thousand pieces of glass launched into the air as the pitcher exploded with the impact.

The sound was loud and startling.

Wait, what?

Hannah was confused. The silky voice of Nat King Cole played as the glass skittered across the floor. Water dripped from the table, the clock resumed its ticking, and the fire regained its crackle. The room no longer felt like a deep freezer, and beyond the impossible that she just witnessed, everything appeared to be back to normal.

Almost everything.

If she thought anyone would react to what just transpired, Hannah was mistaken. This was more confusing than the ghostly visit. There were no sighs of relief, cries of surprise, discussion of events, or anything. Just the family members scurrying around with a broom, dustpan, and towels to clean up the mess.

Hannah was flabbergasted.

The only other person still seated was Grace's husband, Rick. When their eyes met, he raised his eyebrows, but no explanation was offered. That was invitation enough for Hannah. She was by his side in a heartbeat.

"What was that? I mean...what the hell just happened?"

"Keep your voice down. We never discuss this here in the house." Rick hesitated as he glanced around the room before leaning in. "But I'll try to answer your questions. *What was that?* That was the Brody family Christmas Eve tradition no one talks about. It's an annual event."

"Wait, you mean this happens every year?"

Rick nodded. "I've been with Grace for five years and every year it happens. Christmas Eve with the ghost of Christmas past. I take it Liam never told you."

Hannah shook her head. "I love him, but nothing negative ever comes out of his mouth. His family dog dies and not one word about it."

"That seems to be a family dynamic. Grace is the same way. She never mentioned the ghost either. I've just learned to endure the experience every year."

"But, why? If he shows up here every year, why not go

somewhere else? Maybe Aunt Catherine should host next year. I bet there would be plenty of wine."

Rick took a deep breath. "Yeah, they've tried that. But, there's one important distinction you're not getting. The ghost isn't haunting this house. He's haunting the Brody family. If I had to guess, I'd say the previous owner of the house still hasn't gotten over how he lost it."

"I figured there was a story there. Talk about carrying a grudge from the grave." Hannah shook her head.

"But, what if they skipped Christmas Eve or even Christmas altogether? Just stayed home or went to visit friends?" she asked.

"That's been tried. But he shows up wherever they go. Do you really want that angry man storming around your Uncle Bill's house with his little kids around?"

Hannah shook her head slowly.

"No, you don't. It's a lot worse that way. And trust me, wherever they go, he'll find them."

Hannah sat in silence, processing things.

Rick cleared his throat quietly, and Hannah glanced up at him. "Let me ask you a question. Do you really love Liam?"

"Of course, I do."

"But, how much do you love Liam? Before you answer that, think about this. When you marry him, you're marrying into this family."

Hannah swallowed.

"You'll live with that nasty man coming every single year. You'll never get away from him no matter where you go."

Hannah didn't say anything.

"Let me ask another question. Are you two going to have kids after you're married? If you do, they're going to inherit his undying wrath as well."

Hannah fought back tears, but she wasn't being overly successful. She stood and looked around the room at the Brody family. Grace, Catherine, Joanna, and Liam cleaned up the last of the glass. Liam's father had left the room. These were such nice people, but they clearly came with some serious baggage. It was so frustrating the ghost wouldn't let them alone. Ever.

"Why does that man have to ruin Christmas Eve every year?" Hannah asked.

Rick put his hands on his knees, took a deep breath, and slowly raised his gaze to Hannah. His eyes were the eyes of a haunted man.

"If you think Christmas is bad, you should see what he does on Halloween."

THEY'D PACKED up the suitcases and gathered their presents and leftovers before saying goodbyes with the promise to stay in touch this year. As soon as they were in Liam's car, Hannah turned on him.

"Why didn't you tell me?"

Liam started them down the road as they left the Brody family house behind them. As much as Hannah had been excited to visit, she was relieved to have it in their rearview mirror.

"It's just something we don't talk about. We all put it out of our minds. It's like that drunk uncle that everyone seems to have. You don't think about him until you get together and then you know he's going to cause a scene. It's like that."

"It's not like that at all. Not one bit."

"But—"

"No. Not even close."

Liam sighed and nodded. "I'm sorry. I should have been upfront with you from the beginning."

"Do you think?" Hannah folded her arms. "Just so there's nothing else."

Liam grinned. "That's all. Nothing else strange. But, I agree, I should have told you."

"I'm not sure I would have believed you if you had. I'm convinced it would have been easier to swallow if you'd told me your uncle was a bigfoot."

"He does wear a size twelve shoe. True story." They both laughed.

After a moment, Hannah said, "I really like your family. They're all so nice and so funny."

Liam laughed. "And so loud."

Hannah grinned. "That they are. Well, except for your father."

Liam didn't say anything for an uncomfortably long moment as the car drifted over the center line. "I'm not sure what you mean. My father died two years ago."

Hannah covered her mouth and choked back a gasp as a chill went through her. She shivered but couldn't think what to say.

"But before he died, my father kept up with the group just fine," Liam said as he moved the car back into its lane. Hannah's eyes were riveted by the center line. "The holidays are not the same without him."

She wondered if that were true, thinking of Conor Brody still joining his unsuspecting family for the holidays.

"But we'll always have his memories," Liam said as he turned on the radio and the sound of Bing Crosby's White Christmas filled the car. "So he'll always be with us."

Hannah felt the truth of that statement as she glanced in the rearview mirror, and kind eyes looked back at her.

TE AMO, MAMITA

BY SARAH E. SEELEY

The barely teenage Eloida wasn't supposed to be out of bed, but it wasn't the excitement of *Buena Noche*, Christmas Eve, that had deprived her of sleep. She'd had another nightmare about her parents, and she'd awoken to what had struck her distinctly as her mother's footfalls on the wooden stairs leading up from the basement where she slept. As absurd as the notion was, she got up and followed the sound, chasing the yearning tick in her throat with the growing skepticism of wakefulness. It wasn't Mama. She was gone. It had to be one of Eloida's cousins, or one of the grown-ups. But she had to know who it was, whose footsteps sounded just like her mother's back home.

The grand Del Lago house was dark and quiet, except for the yellow flicker of electric lights made to look like dripping candlesticks that had been lovingly arranged around the family's *Nacimiento* scene on the broad foot of the stone fireplace. The central room, with its tall windows hidden behind even taller curtains and a high ceiling that opened up to a library attic and other rooms on the third floor, glowed with strings of twinkling white lights from the banisters above. Loosely folded piles of blankets graced the loveseat and sofa in front of the fireplace. The central room flowed seamlessly along a shared wooden floor to the open kitchen. The whole house still smelled of the delicious spices and umami of the stuffed turkey, tamales, bunuelos, and pineapple upside-down cake—*volteado de piña*—that Tio Roberto and Tia Julinha had made many hours ago. Extended family brought empanadas and various side salads to celebrate the ninth day of *Posadas* on the calendar.

Close to where the girl stood, a North American blue pine tree, decorated with ribbons and another string of lights, was situated next to the stairs that led to the basement, adding its own rich spice and blended cultural aesthetic to the atmosphere. Across the room, an aluminum softball bat lay propped against the wall next to the fireplace. A host of children from the extended family had used it over the last four days to break piñatas. Eloida could spy stray ribbons of paper mâché on the floor in dark textures, here and there around the room, despite the grown ups' efforts to tidy.

A figure stooped next to the two-foot-high wooden statues of Mary and Joseph, fingering the red poinsettia leaves that were dark with shadow in the evening glow of the lights. The figure seemed to take in their perfume. Then she stood up, perusing the picture frames of various shapes and sizes that featured photographs of the Del Lago's family and friends. She looked so normal in some ways, dressed in a white blouse, dark pants that cut above her ankles, and an outline of simple, flat dress shoes on her feet that nearly blended away into the natural light and shadows of the room. Her long, dark hair appeared to be pulled back from her face with a red hair ribbon, neatly braided across the top like a headband.

Eloida stood frozen, not daring to move as she watched the faintly glowing specter trace the nearest stonework of the fireplace with translucent fingers. The spectral figure paced slowly across the room, seeming to take in the Del Lago's splendid *Nacimiento* decorations with an expression of wonder on her shining face, accompanied by a twinge of a frown that made her look uneasy. Then the figure returned to the fireplace mantle, glancing at the scene of the Holy Couple kneeling over the wooden statue of Jesus inside a wooden box filled with actual straw.

"*Mamá?*"

The figure responded to Eloida's strained whisper, meeting her gaze with soft, dark eyes and a face filled with a lifelike warmth that was free from pallor. The girl shivered. She wanted nothing more than to run up to the figure, this essence of her mother, or whatever it was. Throw her arms around her, and weep for hours into her bosom. But the figure had vanished the last time she tried to come close. So she stood where she was, and the figure stayed where she was, the two of them caught by whatever ethereal mechanisms allowed them to see each other on opposite sides of life and death for these small glimmers.

The girl waved. The figure waved back, growing a sad smile.

"*Te amo, Mamita,*" the girl said, just a breath above a whisper, "I love you, Mommy, and I miss you a lot. I need you a lot... Can you stay and talk to me? Fonzo's so scared. He's having a really hard time, and I don't know how to help him figure all this out. I don't think the other grown-ups know either."

The creak of the stairs made Eloida jolt. She turned, expecting an older cousin to scold her for being out of bed. But it was just Alfonzo.

"Elyi?"

"*Sí, Fonzo, aquí,*" she whispered, "I'm here, Fonzo."

Her eleven-year-old brother bounded up the last few steps and threw his arms around her waist. He clung to her, squeezing her tight. He was a little shorter than her still, a little bony, and very strong for his size.

"Couldn't sleep either, eh?" she whispered.

He sniffed.

"You've been crying."

He said nothing.

"It's all right to cry, Fonzo. You know I won't ever tease you for it. Not like the others."

"I hate being here," he said. "We don't know these people, and they don't know us."

"They're Mama's cousins. We never really got to meet her side of the family because, you know..."

"Papa," he said, "and Abuelo Ramiro, and..." he gasped, trying to stave off more tears. Eloida stroked his back, trying to soothe him, to listen. To think of anything to say that only he would understand, that they would understand together.

"It's a really nice house, don't you think? It's got all kinds of smart technology, yet it's old, and vast, and full of history that makes it a little bit mysterious. And we can go anywhere. We don't have to worry about whether the facility people have had their cigarettes before we have lessons or sports; don't have to worry about getting yelled at for sneaking extra food; don't have to do extra chores or push-ups if we forget to make our beds in the mornings. We've got our own rooms. And Tio Rob has a really cool job working on spaceships for NASA."

She glanced back at the fireplace, finding the space empty of mother's essence once more. The room felt a little dimmer, colder, the colors of the decorations fading to a void of meaningless paper, plants, and fabric that were no more inviting than the dreary mists and rains of Northern California winter.

"If I'm not good enough at school here, will the patrol people pick me up and send me back?"

Eloida frowned, peering in thought into the dark maw of the kitchen. "Is that what you've been worried about? Getting sent back to Abuelo, and Tios Onofre and Erasmo?"

"Aren't you worried about it?"

She didn't answer.

"What if I can't learn English?"

"You'll learn English, Fonzo. We'll both learn English, and we'll be fine."

"It's so stupid."

"I know. But at least our *tios* here actually want to help us."

Alfonzo shook his head, burrowing into her shoulder. "They all hate us, all the cousins. Even the ones who can talk to us."

"They don't hate us. They hated our papa's family. They're just scared."

They were both silent a moment.

"Do you think Abuelo will send someone to hurt them because we're here?"

Eloida sighed. "I honestly don't think we matter enough for Abuelo to bother with us. Maybe when we're older he'll care, but for right now we're just a couple of kids who are out of the cartel's hair."

Alfonzo's ribs puffed against her with the emotion of confessing his deepest fears. "You know we don't belong here. We're not like the other kids, the kids who lost their parents or got separated from them because of people like Papa. The kids who had to stay at the camp a long time because they didn't have someone with influence like our *tios* to come get them. We're not the good kids..."

She squeezed her brother a little tighter. "Stop, Fonzo. We haven't done anything wrong, and we're with family now. Good family. We can be whatever we want to be here."

"I don't want to be separated from you again."

The soft clap of metal clattering to the wooden floor made them both jolt. The two children let go of each other, and Eloida went over to a small standing frame that had fallen off the mantle. She picked it up, studying the picture it held. Tia Julinha had told Eloida and Alfonso that the old black-and-white picture inside it was of their mother's grandfather and grandmother. They lived in Iztapalapa and ran a big hotel in the 1930s. These were the closest relatives on their mother's side, linking them to the cousins with whom they were now living.

Eloida looked around the room, searching for the specter of her mother, for any hint of meaning this photograph held beyond a coincidence that it had merely collapsed on its own.

"What is it?" Fonzo asked, coming up to her and following her gaze around the silent room.

The girl shrugged, feeling the ache of emptiness in her heart that she tried to push away from her thoughts again. "Nothing, I guess." She glanced back at the photograph.

Alfonzo took the little frame out of her hands and frowned at it with her. "Do you think Mama's parents are still alive?"

"I don't know."

"Do you think Tia has any pictures of them? It would be nice to see what they look like."

"We could ask tomorrow."

"*Ei*, what are you two doing?" *Primo* Javier called as he emerged from the blackness of the basement stairs. "The whole house can hear you shuffling around out here."

Alfonso quickly set the picture of their great-grandparents back on the mantle with the row of others.

"Sorry," Eloida called back, "We both had nightmares, so we were just talking."

"Nightmares? Ridiculous! Only naughty children have nightmares on *Noche Bueno*."

The girl and her brother looked at each other.

Javier chuckled and flipped on the light in the kitchen. He got a glass out of one of the cupboards and pulled out a white jug with a picture of an orange on the label. He was Tio Roberto and Tia Julinha's oldest son who was back visiting from university for the holidays. Their other two boys were staying overnight with other relatives. He was only about a head taller than Eloida, but he was fit and agile from military training. He wore a pair of dark sweat pants and a gray t-shirt that said ROTC on it.

Eloida saw the agitated pinch in her brother's brow and took his hand. "We didn't mean to bother anyone. Is it all right if we go talk downstairs in my room a little while? We'll be very quiet."

"You'll go to bed, both of you. And you, Alfonzo, have got to quit sniveling about every little thing that doesn't go your way. If you can't sleep in your own bed and tough it out on your own on Christmas Eve, then there's no hope for you ever growing up to be a man."

Alfonzo's hand slid out of his sister's grasp and he looked down at the floor. He clenched his hands into fists. Eloida reached out to put her hand on her brother's shoulder, but he shrugged her off.

Javier finished guzzling his orange juice and turned to put the white jug back in the refrigerator. "Come on, you two. Back to bed."

Alfonzo grabbed the aluminum bat propped against the mantle and began smashing everything in reach—the picture frames, the poinsettia planters. The popping of glass, plastic, and pottery was sharp, jarring. He knocked the fake candles over and smashed the bulbs. Then he knocked over the wooden figures of Mary and Joseph, flipping the manger and beating the bat against the wooden box while he screamed in a fit of tears and anger.

Eloida watched him, stunned, and terrified at how the family was going to react.

Javier ran across from the kitchen, cursing English words the girl recognized, and tried to grab the bat out of the eleven-year-old's hands from behind. The boy spun to face him. One swing of the bat made their grown cousin back up a pace.

"Don't touch me!" The boy screamed. He swung the bat back and forth as Javier advanced on him in a slow circle around the couches.

"You need to stop this...right...now..." Javier lunged as Alfonzo brought the bat up over his head again to swing. Javier ripped the bat away and threw it down, keeping a grip on the boy's wrist. Then he pulled Alfonzo to the ground, pinning him face-down on the rug with his arm wrenched to keep him from wrestling. "Did it feel good breaking things that don't belong to you? Threatening people? Because you're not going to get the chance to do this ever again, do you understand? If you can't handle someone with authority telling you to go to bed, my parents aren't going to let you stay here. You can spend Christmas Day at the police station instead of having fun with us."

The whole house was stirring. The full lights came on in the room. Tio and Tia came out of their rooms upstairs, followed by the other adults. "*¿Que pasa?*" Tio and Tia both asked as they hustled down the steps. "What's going on?"

"I told these two to go to bed," Javier replied to his mother, carrying on in Spanish, "but Alfonzo decided he didn't like that, so he started smashing everything with the bat."

"You told me to act more like a man!" The boy screamed.

"You definitely don't get man points for acting ten years younger than your shoe size."

Alfonzo struggled against his grown cousin's grip, his face red and wet with tears as he continued to howl and weep.

Tia Julinha put her hand on Tio Roberto's shoulder when they reached the bottom of the stairs. The two of them paused, glancing over at the fireplace, then at each other with shocked and worried faces. Tia whispered something to Tio and patted his back, folding her arms and letting her fingers rest over her lips as he crossed briskly to the two boys on the floor. Tia's brother put his arm around her, and her sister-in-law whispered with them as they surveyed the chaos and watched. The children belonging to extended family who were staying overnight at the house looked down from the balcony upstairs, whispering to each other until Tia's brother went back and ushered them back to their guest rooms.

"Let him up, Javier," said Tio Rob.

"You might want to grab the bat first," Javier replied.

Eloida stepped forward, picked up the bat, and handed it to Tio Rob.

Her uncle seemed a little surprised. "Thank you, Eloida. Please stand out of the way for a bit."

She wanted to plead with him not to call the police like Javier had threatened, but she was too afraid to say anything. She stepped back again, pressing her back against the wall next to the tree. A part of her wanted to disappear. Her brother probably wished he could disappear right now, too. They were going to be in a lot of trouble for this.

Tio Rob squatted down in front of his son and Alfonzo, holding the bat in his lap. "I'll take it from here, Javier."

Javier let go, and Alfonzo sat up, swinging punches at his retreating cousin a few more times before Tio called his name. "Alfonzo."

The boy sniffled and turned his head. His face bore a deep scowl that oscillated between terror and frustration, and he wouldn't look Tio Rob in the eyes.

"Did you break all these things with the bat?"

Alfonzo nodded.

"Why?"

Eloida's brother hung his head, rubbing his eyes. "Because I hate all of you," he spluttered. "No one here understands me, and it makes me angry. It hurts."

Tio nodded. "Do you want to talk about it in private? Just you and me?"

"No," Alfonzo growled. "I just want everyone to leave me alone."

"Right. Well, I want you to understand some things. Your tia and I know that there's a lot going on in your heart that no boy your age should have to deal with. We love you. We want you to feel safe here." He gestured at the fireplace. "Those pictures mean a lot to your tia and me, and the decorations mean a lot to us too. They're full of memories about times we've spent with people we love in this house, and they represent our religious devotions. It hurts us a lot that you chose to damage those things."

"I wasn't...wasn't trying to hurt anyone," Alfonzo huffed. "I'm... I'm sorry. Please don't send me back to my *abuelo*."

Tio Rob looked over his shoulder, exchanging a serious glance with Tia Julinha.

Tio rubbed the neatly trimmed stubble on his face. "I want to talk to you tomorrow morning about how we can help you find better ways to deal with this anger you're feeling. Will you promise me you'll do that?"

"I don't want to talk about my parents with you."

"We don't have to talk about your parents. We'll just talk about you."

"Do I have to go to the police station?"

"The police station?" Tio asked, confused.

"Javier said you were going to call the police to take me away so I can't do anything tomorrow..."

"That's not what I said—"

Tio Rob raised his hand to acknowledge and quiet his son, nodding. "I'll talk to him. But let's make a deal. How about we make breakfast together for everyone first thing in the morning, you and me? I'll come get you up at seven to cook the eggs and potatoes, and we'll put smiles on everyone's faces to make up for the drama tonight. What do you think of that?"

Alfonzo nodded. "I'd like to help."

"I thought so." Tio turned his palm up and waved his fingers. "Come here."

The boy slid over to his uncle and hesitantly put his arms around the man's neck. Tio Rob held him for a while, patting the boy's back. "You have a good heart, Alfonzo. Please be patient with us. It's going to be all right. Go apologize to your *tia* and help her pick up the glass, please."

"Yes, sir." Alfonzo got to his feet, pulling his shirt up to wipe his nose as he went over to Tia Julinha. Tia embraced him, then she led him over to the fireplace with her arm around his shoulders. Ben, Clara, and Gabriel went to the kitchen, getting out the broom and dustpan, a trash bin, and a shop vacuum from the far closet to help clean up.

"It's an act," Javier whispered to his father. "He doesn't care. He did that for attention, and he'll do it again."

"Let me parent, son."

"You'd never let me get away with something like that. It's outrageous. You know he literally has tantrums every time you, or anyone else, tells him something he doesn't like to hear. It doesn't matter how small it is. He's going to hurt someone one of these times."

"He needs some help. Mama and I are looking into it." He put his hand on his son's shoulder. "Thank you for your help. I'm sorry this happened, that he got triggered and you had to intervene. I think we need to move him to a room upstairs, near us, so we can hear him when he gets up." They continued the rest of their conversation in English.

The girl caught a flicker of movement out of the corner of her eye. She looked past Tio Roberto and Javier to the kitchen, glimpsing the faintest glow of her mama pacing back and forth. The vague apparition stood with a hand over her mouth, looking worried in just the same way Tia Julina had a moment before. Then the figure faded away.

The girl whispered. "I'll take care of him, *Mamá*. I promise."

Tio Rob's hand lighted on the girl's head and she started.

"Lo siento," he said. "Sorry, dear Eloida." He took her hand and peered into her eyes with a soft furrow in his bristly brows. He wasn't a tall man any more than was his oldest son, so he didn't have to bend much to meet her eye level. "Are you all right?"

The girl nodded.

"I think your brother needs some one-on-one time with me, or I would invite you to make breakfast with us too."

"That's all right," said Eloida. "I'd rather sleep in a little."

Tio Rob smiled. "Very well." His eyes studied her face a moment, darting back and forth. "You have very beautiful eyes, my child."

Her lips turned up, pulling her ears with them, though the grin still felt a little heavy to lift.

He stroked her chin. "And a beautiful smile."

"Thank you, Tio."

He held her hand and continued to gaze deeply at her for a moment, his brow knitting with a soft furrow of concern once more. "Do you need to talk about anything?"

"No, Tio,"

He nodded. "You can always talk to me or to Julinha any time, all right?"

"All right."

His eyes smiled, and he kissed her forehead. "Off to bed, then. *Buenas Noches*—Good night, and happy Christmas."

"Happy Christmas."

Tio pulled away, joining his wife, Alfonzo, and the other adults who were salvaging photographs from the broken frames and sorting how best to put everything back into place. Eloida cast one last glance at the kitchen. Mother was not there, of course. "Happy Christmas, *Mamá*," she whispered, feeling a little sick inside for wishing a "happy" anything to anyone. "Hope you'll come back." Then she turned and retreated back down to her room in the basement.

Eloida felt the cool muzzle of Tio Erasmo's gun pressed under her chin, his hand tight on her arm. The distinctly earthy smell of Cuban cigars mingled with his cologne.

"We heard you were disappearing without fulfilling the exchange with Lisandro. That puts the whole route at stake. You know how dangerous that is for the rest of us, don't you?"

Eloida's father leaned with one hand on the kitchen counter, his face haggard, looking down at the floor. He had Alfonzo under his other arm; the boy clinging to his shirt like a child half his age. "I'm not leaving."

"Where are all your things? And what's this?" Abuelo kicked one of two large black rolling suitcases filled with clothes, the children's toys, and their mother's possessions. Then he waved the family's plane tickets in Papa's face. "And don't tell me you're flying from Acapulco to Los Angeles for *vacacciones*."

"I'm leaving David," Eloida's mother confessed. Another man from the cartel had her in the same threatening grip, an arm around her waist, with a gun pressed to her throat.

Abuelo laughed, pacing back to her. "I never liked you much, Amalia. My son gave you everything you wanted. You took his money, and you always caused trouble." He tucked the plane tickets into a pocket inside his blazer. Then he rummaged through Mama's purse, pulling out her wallet, everyone's passports, other papers. "Very well, *mi hija*. You can go. But you're going to carry something for us to our contacts up north. And whatever you can't carry..." he pointed at Eloida, "this one will carry," he pointed at Alfonzo next, "then this one." He waved his hand.

The man holding Eloida's mama put a cloth over her mouth, then carried her limp body over to the kitchen table. The man tied her down with ropes while Tio Onofre put a paper mask over his mouth and pulled on a pair of latex gloves.

Eloida's father pulled Alfonzo a little closer and spoke, "Papa, we can do this another way."

"You don't get a choice here."

"You don't need to cut the children."

"What's the matter, son? We know the boy isn't yours." Alfonzo looked up, meeting David's uneasy gaze, confused.

Abuelo paced over to Eloida, glaring at the girl with such cold detachment and disdain as he perused her face it made her shiver. "And I'm not convinced about this one either."

In the dream, Abuelo Ramiro reached for her.

"Elyi, wake up. Your brother is in danger." The girl jolted and threw her eyes open, slowly gathering the shape of her room at the Del Lago's house from the darkness. She wiped the dew of cold sweat from her face with her comforter, shaking. What was that thought she'd had about Alfonzo being in danger? Was it just part of her nightmare? She sat up and peered across the room from her open door, into the deep shadows of the hallway past the stairs.

A pale indigo nightlight beamed from an outlet opposite Alfonzo's room. His door was shut. Everything was still. Then the nightlight flickered. *"Elyi, ayuda me,* Elyi, help me. Hurry. Please." It was an airy sound, not exactly a whisper, not quite a voice.

"Mamá?" Elioda slid out of bed and hurried across the coarse carpet to the doorway. She paused there, her pulse ticking in her

throat and ears once more. She called for her mother again. But she saw nothing, heard nothing more. Primo Javier's room was right next door to Alfonzo's. His door was open, and he had sharp ears. She knew that if she stepped out onto the cement in the hallway, there was a good chance he would hear her footsteps and tell her to go back to bed, even if she tiptoed very carefully. Surely he would hear if her brother was crying, or if anyone came down to bother him, too. *No one will believe me if I tell them mother got me out of bed,* she thought. But the haunting call from the shadows made her anxious.

The cement was cold on the balls of her feet as she darted down the hallway, trying not to patter. She opened the door to Alfonzo's room, cringing as the hinges squeaked. She shot a quick glance at Javier's doorway, then pushed the creaking door all the way open and stepped onto her brother's carpeted floor.

Her brother sat on the middle of his bed, on top of his covers, with his back to the wall next to the window well. He shifted his knees up and slid his hands underneath like he was hiding something. "Fonzo," she whispered, "I still can't sleep. Can I come sit with you for a little while?"

He didn't say anything, but she crossed the floor and moved his pillow out of the way so she could slide up next to him. She sat close to him and pushed his arm with her elbow. "What were you looking at before I came in?"

He hung his head, shifting his hands so he was sitting on them. He still said nothing.

She let him sit in silence for a while, then she prompted, "Are you all right now, Fonzo? You were really upset earlier. I wish Javier had said different things, too. But Tio Rob and Tia Julinha don't seem to be angry with you."

"It's not about them," he said.

"What's not about them?" She put her arm around him, worried he might pull away. But he let her pull him close. He curled into her, resting his head on her shoulder.

She whispered in his ear. "Will you show me what you've got in your hand? You know I won't tell anyone."

He hesitated a little longer, then he took his hand out from under his seat, passing something round and heavy into her upturned palm.

"What's this?" She fingered the polished wood and metal, trying to make sense of it in the shadows.

"It's a fancy folding knife; a hunting knife, or something." Her brother's voice quavered a little. "I was just looking at it."

"It does look fancy." She caught the gleam of filtered moonlight on it through the window well. "What do you find most interesting about it?"

He shrugged into her. "I don't know."

"You don't know?" With her arm still around him, she took the knife box in one hand and felt along the edge for the finger tab. The blade was heavy to lift out.

Her brother's hand came down on top of hers. "Don't open it," he said. "You'll...you'll cut yourself..."

"I know how to open knives without cutting myself," she said. "But I won't open this one if you don't want me to." She took the closed knife back into her dominant hand and rested the weight in her lap with her fingers curled around it. "Where did you get it?"

"I found it in Javier's room. In his bag."

"Oh, we'd better put it back in the morning so he doesn't miss it. Is it all right if I hold onto it? I'll put it back for you."

He nodded.

She rested her cheek against his head. "Brother, can I ask you a scary question?"

"All right," he said.

"Did you want to hurt someone with the knife?"

He was quiet a long time. "I wasn't going to," he whispered. "I was just thinking about it."

"Who did you want to hurt?"

"Just myself," he said.

"Were you thinking you'd hurt yourself just a little bit? Just to see what it feels like? Or were you thinking you wanted to hurt yourself a lot?"

His breath shivered as it went in and out. But he didn't cry. "I don't know... But I think just a little bit." He sniffed and rubbed his nose.

"Are you unhappy that Tio's making you get up to cook breakfast?"

"I told you it has nothing to do with them."

"What is it, then? Can you tell me?" She waited for him, stroking his arm.

He let out a deep breath. "I feel like I'm stuck in a nightmare and can't wake up. I'm angry all the time. I don't know who I am. I feel like I don't know where I am. I think about my friend, Ikal, who's probably still stuck at the facility without his mama and papa. And talking to people here just explodes into a big fight or a big mess, every day. Tomorrow isn't going to be any different, except that it's the first Christmas not knowing who my papa is, and not having Mama there to spoil us and tell us we're her favorite people in the whole world. We're not anybody's favorite people anymore. We're just cockroaches now, like Abuelo said."

"You're still *my* favorite person in the whole world," Eloida whispered. "I wouldn't have made it to the wall without you."

"Yes, you would have. You're a lot stronger than me." He kneaded his fingers into the legs of his pajama pants. "Nobody needs me. And these days the only thing I do is cause trouble."

"I'm sorry this hurts so much," she said. "I'm still trying to get used to living here, too, and I wish you knew how much I need you. Besides, don't you want to keep your promise to Tio Rob to help with breakfast? I can come with you, if you want, so you don't feel embarrassed or ashamed."

"I'm not sure he's punishing me," said Alfonzo. "He asked me so nicely, and it sounded very nice that I could do that, and then everything would be all right again."

"Well, I think you should at least give it a try."

Alfonzo breathed out a laugh, as though relieved.

She left the folding knife in her lap and put both her arms around him. He clung to her, like he had earlier when they were upstairs. "It's all right to cry," she repeated.

"I know. I am crying, just a little bit." He wiped his face again with his hands. He bounced his foot up and down, shaking the bed a little with the tick. "How did you know?"

"How did I know what?"

"That I had the knife."

Eloida shivered, thinking about the warning in her sleep, the wisp of her mother's pleading voice in the hall. "Can I tell you a secret?"

"All right," he said.

"I saw Mama tonight."

He let go of her and relaxed a little, scratching his chest. "Was it a good dream?"

"No, it wasn't a dream. I went upstairs earlier because... Well, I thought I knew what her footsteps sounded like, even though we've never been to this house with her. And I saw her ghost over by the fireplace, smelling the poinsettias."

"Why would a ghost smell poinsettias? She wouldn't have a nose."

"I don't know. That's just what I saw. I waved at her... And she waved back."

The sound of Javier's bedsprings creaking traveled through the wall. The two children went silent. Alfonzo stopped bouncing his foot, and they were still. But they heard no more movement or sound from their cousin's room after a while.

"I wish he snored so we could tell better if he was asleep," Alfonzo whispered, very softly.

"Me too," said Eloida.

"Was it scary seeing her...you know...all bloody and cut up?"

The girl shook her head. "She didn't look like that."

"What did she look like?"

"Just normal. A little lost, maybe, or worried. I couldn't tell. But she had her red ribbon in her hair, the one she always wore for *Navidad.*"

Alfonzo seemed to ponder this, his eyes looking bright again where the moonlight caught them. "I wish I could see her."

"Maybe you will."

He sat up and proffered a slight smile, scratching his head. "Why are you telling me this story?"

Eloida bit her lip. Of course he wouldn't believe her. It sounded absurd. "You asked me how I knew you had the knife. I didn't know. But she knew. She woke me up and told me you were in danger. She's here, and I think she knows some of the things we're thinking about somehow."

"Do you think she saw me break everything, then?"

"She did. She looked sad."

He seemed to be expecting a different reaction than that. Perhaps he meant to make her laugh. His small smile sank back to a frown, his brow pinching. "You don't have to tell me silly stories, you know, to make me feel better. I'm not seven."

"Right." She sighed. "I thought you were liking the story, so I just kept going."

He nodded. "Sorry. Yes, I do like it. It's nice to think of her being here, looking normal, like you said. Watching over us, that sort of thing."

"Don't you think she could come watch over us?"

"I don't know. The only ghosts I've seen are in nightmares. I don't think I'd want to see one in real life. It'd probably end up being somebody Papa killed, coming back to get revenge on us or something. You know? I'd rather just not believe in the dead living on that way, coming back to bother us."

"Oh." She felt crestfallen, and her demeanor seemed to show it enough for her brother to notice.

"You really think you saw her, don't you?"

Eloida nodded.

Alfonzo nodded in turn. "Well, that's all right. I'm glad it wasn't too scary, anyway."

"It was a little scary. Mostly just because it was weird, because...*ay,* she was in a lot of pain and things when she died. But she's not that way now. It feels off that way. And sometimes I think I can hear her voice, but other times it seems like she can't really talk to me or touch me. I saw her a few times when I was at the facility too."

The girl's brother shivered. "Is it all right if we stop talking about Mama?"

"Yes. That's all right."

He smiled again, rubbing his ear and returning to bouncing his foot. "Elyi, do you think I'm an affair baby or a rape baby?"

She frowned at him. "What?"

He uttered a nervous giggle and covered his mouth to hide the sound.

"Goodness, Fonzo, why are you thinking about those things?"

"I don't like thinking about Mama getting hurt." He bit his lip and scratched his face, making it clear his laughter came more from embarrassment than amusement at the concepts he'd proposed.

"Oh, I see." She patted Fonzo's knee. "You didn't hurt her, though."

"But maybe I'm not supposed to be here. Maybe I have more genes that make me angry, or violent, or...or something like that."

"I don't believe that." She thought for a moment. "I was an affair baby, you know. Sort of. They weren't married to other people, but they weren't married to each other either."

"Yes, I know that story," he said. "That's how Mama and Papa... or David... How they got together in the end."

"He's still your papa, silly. He raised us both, with Mama."

Alfonzo shrugged. "I just didn't know I was *adopted.* I wish I knew my story."

"Well, we'll just have to figure it out then. But we have to let Tio Rob and Tia Julinha help us."

Alfonzo looked thoughtful, his smile returning again. "Didn't our other *abuelo* insist on Mama and Papa getting married? I can't remember."

"No, not at all. I think Abuelo Pepito knew Papa's family, and he was against it. But Papa felt like he needed to take care of her, and me. So he did."

The sudden squeak of Javier's bedsprings made the children both gasp. Eloida let go of her brother and scrambled to hide the folding knife in the waist of her pajama pants. She wished very much that she had brought a sweatshirt with pockets. Javier pushed the door to Alfonzo's bedroom open wide. "Eloida, why are you in here?"

She said, "We were just talking about our parents, *primo*."

Javier sighed, the silhouette of his form in the doorway rubbing his brow in weariness. "All right, *chicos*. Alfonzo needs to get up in the morning to make breakfast. And you don't want to be so tired on *Navidad* that you sleep all day and miss celebrating with everyone, do you, Eloida?"

"No, Javier," the girl said.

"Go back to your room, please, and let your brother sleep. You can talk all day tomorrow."

"*Sí.*" As she stood, the weight of the folding knife slid down her pant leg and thudded on the carpet.

"What's that?"

Eloida bent down, picking up the knife. She was tempted to say "nothing," but she didn't try to explain anything at all. How she wished she had pockets right now.

"Eloida, what do you have? Bring that to me."

The girl hesitated, staring in the dark at the weight and smoothness of the dangerous implement she held. She couldn't hide it now. She promised her brother she would put it back without telling anyone he'd taken it, and now they were both going to get into trouble. The girl steeled herself and crossed the room. Then she placed the folded knife, and all its weight, into Primo Javier's beckoning upturned palm.

He held it up close to his face. "Is this...?" He flipped on the bedroom light. Eloida blinked at the sudden brightness, her older cousin scowling as he confirmed the object's identity. Then he looked her in the eyes with that same weary scowl. "This is mine. You took this out of my bag, didn't you? Why do you have this?"

"I took it."

Eloida looked over her shoulder at her brother, who had slid out of bed and stood behind her.

"Don't be mad at her. She took it from me." The boy's whole face twitched with the depth and turmoil of his emotions, his eyes turning glossy as he kept gaze with his older cousin, seemingly willing himself not to cry. He kneaded the front of his pajama t-shirt with both hands. "I wanted to cut myself."

Eloida marveled at her brother's frankness. She wasn't expecting to feel relieved, but she did.

Javier sighed and scratched his forehead. "You're coming upstairs with me, both of you."

"She didn't do anything," her brother growled.

"Don't do this right now, Alfonzo. I'm not your enemy. Come on. We're going to talk to my parents."

"I know they're going to send me away after *Posadas* and Three Kings Day," Alfonzo huffed. "I've heard them talking about it a lot, how they can't keep me here."

Their cousin nodded. "Listen, nobody's sending you back to the border camp, and nobody's sending you back to your *abuelo* in Acapulco. You're here with us now. But you need some help. All right? My parents need to be able to sleep at night knowing they're not going to find you dead in your room because something happened during the day that frustrated you. We need to go talk with them now."

"Eloida doesn't need to get in trouble."

"This isn't something we need to argue about," Javier growled, failing to hide his growing exasperation. "Come on."

The girl extended her hand to her brother. He hung his head and walked past her, ignoring her gesture. Javier let a guiding hand fall on

Alfonzo's shoulder from behind. The young boy curled his posture in apparent discomfort at his cousin's touch of authority mingled with any affection it meant to bear. Javier flipped off the room light, plunging the three into darkness once more as Eloida headed their march down the hallway and upstairs from the basement.

"*Elyi, ayuda me,* Elyi, help me…"

The girl halted at the top of the stairs, heart racing a third time at the airy, distant sound of her mother's call. She shot glances back and forth, hoping and dreading to catch her translucent form moving across the grand, open floor once more.

"*Elyi, watch your brother.*"

"Why are you stopping?" Javier asked.

The girl turned, pulling her brother up the last step and into an embrace he seemed reluctant to share in front of their cousin. "I love you," she whispered in his ear.

"Come on, this isn't a firing squad," said Javier. "We're just talking to Tio Rob."

"I can't stay here," Alfonzo whispered back to his sister. Then he pushed her, slipping out of her embrace. He ran through the kitchen, and past, towards the back rooms of the house that were veiled in darkness.

"*Ei!*" Javier called, apologizing as he pushed past Eloida with a look of utter perplexity on his face.

The back door squealed and smacked shut, making the young man jump to a sprint. The door smacked a second time. Eloida rushed through the eeriness of that black space. When she reached a window next to the mudroom door, she lifted up one of the heavy blind slats. Her cousin dashed barefoot out beyond the reach of the porch light, into the misty woods. He cupped his hands to his mouth in a gesture of crying Alfonzo's name. After searching in vain without a flashlight a brief while longer, Javier rushed back to the house.

When the door swung open, he ran right past the girl without noticing her, then he halted in the grand room. He hollered, "Eloida! Where did you go!"

"I'm here," she called, rushing to show herself.

When he caught a glimpse of her, he took her shoulders in an earnest grip. "Stay here. Maybe sit over there on the couch. I need to get my parents up, and then we might need to call for help."

She nodded and replied, "*Sí.*"

Her cousin let go and scrambled upstairs, greeting Tio Gabriel who had come halfway down. Then the two of them hurried back up together.

She turned to go sit down like she'd been asked.

"Elyi, get your shoes and your coat."

The voice chilled her. She wanted to say that she didn't know where her brother went, that she wanted to trust Tio to find him, not make things more complicated. But something in the pit of her stomach told her there wasn't time for that. So, with a last glance assessing the noise of gathering progress among the adults upstairs, she turned back into the shadows, slipped on her running shoes, and took her rain jacket out of the closet as quickly as possible.

"Eloida!" Javier's voice called again from the front of the house as feet thundered down the steps from the upper floor.

"Take your brother's coat and shoes," the disembodied voice whispered, close enough the girl almost thought she felt her mother's breath upon her ear.

The girl took them, then she slipped out the back door, shutting it behind her as quietly as she could. Then she raced off into the misty tree line past the yard.

ELOIDA REACHED out to touch her mother's knee, where the woman lay handcuffed to the floor of the van under a dark blanket in the space between the seats. Her mother had been given drugs to make her sleep most of the time, but now she groaned every time the vehicle hit a bump—a rock, vegetation, dips and juts in the landscape. The van was a rugged old thing that rattled terribly, stinking of diesel.

It wasn't like Abuelo Ramiro's nice cars that he kept in his fancy garage at Puerto Marques.

Abuelo took Papa with him into another van so they could talk business "in private." He said Papa was a weak man, and he didn't want Mama's groans and the children's tears to "distract them and exploit their sympathy." Eloida didn't ever find out what the two men talked about, with yet more cartel fellows in their company. She felt certain, however, that Abuelo was trying to convince Papa not to love his wife and kids anymore, not to care what happened to them anymore because the older man hated the girl's mama so much. Mama had been trying to get Papa to leave the cartel for a long time, and Papa hadn't ever been able to figure out how. It made the girl sick with dread. What if Abuelo succeeded? What if he found just the right words to say, and the next time she saw her papa he wouldn't want anything to do with her, or her brother, or her mother? The girl prayed that her papa would still love them and want them, that he would still fight to care for them, no matter what Abuelo said to him.

The girl sat in the back, her mama lying in the aisle beside her, between the four back seats. Tio Erasmo sat in the matching bucket seat next to the van door, to the side of the girl and where her mother lay on the floor between them. He wore his dark hair a little long, past his ears, but always clean and neatly parted. He and his twin, Tio Onofre, kept their goatees close-shaven to their faces. They were both robust individuals who looked a little pocked from steroids, but enjoyed muscle shirts on days at the beach. On this occasion, they were both dressed in button-down shirts with no tie, fine slacks, and Sunday shoes that had grown a little dusty and cracked from use beyond this excursion.

Alfonzo was buckled into the seat ahead of his sister, with Tio Onofre to his side. The nasty surgeon kept his hair very short to his scalp, almost bald in appearance. And the man had a dark purple port-wine-stain birthmark that sprawled across the left side of his face, under his eye.

Two men from the cartel sat in the front, driving. Abuelo and

Papa were in a second van, leading the way ahead of them. They'd been driving for almost three days now. Mama was terribly sick after the forced surgery. She ate very little, and said it hurt to eat whenever they took the tape off her mouth to feed her or give her water. The girl hoped no one from the cartel would notice the modicum gesture of comfort she extended to her very shaken and miserable mother. Or, at least, that they wouldn't care where she rested her hand.

They'd driven off-road for hours when the vans finally stopped. Tios Onofre and Erasmo slid the door open, then escorted the children past their mother and out into the hot evening air. They set foot on a windy, red, dusty landscape covered in sagebrush and a thousand varieties of cacti. There were no tall trees, no buildings, and no roads. When Papa and Abuelo emerged from the other van, Tio Erasmo grabbed the children's wrists and jerked them forward as he escorted them over. Eloida clung to the unhappy man, her father. Her brother stood just out of Papa's reach. The boy folded his arms, looking down at his feet and shooting glances back at the van from which they'd emerged.

The cartel opened the back door of the first van, throwing back the mere blanket hiding her condition from any eyes outside. They took off handcuffs, ripped the tape off her mouth, and slid her out from the aisle between the bucket seats, letting her collapse on her hands and knees on the natural gravel. Abuelo and others from the cartel spit on her, calling her names, calling her *perra,* a bitch and a whore. "You can scuttle to the North Americans like the other cockroaches who have nothing," he said.

Then Abuelo told Papa to take Mama, whom he referred to as "*mula,* that mule," to a certain checkpoint on the United States border to "retrieve the cargo." He instructed Papa to use the paper map and call someone on the burner phone he'd been given when they got there. He discussed how things would not be good for Papa, coming back to Acapulco, if the cargo didn't make it. Then Abuelo laughed and gave Papa a loaded pistol, "in case he needed it for the wild animals."

Mama couldn't get to her feet at first, so she crawled away from the van, toward her children, toward Papa. Papa pulled her carefully to her feet and walked briskly away with his arms around her, into the wilderness, calling for the children to follow. When the vans had turned away and they were alone, Papa stopped, steadying Mama. He buttoned up the front of her shirt, attempting to restore her dignity and hiding the lumpy distention bulging against a couple of large incisions that had been stitched and cauterized. Everything Mama spoke was slurred and wispy, but she asked Papa if he would come with her. She'd asked him this before, under very different circumstances. He assured her that he would walk with her, saying he had to get her to the checkpoint. But he said once more that he could not stay in the United States with her because he had too much blood on his hands.

The family walked until the heat of the day began to fade. Then Mama clutched at her abdomen and couldn't walk anymore. Papa carried her a short way until he found a soft patch of ground to set her down. She said, in a tone still riddled with physical and emotional trauma she would never recover from, that the bags were leaking. She asked him if the bags were important to him. When he said no, she asked him to take them out. He said he was afraid to do it because he wasn't a doctor or a surgeon. He didn't want to cut the bags by mistake, and he didn't know how to sew her stomach back up afterward, didn't have a way to do it. But when Mama began to shake with violent tremors and couldn't talk anymore, he cut the stitched lines in her flesh. She shrieked when he started, perhaps in pain, perhaps at the unnatural sensation of having someone plunge their hands into her guts, or the way the bags pinched things as Papa pulled them out. But she stopped groaning, stopped moving before he finished.

Papa cried out for a long time. His arms were dark with Mama's blood in the setting sunlight. He gave Eloida the backpack full of water, snacks, and some first aide supplies that Abuelo had let the family take with them. He said he would be along soon. Then a shot rang out, piercing the growing shadows of nightfall. Eloida had to lead her brother away, in the opposite direction from the silhouettes of Mama and Papa's lifeless forms on the landscape.

It was a long, windy night, and they didn't have a flashlight. Fonzo got stung by a scorpion and cried. Then he shook her when morning's light came, urging his sister to wake up, to not be dead like their parents, not to leave him all alone.

ELOIDA LAY winded and dazed at the bottom of a rocky ravine. She slipped and fell chasing her brother, while he screamed that he wasn't going back to Tio Rob's house ever again. Her head throbbed with a dull pain that made her nauseous. Her whole body felt heavy to move, and everything ached terribly. She heard the voices of Tio Rob, Primo Javier, and others calling to them below to wait, to hold on while help came for them.

"Elyi?" Fonzo's broken voice called to her. His hand shook her shoulder. His motion was cautious, like he was afraid he might hurt her or break something if he moved her too much. The air was damp, and she trembled with the chill of the northerly winter atmosphere on her skin through the lightweight cotton of her pajamas, despite the jacket. The earthy smell of mud and mountain trees filled her nostrils, and the sound of birds welcoming an impending sunrise filled the dark, misty canopy above.

The boy sat by his sister on the mud-slicked cobbles. He'd pulled on his coat and shoes that she had carried, but his hands shivered all the same as he pulled at the collar of her coat and stroked her muddy hair and face.

She groaned her brother's name.

He sniffed and wiped his nose on the back of his hand. "It's me," he said. "I'm sorry, Elyi. You weren't supposed to come looking for me. You weren't supposed to get hurt... I just wanted to go away and stop causing everyone trouble."

She reached for his coat and pulled him to lie on her chest, embracing him. "Please don't go away," she said. "I don't care how much trouble you're causing. You're my brother, and I love you so much. The grown-ups will figure it out. And I'll always be right here with you."

"Not always," he said. "I think you have to go to the hospital now. And I think I have to go...wherever Tio Rob and Tia Julinha were going to send me. And maybe to jail for a little while."

"I don't think you're going to jail, Fonzo. I think it's just therapy. They want you to figure out who you are, and they want you to be calm and happy here."

"I'm scared that I won't ever figure it out, and then I won't ever be able to come back." He kissed her cheek, pushed himself up, and took hold of her hands. "You'll be all right, though, Elyi. You'll be all right. You just hold still for now. I won't go anywhere until they come down to get you. I promise." He let go just a moment to wipe his face with his sleeve as he had done so many times that evening. He looked exhausted, his face reddened with cold and pained with the same expression of terror and sorrow that had driven him from one miserable state to another all night.

A flicker of movement caught the girl's eye. She looked past her brother, heart leaping for a moment with fear that a wild animal might be stalking them. But it was something far stranger than an unknown peril. "Mama's here," she said, quieting her voice. "Behind you."

Fonzo glanced over his shoulder. He gasped and jerked as though he meant to back away. But he didn't let go of his sister.

"Can you see her?" Eloida asked.

"*Sí*," her brother whispered.

The faintly glowing apparition approached them in silence, her form and identity growing more distinct as she came closer. The essence hesitated a moment, as though testing some threshold before her. Then she came closer than Eloida had ever experienced before. Mama crouched down beside her, right in front of Alfonzo. He shook like he'd just gotten out of cold water. His clasp turned clammy in his sister's hands. The three of them were silent for a moment that was as still and deep as a lake after a storm.

"I'm sorry I keep failing you," Fonzo said to the apparition. "I don't know how to be strong, and I don't want you to be sad because of me." He bit his lip and shot a guilty glance at his sister. "Have you come to take Eloida away with you?"

"Not for a while, *mi hijo*. It's not time."

The girl shivered, hearing her mother's voice so clearly. Alfonzo put a hand over his face, weeping once more. "Are you here to tell me not to behave so badly anymore?"

"No, *mi hijo*. I'm trying to find my way to you. I can see all your tears from here, yours and your sister's. But I can't always touch you. Will you let me look at your face?"

Fonzo rubbed his eyes and met the apparition's gaze once more. The figure reached out her hand, brushing the boy's cheek with ethereal fingers. Maybe Fonzo could feel her touch, because he shivered and reached his hand to his face. But his searching fingers and earnest frown seemed to show that he could only find his own skin. The figure took her hand away again.

"I miss you, Mama," he said.

"I miss you too, *mi hijo*."

"They hurt you a lot. I couldn't do anything about it. I couldn't even come hold your hand to make you feel better like Elyi did when you needed to rest. And I didn't get to say goodbye."

"I know you love me, Fonzo. I know it from the bottom of my heart. Nothing you did when I was in pain was cold, or cowardly, or heartless." Mama sighed, gazing at her son with so much pride and warmth even Elyi felt it from the top of her aching skull to the tips of her toes. "You are so precious to me, son. One day, you will be all grown up, with a family of your own. You won't know everything you wish you knew. No grown ups ever do. But if you let yourself trust Tio Rob and Tia Julinha, they will help you heal and bear the grown-up things you were never meant to carry. Then you'll know what to do when you're an adult. And all I need you to be right now is my little boy who loves football and hates olives. Or whatever pleases you, as your interests change... Fonzo, can you see that I'm all right? Can you see that there is nothing you did to hurt me?"

Fonzo nodded, wiping his nose inside his shirt collar in another usual gesture. "I cared about you. I just didn't get to show you."

"Yes, I know you cared very much. I know you still do, that you always will." The apparition smiled. "I wish I could hold you, *mi hijo*. But I will hold you again someday when it is the right time. Stay close to your sister, and let your cousins get close to you."

The apparition reached for Eloida. Fonzo moved his hand away so she could feel it. Her mother's touch was warm, not cold like she expected. But it felt more like a feather or a gust of air than a hand. "You'll be all right, my sweet one. Thank you for helping me. Thank you for listening, for keeping your brother safe until I could come closer. I will visit you both again."

"*Feliz Navidad*, Mama," said Eloida. "I look forward to seeing you." The feathery touch of her mother's hand vanished, and the girl sank out of consciousness once more.

A LOT CHANGED IN A YEAR. Both children had learned how to say many things in English from school and tutoring. Eloida had taken up piano lessons and a love for metallic gel pens, and Fonzo had started a model car collection like his cousins. Fonzo even wore one of Javier's old ROTC t-shirts with his pajama pants on *Buena Noche*. He'd grown very close to the other Del Lago boys with whom he used to fight when the children first moved in. He'd grown very fond of Javier especially, emulating him in every way he could. Things were not perfect. The memories of how Eloida's mother died still hurt Alfonzo sometimes. They hurt her, too. These things would not go away. But they also knew that they would continue to grow, and to heal, and they knew that they were loved. And Fonzo knew that Tio Rob and

Tia Julinha had a special package to give him on Three Kings Day that would tell him more about his DNA ancestry.

All the family photographs still sat on the fireplace mantle, arranged around whatever seasonal decorations the family featured there from month to month. But they were all in newer frames that matched in color and trim. The wooden *Nacimiento* scene was centered on the foot of the fireplace again for *Posadas*. More rugged than the old picture frames, it had remained intact after last year's outburst. A fresh batch of poinsettia planters were arrayed in front of it.

The family let Eloida and Alfonzo stay up to talk, even after all the grown-ups had gone to bed, as long as they were quiet. So Alfonzo came down from his room on the third floor and Eloida came up from the basement. The two of them leaned on each other, waiting in the balmy chill of winter that blanketed the sleeping house full of distant cousins who had all become close family. They waited in the shadows amid twinkling white lights that arrayed all the banisters, and even the mantle itself.

The lights over the mantle dimmed and crackled. And there she was, wearing a white blouse, her favorite crop pants, and a red ribbon in her translucent hair. Mama crossed the floor from the kitchen to peer at the carvings of Mary, Joseph, and baby Jesus. She stooped to touch and smell the poinsettias, then she turned to her children and waved at them. She shared a long, silent glance to where they sat. Then, when she seemed satisfied that they were all right, she turned and crossed the floor again, disappearing into the shadows that went to the back of the house.

Every year thereafter, until they were grown, Eloida and Alfonzo saw their mother on *Buena Noche*. They waved her a silent goodnight, and when she vanished they always whispered to her, *"Feliz Navidad,* Happy Christmas, Mama. We'll be all right. But we love you, we miss you, and we hope you'll come again."

SOLSTICE FIRE

BY JODI LYNNE CHASE

Wandering through antique stores had always been a favorite pastime. It was late in the day when Lily entered the small shop with a heavy wooden door.

"Good afternoon," a voice spoke from behind a stack of books. "Welcome to my shop." Peering around the corner of the pile was a woman that appeared to be as antiquated as some of her merchandise. "Feel free to browse through the aisles."

Lily smiled and thanked her, and started back through the closely packed stacks of treasures. Several old dressers stood along one wall. A few dining tables were bunched together in the center. Around the edges were several armchairs, each draped with linens that had seen better days. Up and down each aisle she would find bits and pieces of bedroom sets. There seemed to be little organization to the inventory, and she had just decided there was nothing to find, when a fur-tipped fold of fabric caught her eye. It peeked from behind a large gilt-framed mirror as if it had been hidden. Lily carefully edged the mirror to one side and revealed an odd figurine. It looked like an old Victorian Angel. It was nothing like you would expect from a modern tree adornment, but Lily was captivated. The Angel wore a pale linen gown with gray fur trim. Rather than a halo, it sported a cape with a hood that was also lined with fur. Holly berries and twigs sprouted from the waist to rise behind in an approximation of wings. Its hair fell in auburn curls down over its shoulders.

Lily gently picked up the figure and took it to the front of the shop.

"Are you certain this is something you want?" The old woman seemed unsettled about something. "I have much more elegant figures to adorn a tree. This Solstice spirit is intended for use while burning the Yule log, not to brighten your Christmas holiday. To use it there is not wise."

"No, this seems exactly what I need."

"Please," the old woman quavered. "Let me help you find something more appropriate." Reaching into the grouping of mid-century decorations on display, she offered an alternative. "This beautiful Angel with the silver gown and golden wings is much more pleasing."

"I want this one." Lily was determined.

With a sigh, the woman conceded. She silently wrapped the figure in brown paper and string.

As Lily walked out the door, the old woman called after, "Have a care with the Solstice Spirit," she warned. "It will not appreciate the honor of adorning your tree."

A traditional Victorian Christmas tree. It was amazing. It looked like something out of a fairytale. Her first house, and it was perfect. The years spent studying architecture and art had given her a detailed picture of what she wanted. She hadn't settled for anything less. Lying back on the sofa next to the fireplace to take in the image, she felt a glow of satisfaction. Blown-glass ornaments and holly-berry garland with candles scattered throughout the branches. Of course, she had replaced the traditional wax candles with artificial ones. Much safer that way. But everything else was authentic. And the Angel was the crowning glory. The effect was enchanting. The soft light and the warm atmosphere were the perfect makings of a dazed reverie. The warmth of the room grew and pulled Lily deeper into slumber.

In her doze, it seemed to Lily as if the Angel was coming down off the tree. As it moved, the room melted away into a wooded area. The Angel gestured to her, inviting her to follow deeper into the grove of evergreen trees. It was cold. Mist rose from her lips. In the winter landscape, the trees scratched at Lily's arms and face as she tried to move closer to the center where a light burned. Stepping into a clearing, she saw the traditional Yule Log blazing. Small, crooked figures danced around it. The Angel hovered in the center, above the flame, beckoning. Lily's surroundings became colder, and yet the fire rose higher. The Angel reached out toward Lily with a smile on its lips. With eyes glittering black, the figure began to grow. The fire raged, and yet the cold became intense. As it grew, the Angel changed, becoming pale and thin. It was as if all the color in it was stretched and faded away. The once fiery, lustrous hair dulled into stringy, ashen locks that writhed with an unearthly life of their own. Then it wailed. A high-pitched shriek of pain and sorrow. Like a lamentation for lost life and a warmth it could not feel. It reached toward Lily.

Starting awake, Lily found herself in a living nightmare. The room was an inferno, fire surrounded her. Above her floated a wraithlike figure who wailed as it clawed at her throat with cold, stiff hands. The tree had fallen across the sofa and lay across her chest. Heaving with all her strength, Lily dashed to the front door and threw it back toward the window. Flames leapt to encircle the opening. Turning back to the room, she saw the Angel floating toward her. Gray and cold. Its mouth opened wide in a shrill cry. Throwing her arms over her head, Lily raced into the dark beyond.

Sirens wailed in the night. The local fire department had fought the inferno for more than an hour before calling it a total loss. The best they could do was keep it from spreading.

The next day, the fire chief came to the hospital to check on Lily.

"How are you feeling?"

"Ok," she mumbled.

"I'm sorry we couldn't save the house," he sat a brown paper bag in the chair at the foot of her bed. "But we did find your Christmas Angel. I guess it was thrown out when the tree fell through the window."

Lily went silent. She couldn't look at the bag.

"Thank you." Shuddering, she sank lower in the bed.

Three days later, when Lily was released from the hospital, she ignored the small brown bag in the chair. She went in search of the old woman who had warned her against purchasing the angel.

The sign said the shop was closed, and the heavy wooden door was locked, but Lily could see lights in the back and pounded on the door until the old woman opened it.

"You knew something would happen. How did you know? I nearly died, and my house is burned to the ground," Lily couldn't yet admit what she had seen. "A simple figurine would have burned with everything else."

"The spirit of the Solstice is not a simple ornament," the old woman looked weary. "It has a life of its own, and it desires to return people to the practice of the old ways. You angered it by using it within another tradition."

"Why would you have something like that for sale in your shop? If it is dangerous, why didn't you destroy it?"

"I have attempted to do so many times," shaking her head, the old woman sank into an armchair. "I did not place it for sale in my shop. Last January, I had sealed it in a wooden crate and buried it far from here, in a place I hoped it would never be found. After you left, I returned and dug up the crate. The crate was there but the spirit had escaped. It will always follow the last to have seen its fire. I have been trying to escape it for many years now. I am sorry it has passed to you."

"I KNOW IT WILL COME," Lily stood at the base of the stairs. "It always does, but I will be ready this time."

The figurine stood on the mantle in a sealed glass case with a large lock at the top.

It had been ten years of running. Every Christmas the figurine reappeared. Many times she had left it behind, hoping she could escape. Wherever she ran, it found her. She had not celebrated Christmas again, and it had not attacked. But she had studied. She read of Solstice traditions, and a glimmer of hope dawned. This time she would face it. This time it would end.

She had chosen this house carefully. A homestead set far from town. It had been part of a large ranch, but after the family had sold, the home had been abandoned. It was built primarily of wood. Sturdy walls that could withstand a battering. She had talked of loving old houses, of having it remodeled, and the agent had accepted her story at face value. There were no remaining furnishings when she bought it, and she only had the windows replaced on the main floor to keep the area dry. The pantry, right in the center, was just large enough for her purpose. She spent the days afterward preparing.

Lily had wandered in the nearby thickets, trying to find a dead tree to use for her yule log. A large pine was nearest. A two foot section of the trunk had broken away. She had wanted something larger, but was limited by the doors she had to go through. She trimmed off most of the branches before hooking the log to the back of her rented truck. It took most of a day to drag the dry pine log to the house, and another day to maneuver it into the pantry. It would play the part of the traditional Yule log of Solstice. She hauled in several large garbage bags of dry pine needles and emptied them around the room. The fire needed to be hot. She completed her preparations on the eve of the Solstice. As the sun set, she placed the glass case next to the tree in a hollow in the needles. She carefully opened the top. After quickly filling the space around the figure with gasoline and pine needles, she slammed it closed. With shaking fingers, she leaned in to lock the case. The key slipped out of her hand and down between the floorboards. She could see the skirt of the figure through the needles. Was it moving? She didn't have time to look for the key. She placed the gasoline tank on top of the glass case. Stepping back, she tossed a candle into the room and closed the door. Waiting outside of the room, she could hear the wail of the spirit. She stood her ground, waiting to see if the spirit found a way out. The walls began to smoke, but Lily didn't budge. She wouldn't let it escape again. No matter what it cost her. Scraping sounds came from the door, but it held. The wails and scratching ceased. She had won. Overcome with smoke, Lily fell to the floor.

THE FIRE CHIEF walked through the remains of the house. The only part that showed real damage was a windowless room in the center. The door had been locked, and they had to batter it down to examine what had happened inside. The fire had raged hot here, scorching and melting the contents of the room, leaving the walls and floor charred, but intact. All he found were the remains of a shattered glass box with a scorched substance melted to the shards. There had been gasoline poured on the floor and rags stuffed under the doors. The remaining rooms only had minimal damage, mostly from smoke and the water employed to douse the flames.

Lily, lying on a stretcher, struggled to breathe. The paramedics had wanted to take her to the hospital, but she had refused.

"I need to wait, she wheezed. "I need to know."

"This was no accident." The fire chief and several police officers stood next to Lily as the paramedics tried to get her to keep her oxygen mask in place. "That fire was set for a reason."

"I knew it would come," Lily tried to rise, too weak to lever herself up. "It always does, but I was ready this time."

"What came?" the fireman asked.

"Did you find anything?" She glanced at him, and whispered, "Did anything survive? Anything from the room?"

"Nothing could survive inside that," he snorted.

The paramedics started to lift the gurney into the waiting ambulance.

"It's gone," with relief on her face, Lily leaned back on the gurney. "I can rest now." Her eyes drifted closed. The labored breathing ceased.

The paramedics leapt into action, the sirens wailing as they rushed to the hospital.

As they continued cleanup at the site, one of the volunteer firemen came up carrying a small bundle. "Hey, chief, I found a doll in the backyard. Ever see anything like this before?"

It wore a pale linen gown with gray fur trim. It sported a cape with a hood that was also lined with fur. Holly berries and twigs sprouted from its waist to rise behind it in an approximation of wings.

"Maybe it's an Angel."

THE GHOST OF CHRISTMAS LOST

BY L'REN BECK

"It's the most wonderful time of the year," Allie said. She huffed and turned up the volume on her headphones to drown out the noise coming from downstairs.

December was supposed to be a time filled with Christmas cheer, a time where people put extra effort into being loving and charitable. Maybe for some people it was, but it wasn't here. Who knew what her parents were going on about this time? Finances? Another miscommunication? The dog?

Allie subconsciously scratched the corgi behind the ears with her hand that wasn't busy sketching an idea for a cosplay, a lavish gown from her favorite anime. She didn't know if she'd ever be able to pull it off. Right now, her crafting abilities were limited to ordering costume pieces on the internet and trying to sew with disappointing end results—not quite the level of skill needed to do this cosplay well.

She reached for her pencil sharpener, stretching perhaps too far for one with a dog on her lap. Sadie, still asleep, didn't seem to notice. The dog didn't seem to notice the torrent of angry words lashing about downstairs, either, or if she did, she didn't care. Allie told herself she didn't care, either. If her parents wanted to bite each other's heads off, fine.

Then why did it bother her? She swore she wouldn't let it get to her, but it did. That she wouldn't be angry about it, but she was. She tried to be optimistic, telling herself that at least they were yelling at each other and not her. If she had a penny for every time they'd gotten mad at her—often for things that weren't even her fault—she could skip college and retire fresh out of high school.

Try though she might to ignore the argument, it wore on her until she was too frustrated to think of anything else. Time to intervene. That usually did little to quell an argument, but the possibility of earning a few hours of peace was better than doing nothing while her parents went on for who knows how long.

Allie threw down her pencil and shoved the dog aside. She pushed harder than she had intended. Sadie tumbled to the floor and whined. Allie grumbled an apology before storming downstairs.

"Can you two quit it?" she said, raising her voice to compete with the high decibel level, which seemed to shake the house.

This caused a cease fire for all of two seconds before her parents redirected their aim and opened fire on her.

"Watch your tone, young lady," her dad said. He was no longer shouting, but he made no effort to disguise how irked he was.

"You're one to talk," Allie said. She made no effort to hide her true feelings, either.

Her mom looked like the accusation had been a bullet wound. "Alison Jane Parker, you listen here—!"

"No, you listen! I get it; you hate each other, but you don't need to make everyone else under this roof miserable because of it!"

"You don't like being under this roof? Then leave! A few more months of high school, then you'll be able to go wherever you want," her mom said.

"I will!"

For now, Allie needed to get out of here, if only temporarily. She stormed back to her room. Sadie greeted her with a wagging tail, having already dismissed the earlier incident. What Allie wouldn't give for her parents to be more like the dog. Sometimes, Allie questioned if they even cared about her or if she was just another thing for them to get angry about. Sadie, on the other hand, loved Allie no matter what, always bouncing back to being her best friend even when she made mistakes.

"Good dog," Allie said. She gave Sadie a quick pat on the head. "I'll be back. Eventually."

After snatching a coat, her keys, and her purse, Allie braved going downstairs again. She ignored her parents' demands to know where their belligerent daughter was going as she escaped through the garage, and after getting into her car, she put her phone on airplane mode so they wouldn't be able to track her. Truth be told, she didn't know where she was going, but as long as it was away from here, she couldn't think of a better place.

For a time, she just drove, letting the tires crush her problems beneath all three-thousand pounds of the car's weight as a gentle snowfall billowed around her. Enclosed within the four walls of her car was like being sheltered within a separate world, a world where she was completely in control of what she wanted to do, where she wanted to go, and who she wanted to be. Today, Allie would be the greatest singer in her world. The popstar flipped on the radio and vented her steam with each note of the Christmas songs she sang along to.

As though encouraged by her rendition of "Let It Snow," the weather outside became frightful, and the snow intensified until it plummeted down like a white waterfall. Allie thought about turning back but dismissed the thought as soon as it crossed her mind. She knew how to drive in the snow, and she wouldn't need to worry about people who didn't. She rarely saw cars on this strip of the rural highway. Besides, she wasn't ready to go home yet.

When the radio channel reached a commercial break, Allie tuned in to a different station. This song was less upbeat than the previous few. It was like the DJ was reading her mind. Sometimes, it took a good cynical song to drive the cynicism from her. She didn't know the lyrics to sing along, so she listened in silent appreciation of the artist whose song resonated with the anger in her heart.

> *"And in despair I bowed my head:*
> *'There is no peace on earth,' I said,*
> *'For hate is strong and mocks the song*
> *Of peace on earth, good will to men.'"*

Allie thought of her parents, always in conflict. She thought of the chaotic state of the world. There was no peace on earth. Any guise of it was the work of those who put on their masks as they pranced about, ensuring that people only saw what the charlatans and hypocrites wanted them to see.

The next verse of the song turned hopeful. Allie glowered and switched off the radio. Commercials on one station, a song that tried telling her there was hope on the other. Even when there wasn't seasonal music, these were her default stations. She tried to think of other stations she knew about. Classical—no. Oldies—gross. Country —definitely not. Country songs were only about horses, girls, and trucks.

Then Allie saw it—two lights approaching. She watched, unconcerned, as the lights came toward her. Too late, she realized the truck was in the wrong lane. She screamed and swerved to avoid it. Her car slid on the ice. Grasping the wheel, she fought to regain control. She couldn't. The car went skittering into a ditch. Allie braced for impact and screamed again when the car plummeted off the road.

Time slowed. Allie looked around with eyes wide in terror. She saw the snow surrounding her windows. She saw the vapor of her breath. All was still. The only sound was that of her timorous breath. Somewhere in the back or her mind, she heard a bell toll three times. Then time returned to normal.

Allie was so stunned that she couldn't move. She could scarcely process what had happened. What had that truck been doing in the wrong lane? Why hadn't it seen her sooner? Why hadn't she seen it sooner? Some people had trouble driving in bad weather. Not her. Sun, rain, or snow, she never had any problems. Why had this time been different? Going on drives through the country was supposed to free her from her problems, not create half a million more.

Fearful tears welled up in her eyes. She fought to hold them back. This was no time to be hysterical. She focused on slowing her breathing and thinking about anything other than the crash, and after a long while, she calmed down enough to assess her situation. The impact must not have been as bad as it had seemed in the moment; she wasn't injured. Her airbags hadn't even deployed. Her seatbelt had locked, though. She unbuckled it.

The car tilted down at an angle steep enough that the frightened teenager knew reversing wouldn't be an option, and she doubted she'd be able to push it out on her own. Maybe the truck driver would be able to help her? First thing first, she needed to get out.

Allie pulled on the door handle and pushed to open the door. It wouldn't budge. Despite her resolve to remain calm, panic lumped in her throat. Choking it down, she shoved the door repeatedly, each attempt harder and more desperate than the last, but the door remained jammed shut by the snow.

"No!"

She moaned and slumped forward, her forehead pressed against the foggy window.

The window.

New determination coursed through her. The door was stuck, but there was another way out. She rolled down the window, threw on her gloves, and dug. With nowhere else to go, the snow seeped into the car. Allie couldn't care.

The cold nipped through her coat and gloves, and the snow clung to her face and endeavored to get through her squinting eyelashes. This discomfort combined with Allie's lingering terror rendered her more and more desperate. She dug faster, now deliberately shoving snow into her car to get it out of her way. Why was it taking so long? Was she digging the wrong direction? No, that couldn't be. If her car had crashed upside down, gravity would have pulled her to the ceiling.

"Help!" she said as she burrowed through the snow.

If anyone was there, they didn't hear this or her subsequent calls.

Allie couldn't hold back the tears any longer. She couldn't get out, and it was so cold. Still, she kept digging until, at last, she broke through the surface. Her tears morphed into those of relief until she looked at the road through the blizzard. It stunned her to the point she stopped crying.

She was alone.

Allie had expected the truck driver to stop and help her. Instead, she was on an insignificant road in the middle of nowhere, stranded.

She pulled her phone out of her pocket and eyed it, frowning. The last thing she wanted to do was call her parents. If they found out about the crash, that would likely start World War III, even if it had been an accident and the fault of the truck driving in the wrong lane. But who else was there? Sadie couldn't very well come rescue her.

Allie turned off airplane mode and waited for the phone to pick up a signal.

No service.

Allie refused to believe the error message.

"Come on," she said, never having pled to an electronic device with that level of fervor.

Nothing.

She begged a few more times before giving up and stuffing the phone back into her pocket.

"Now what?" she said to the deserted expanse before her.

Maybe someone would drive by, and she'd be able to get their attention. On this road and in this weather, it was unlikely, but she had to hope.

Curling up on the roof of her car with her knees to her chin, she waited. It would have been warmer inside, but the road would be out of sight from there. All was still except for the raging snow.

Wait. Were those lights off in the distance? Maybe she was imagining it, but if they were, she couldn't let this opportunity pass. Her hazard lights alone would likely not be enough to catch their attention. Scurrying into her car, she honked the horn—three short, three long, and three more short—and she kept honking in the same pattern. She silently begged them to stop, but enough time passed that either they hadn't bothered to stop or the lights had been but a figment of her desperate imagination. She climbed back out of the car and was about to fall into despair when she saw the elderly couple getting out of their car and running toward her.

"Are you all right? Come here, you poor thing. You must be freezing." The woman wrapped Allie in her arms and rubbed her shoulders. It did little to coax warmth back into Allie's arms, but it coaxed hope back into her heart.

"I—I think I'm fine," Allie said.

She was shivering, more so from fear than the cold.

"The first of the solstice," the woman said to her husband. It sounded like a lament, but Allie wasn't sure what it meant. "Do you think—?"

"Shh!" the man said.

A silent conversation passed between them through a series of exaggerated expressions. To Allie, it looked like the wife wanted to do something, but the husband urged her not to. At last, they reached an agreement.

"Come inside where it's warm," the man said to Allie. He gestured to the car.

Under any other circumstance, Allie would have turned down the offer, but the couple seemed genuine enough. She clambered into the back seat. The warmth was refreshing. The woman turned up the heat, which made it even better.

"Thank you," Allie said.

"Of course." The woman gave her a smile that was as warm as the car.

"We need to get somewhere with cell service. I'll call a tow truck so we can get your car out of there," the man said.

"There was a town not far back. Would that be all right with you, sweetie?" the woman said to Allie.

It was, so the three braved the blizzard, continuing the way Allie had been heading until they reached the town. The man called a tow truck, which could be to Allie's car in around an hour. Meanwhile, Allie tried to call her parents. They didn't answer, and she was still too frazzled to bother with leaving a message.

"I'm so sorry," the woman said. The pained sympathy in her voice seemed extreme, even for the circumstances. The crash left Allie feeling shaken, and she couldn't get ahold of her parents, but she was safe.

"I'm going to go wait by Allie's car. You take care of her?" the man said.

His wife agreed, and they parted ways.

After the man's car was out of sight, the woman turned her full attention to Allie.

"It's close enough to dinner. Would you like to get something to eat?"

Allie nodded.

They ventured into a festive square spotted with Christmas trees and surrounded by quaint shops. For a small town, the square was buzzing with activity. All the shops had closed for the holiday, but the people were content to wander the square and admire the decorative displays in the windows.

"Come on." The woman led Allie by the hand to a narrow door at the back of one of the buildings.

It looked like it should have an "Employee Access Only" sign, but upon entering, Allie found herself in the front lobby of a small café. It was as festive as the rest of the town. A cheerful carol rang from the overhead speakers. A tall tree covered in blue and silver ornaments stood near the front of the lobby, and all the tables had a silver reindeer statue as a centerpiece that stood atop tablecloths with sparkly snowflakes. There were only a handful of customers occupying the tables.

The hostess greeted the newcomers, but her eyes turned sad when she saw Allie.

"The first of the solstice?" the hostess said.

The old woman didn't answer.

Allie puzzled at this. The woman had said the same thing upon meeting her.

"The first of the solstice?" Allie echoed.

"Nothing to trouble yourself with, dearie," the woman said.

The hostess adopted her best customer service voice. "Right this way, please."

She took them to a small, circular table and gave them menus before returning to her post at the front of the café.

Allie skimmed over the menu, and, when a server came by the table, ordered a slice of quiche.

She didn't taste the food, and she didn't hear the woman's attempts at starting a conversation. The girl finished her meal not long before the tow truck arrived with her car.

She kept out of the way while the trucker eased her car off the truck's bed and parked it in front of the square.

"Not a scratch," the old man said, patting the vehicle.

Allie circled her car to verify this. He was right. That came as a relief.

"Thank you for all your help," she said.

"Of course," the woman said.

She and her husband entered their car and drove away. Allie was about to follow them when she saw him.

He wore a tattered robe of a dull, white fabric. His white hair was short and spiked, iced in place. His skin was frostbitten from head to toe, withered and discolored with some areas blackened and others scattered with bits of peeling flesh.

The macabre sight made Allie shudder, but it was nothing compared to the dark sockets where his eyes should have been. He seemed to have sight despite being eyeless. The sight penetrated all the way to Allie's soul.

Unsettled, she looked away, but her curiosity pulled her gaze back. He was no longer looking at her. Rather, he roamed the square. As he crossed paths with a middle-aged woman, he placed a hand over her heart. Icy tendrils crackled as they seeped from his spidery fingers. When he pulled away, a web of ice in the shape of an eerie snowflake coated her chest.

Surprised, Allie blinked. How did he do that, and why had no one else noticed, not even the woman he touched? Were the townsfolk actors taking part in a Christmas show, and their roles dictated they shouldn't react to the specter and his icy webs? No, she couldn't imagine anyone, not even a professional with an unlimited budget, could create such an incredible costume, and she couldn't believe an ice effect like that was possible with anything short of CGI.

The specter stalked toward a boy in the square and, placing his hand over the boy's heart, performed the same impossible effect—the crackling tendrils seeping from his fingers, forming an icy web. Allie, seeing this a second time, could not deny the reality.

She had to know how he was doing it.

"Excuse me," she said, approaching the specter.

He turned, and his cold, empty sockets were upon her once more.

Allie itched to flee his gaze, yet she was awed. Up close, the makeup job was even more grotesque. It took a lot to creep her out, and this succeeded. She would applaud him for his makeup, but first, she asked the question that had brought her to him.

"How do you do the ice?"

He regarded her with derision. When he spoke, his voice rumbled like an avalanche. "I am the Ghost of Christmas Lost. For every deed, there is a cost, and when you hear the bell toll thrice, it then comes time to pay the price." With that he stalked away, his bones creaking like a ship caught between ice.

Allie wasn't sure what to make of that. "Okay? A magician never reveals his secrets, I guess. Cool costume."

He didn't acknowledge her compliment. Rude, but whatever.

Allie admired his costume until he was out of sight. Then, she went home. The house was dark. That would make it easier to sneak upstairs unobserved. She left her car in the driveway to keep the sound of the garage from alerting anyone of her return, but any attempt of being discreet failed when she opened the front door.

Sadie heard the door and raced to it. Seeing Allie, the corgi burst into a stream of aggressive barks intended to scare off an intruder.

"Sadie, what are you doing? It's me." Allie reached out her hand to let the dog smell her.

Sadie nipped at her, but Allie pulled away.

"What's gotten into you?"

Allie didn't stay around long enough to find out. She jumped past the deranged dog and locked herself in her room.

When she went to bed, images of that frostbitten skin and those empty sockets filling her dreams.

Despite the nightmares, sleep did wonders for her mood. In the morning, spiraling off the road seemed but a distant memory, and the acclaimed "Ghost of Christmas Lost" was a nightmare, nothing more.

She went about her day as usual, though she had to avoid Sadie. When she got to school, it was like she was invisible. Everyone she talked to was so absorbed in what they were doing that they didn't respond. No one even looked at her. Or was it her imagination? She dismissed the thought. This was the last day of school before Christmas break, and she wasn't going to make it even harder to get through by fretting over nothing.

Minutes into her first class, the principal made the announcement.

"If I may take a moment of your time, it is with a heavy heart that I must confirm the rumors are true. Yesterday evening, Allie Parker crashed into a snowbank. She is in a coma and may not make it. Our thoughts are with her family at this terrible time. The school counselors are available to any students who may need to—" The principal choked, unable to continue.

Allie listened in disbelief. What was the principal talking about?

"I'm fine. I'm right here," Allie said.

What was this? Some kind of sick joke?

She looked around the room at her classmates. All were silent. Some shifted uncomfortably in their chairs. Her friends were tearing up.

"I'm right here!" she said again.

She searched the faces in the room for anyone who wasn't pretending to ignore her. When her eyes reached the doorway, she found the dead eye sockets returning her gaze.

She recoiled. Then, she leapt from her chair and crossed the room to confront him.

"What are you doing here? Do you have something to do with this?" she said.

The supposed ghost's tone unsympathetic, he spoke. "What the principal said is true. Alone and dying, they found you. Machines control your heart and breath, but you are lost, succumbed to death. Till they decide to let you go, this half-death is all you shall know."

She gaped. "I'd know if I were 'half-dead.' I wouldn't have been able to talk to that couple, the truck driver, or the people at the café. I ate food at the café, and I drove a car."

He chuckled. "The people you met were all ghosts who lied, protecting you from learning that you died. For this, you saw what you wanted to see, but now, you must face the reality."

Dread gnawed at Allie's stomach. "You're lying."

"See for yourself, dear wretched child. I will not have you be beguiled."

He reached for her hand and wrapped his gaunt fingers around hers. She yelped and watched with wide eyes as their hands exploded into a puff of snowflakes. An instant after, Allie's vision fractured. It was like looking at the world through millions of faceted crystals. Stunned, she took a step back. Her feet didn't touch the ground. She didn't have feet. She was the crystals.

If she had a mouth, she would have screamed. Instead, her mass of floating snow crystals rippled, causing an unpleasant tingling sensation as she blew through the wintry air. She couldn't wrap her head around what was happening, mostly because she didn't have a head but also because there was no way to explain this. It had something to do with the Ghost of Christmas Lost. She wanted to pass it off as stage magic, some sort of wild illusion that affected all her senses, but even the rational part of her mind could no longer deny the irrational truth. The Ghost of Christmas Lost really was a ghost.

The ghost mingled his crystals with hers and carried her along on a wind he controlled. She watched the world breeze by through her faceted vision, a disorienting jumble of colors and shapes. The tingling became unbearable, and it worsened when she and the ghost slipped through walls and solid objects unhindered. At last, their journey ended, and they rematerialized. Allie gasped in relief. She never wanted to do that again.

They were in a hospital room where her parents stood arguing over whose fault the accident was, each blaming the other for their daughter storming out of the house and into catastrophe. Allie didn't hear them. She was oblivious to everything in the room except for the girl on the bed. With all the girl's injuries, Allie almost didn't recognize her. She stared at herself or, at least, the shell of who she had been. She was dead, or at least, so far gone that she would die as soon as the machines were turned off—the state of half-death the ghost had spoken of.

The shock slammed into her with enough force that she faltered. She would have fallen over if her icy escort hadn't caught her. Again, he dissolved them into snowflakes. This time, he transported them to a castle that loomed over a forest of pine trees. The castle's towers were sharp spikes of ice that jutted from the earth, and its gates were as empty and daunting as the ghost's empty eye sockets. The ghost led Allie into the sinister structure. Inside, it looked like it had been made by carving into a glacier. Everything was ice—the furniture, the maze of hallways, and the throne room. Here, the ghost sat Allie in one of the two thrones and stood nearby, callous, as she came to terms with her death.

She felt hollow and numb beyond the realm of possibility. It was like she was trapped in a dream, a terrible dream from which she would never awake. She couldn't process anything that was happening around her. She couldn't move.

Searching for something to ground herself, her eyes drifted to the far corner of the room where stood an ice sculpture of a winged woman wearing a flowing dress and a crown of holly. Etched on her face was an expression of grief that matched the pain Allie felt. It seemed an odd statue to keep in a throne room.

The ghost didn't give her time to dwell on it. "The time for sulking's at an end. We have work to which we must tend."

"Work?" Allie said.

She was dead. What was the point in doing anything?

"In life you were nothing, but this, your death, grants you a new purpose," the ghost said. "There is enough anger within your heart that I have chosen you for a great part, to serve beside me as my Queen of Snow and freeze the hearts of men where e're you go."

He waved his hand through the air, and as he did, ice gathered around it and spiraled into a crown of dagger-sharp icicles. The ghost presented it to Allie. Her nose wrinkled in disgust. She wasn't sure what he meant by "freeze the hearts of men," but she knew she didn't want to serve the deathly apparition, and she certainly didn't want to be his queen.

"I'll pass, thanks."

"We shall see. For now, come with me. I shall show you your destiny."

He tossed the crown, which dispersed in a puff of snowflakes, before taking Allie's hand, and they, too, became snowflakes. This time, the ghost blew them into a house that was in disarray. An unfolded pile of laundry sat on the couch. Scattered toys littered the floor, which was in need of vacuuming. Screams of children rang from upstairs. A pile of dishes rose from the kitchen sink and overflowed onto the counter. A frazzled woman was in the kitchen, putting a casserole in the oven. When she stepped away, the Ghost of Christmas Lost approached. Crackling ice seeped from his fingers and formed a web over her heart.

The front door opened, and a man entered. As he examined the chaos, the ghost placed an identical web over his heart.

"Dinner is going to be a bit late today," the woman told her husband when she saw him.

The ghost added another layer of ice over the man's heart.

"You're home all day, and you can't keep the house clean or make dinner? What do you do all day?" he said.

The ghost added another layer to the woman's ice.

"More than you think, obviously," she said. "You try keeping a house in order while keeping a toddler and two kids out of trouble all day."

More ice.

"You try spending eight hours in a call center and coming home exhausted, only to find there's no dinner."

More ice.

"You don't think I'm exhausted? Try spending twenty-four seven as a homemaker!"

More ice.

"I can't do this anymore, Richard!" the wife said through angry tears. "I won't spend all day working harder than you can begin to imagine only to have you come home and tell me I don't do anything. We said we'd support each other, but all you ever do is tear me down. We'll see how much you appreciate everything I do for you when I'm not here doing it anymore!"

She stormed out of the room and up the stairs.

"Laura, what are you doing? Laura? Laura!" Red in the face, Richard kicked over a chair.

Allie was mortified.

"What was that?" she said to the ghost.

"Another Christmas is now lost, and they have paid the heavy cost. I have watched this family for years, learned their struggles and learned their fears. Each day, I came to freeze their hearts. Now, I have frozen them apart."

"But why?"

"Every Christmas that I devour, I add to my kingdom and power. No matter where your journeys wend, I will take you all in the end, and you have made your decision. Your anger caused the collision."

Allie gaped at him. She got in a fight with her parents. That didn't mean Christmas was lost.

But it hadn't been one fight. It was an accumulation of fights over seventeen years, years she spent resenting them. Christmas had been lost, not the date on the calendar but the spirit of Christmas.

"It's the most wonderful time of the year," a sentiment she always grumbled about. If she had that spark of hope, every month would be the most wonderful time of the year like it was for those who embodied the spirit of Christmas, not the mundane crawl from one pointless day to the next she had experienced during her life.

Not having Christmas spirit didn't make her cold enough to be an ice queen, though. Everyone lost sight of it at some point in their lives and most had fights with their parents on their track record. The rest of her track record was clean.

"Why me?" she said. "What makes me colder than anyone else? Wouldn't you be better off choosing, I don't know, a murderer?"

If he wanted her to help him, he was going to be disappointed. Now that she knew who he was and what he did, she would do whatever it took to stop him from ruining anyone else.

The ghost gave a subtle smirk and extended a hand to her. "Shall we continue with our work, my queen? Who knows what other Christmases we'll glean."

Stone faced, Allie took his putrescent hand and allowed him to blow her to their next destination.

They were outside a restaurant. The ghost cast his empty sockets about the street until he saw whom he was looking for, a man whose demeanor was as formal as his suit. He appeared to be in a hurry, but he stopped in the restaurant's reflective window to straighten his tie. He froze, staring into the restaurant. The ghost iced his heart.

"Stop!" Allie said, too late.

The businessman entered the restaurant and strode up to one of the tables where a woman sat with a younger man who looked to be on the opposite end of the spectrum from the businessman—casual to the point of seeming rough around the edges.

"What are you doing here, Gavin," the businessman said, "with our sister?"

The ghost took this as an opportunity to form icy webs over the hearts of Gavin and his sister.

"David," Gavin said in terse greeting. "What's wrong with me having dinner with Sarah?" It was a challenge.

"No, stop!" Allie said. She didn't know what to do. She couldn't let the ghost win. She had to get rid of the ice.

Accepting the challenge, David sat across from his brother. "You know what is wrong with it. Our mother's final request was for you to stay away from Sarah. You're a bad influence."

Allie intended to scrape away the web of ice on Gavin, but the moment her fingers came in contact, the web expanded, and the ice became thicker. She gasped and pulled away. She was making it worse. The ghost sneered at Allie's frustration and added to the web of ice over Sarah's heart.

The siblings hardened. Both spoke at once.

"She was on her deathbed. She didn't know what she was talking about. I'm not going to let a few words during a time of tragedy tear this family apart," Gavin said.

"You think he's a bad influence? What about the man who wants to turn me against my brother?" Sarah said.

"No, you're all turning against each other," Allie said. "You have to stop!"

"Don't justify disrespecting our mother!" David was trying to keep his voice down, but a few heads turned. "If this is what our family has come to, then I don't want to be a part of it anymore."

"Fine," Sarah said, refusing to look at him.

Gavin stared down at his older brother. "Good. Then go."

David stormed out of the restaurant. By now, everyone was staring.

Allie gawked at her hands, appalled and terrified. A spidery layer of frost coated them.

"I did this." She choked on her words.

The Ghost of Christmas Lost placed a gaunt hand on her shoulder. "You did well, but don't take all the glory. Over years, I have woven this story, and now this family has paid the cost. With your help, another Christmas is lost."

She didn't take all the glory. She took all the blame, for her ice had been the final stroke.

The ghost reached for one of her frosted hands. She pulled away. She wouldn't go with him. She wouldn't keep helping him. He seized her by the forearm, transformed them into clouds of snowflakes, and blew Allie along with him to his next destination.

Her cloud shook in response to her unspoken, "No!" The thought of going anywhere with him repulsed her, but she didn't see how she could get away. A cloud of snowflakes had no power over the wind.

If she couldn't escape him, she would find a way to stop him from hurting anyone else. Resolute, she surrendered to the tingling breeze.

Everywhere the Ghost of Christmas Lost went, he placed ice into people's hearts. Some, as with the first two, resulted in Christmases lost. Others, he was still manipulating with his subtle influence, working toward his next victory one icy touch at a time.

At a daycare, two children wanted to play with the same toy. Allie planted herself between the ghost and them. If he couldn't touch the children, he could have no influence on them. Unfazed, the ghost pushed her through the children. Her incorporeal form froze their hearts. A fight broke out between them.

At a department store, a customer was arguing with the manager. Allie, knowing she couldn't touch them, decided she needed to keep the ghost from touching them. She reached for the platter that was the topic of the debate, intending to use it as a shield. Her hands passed right through it. Perplexed, she tried again with no success. While she was distracted, the ghost iced the hearts of both customer and manager, and the debate became heated.

Noticing Allie's bewilderment, the ghost merely laughed a rumbling laugh.

"Unlike the imagined things you beseeched, the mortal world is far beyond your reach," he said.

She couldn't affect the mortal world? Fine. She would have to stop the ghost directly, then.

They came to a street where two neighbors were addressing their concerns about parking since both would have many guests staying with them for the holidays. The ghost stalked toward them. Allie threw herself at him. She seized his arms and held him in place so he couldn't get any closer. His lips curled into a disparaging smirk. With impossible strength, he threw her through both neighbors, creating icy webs over their hearts. She tumbled to the ground, and their discussion devolved into a quarrel.

Allie was uninjured, but she broke inside. No matter how she tried to intervene, she only ended up helping the ghost. She cried bitter tears.

The ghost knelt beside her and presented the crown again. "Even as you try to stop me, you hate. Accept your crown, and thus accept your fate."

Allie slapped a hand through the crown. It dispersed in a puff of snowflakes. "Never. I'll find a way to stop you."

The ghost laughed and then, as though to taunt her, said, "There once was one who could stop me, but of her vexing, I am free. She's lost forever, lost to time, and now this wretched world is mine."

Allie's thoughts turned to the sculpture in the throne room, the lamentation forever etched on its face.

"That statue in your castle. Who is it?"

"An astute observation, my Snow Queen, but it was not a statue you have seen. She was called the Ghost of Christmas Spirit, but even her 'goodness' had its limit. She grew to loathe me, and from this she fell, another Christmas lost with the thrice knell."

Right, cryptic poetry. Allie did her best to decipher it. The only person who could stop the Ghost of Christmas Lost was the Ghost of Christmas Spirit. Something had happened, and now she was only an ice sculpture.

The Ghost of Christmas Lost went about freezing hearts. He must have done this to his archrival, but on a more extreme scale to get her out of his way. Allie just needed to unfreeze her.

The Ghost of Christmas Lost fixed his dead, soul penetrating gaze upon her. "I see that you would try to set her free. Nothing can restore who she used to be. Nothing of her remains within the ice. She betrayed herself and has paid the price."

"We'll see about that," Allie said.

She needed to get back to his castle, but she doubted he would take her there. Rather than ask, she determined to find her own way. She envisioned herself dissolving into snowflakes. This proved to be enough. She exploded into a puff of white powder.

Allie marveled at her new form, a cloud of millions of snowflakes. When the ghost had been in control, the experience had been unpleasant, but this felt exciting, powerful. With that power, she found hope. She was not subject to the whims of the Ghost of Christmas Lost. She would take control of her own path, and she would fight him until the world was no longer subject to his whims.

If she were to melt the ice coating the sculpture, she would need a source of heat. Steering with her thoughts, she guided herself to the forest outside the ghost's castle.

Allie couldn't touch anything in the mortal world, but she wasn't trying to thaw a statue in that world. She looked through the forest for the ghosts of dead trees and gathered an armful of sticks and branches, which she placed at the foot of the statue before returning to the forest to gather four more loads. But how to light the pile? The answer blazed in the sconces on the wall.

Taking one of the torches, she lit the pile. The flame devoured the kindling and licked the wood. The heat coaxed a layer of water onto the floor and nearby wall, but the sculpture held firm. It didn't so much as drip. Allie held the torch near the statue as added encouragement. Several minutes passed. The heat was carving a crevice into the castle, but the statue still showed no change.

"Just melt!" Allie said.

She decided she needed a bigger fire, so she returned to the woods, bringing back as much fuel for the flames as she could carry five more times. She spread the logs and sticks around the statue in a wide circle. After lighting sections with the torch, she watched as the flame grew until a circle of heat trapped the statue. Still, there was no effect.

Not willing to admit defeat, Allie gathered more wood and tended the flames until she had a raging bonfire. The room was scorching hot, and the crevice was turning into an alcove, but it looked as though the stubborn statue wouldn't yield.

There was a droplet of water, then another. Allie whooped in triumph. It was working! She watched and waited for the fire to free the Ghost of Christmas Spirit.

But, after the scorching flames melted through the last of it, all that remained was steam lingering in the air with the smoke.

"No!" Allie said.

This couldn't be. The spirit was in the ice. Melting the ice should have freed her.

This was the wrong statue. It had to be the wrong statue.

Instinctively, Allie knew the truth. There wasn't another statue. The Ghost of Christmas Lost was right. His adversary was gone, and there was no way to bring her back. Seething, Allie slapped the floor hard enough that she hurt her hand, which only added to her vexation. A cold as powerful as the heat had been swept through the room, extinguishing the flame as it did. She expected to find the Ghost of Christmas Lost looming over her, but she was alone in the bleak room with her defeat spread out before her—what remained of the charred wood, a crater in the floor, a hole in the wall, and no Ghost of Christmas Spirit.

She stormed away. Before she made it far, she became a storm. Her snowflake form bombarded the world with her icy fury. Roads turned to ice. Her wind blew over trees and buried them in snow. Allie couldn't control it. She didn't care. Her only thoughts were of the Ghost of Christmas Lost. He said he would always win. He was right, and that infuriated her all the more.

Her rage blinded her multi-faceted vision. No longer did she see the fragmented world spinning about her. She saw only the interior of the ice crystals, which grew thicker and harder until her form was a jumble of hailstones the size of marbles. Too heavy to stay aloft, she clattered to the ground. As each stone hit, she protested and leapt to bounce back into the air, but she soon lost momentum and lay as a mass of frozen pebbles on the ground.

The rush of power she had felt during her flight faded, leaving her exhausted but still angry. She craved to feel that power again, but it would have to wait until she regained her strength. After rematerializing, she sat up and looked around to see where her flight had taken her.

She was on the side of the road in the middle of nowhere. The large indentation she sat in the center of told her she was where it all began, where she had died. Allie shuddered. Of all the places in the world, this was the one she least wanted to be. She pursed her lips. Energy or no energy, she had to get out of here, and becoming a snow cloud was the fastest escape. She closed her eyes, about to envision the transformation, when she heard a familiar voice shout from across the way.

"Don't!"

Allie opened her eyes and saw the old woman running toward her.

"Every time you give yourself to the ice, you speed up the process!"

Allie's eyebrows scrunched together. She would have dismissed this as senile ravings if there wasn't unmistakable clarity in the woman's eyes.

"What process?"

Just a few yards from Allie now, the woman faltered. "I'm not supposed to say."

"Tell me," Allie said, uneasy.

The woman bit her lip, still hesitant, but then, she explained. "The Ghost of Christmas Lost has great powers. Centuries ago, he placed a curse upon the world. The winter solstice is the darkest day of the year, and if, on that day, the first person to die is a young woman with ice in her heart, she will be susceptible to that darkness. It will seep within her and enlarge the ice. Each day she wanders the earth, she will lose more of herself as the darkness warps her. By Christmas, she will be no more than a cruel, cold creature." The woman broke eye contact. "Yours was the first death of the solstice."

All the air flew from Allie's lungs as though the woman's words had punched her. She didn't want to believe it, but it explained her other questions—when the woman and the waitress had lamented "the first of the solstice" upon meeting her, why the ghost thought she would be a perfect ice queen. She wasn't yet, but she would be by Christmas.

"No, that won't happen. There has to be a way out," Allie said.

"I'm sorry, but you are turning to ice." The woman gestured to Allie's arms.

Looking down, Allie found hands that were white and sparkled like snow in the morning sun. Rolling up her sleeves, she found that the whiteness had overtaken her arms.

Her stomach twisted into a knotted rope, and tears streamed from her eyes, but they froze on her face before they could roll down her cheeks. Desperate, she tried to think of something that could save her. The Ghost of Christmas Spirit might have been able to, but she was gone. Then Allie had an idea.

"I'm only half-dead," she said. "What if I die before Christmas?"

The woman pursed her lips and thought. "That might work."

Allie took that "might" as a "yes." It was her only chance.

"I need to get to the hospital," she said.

"I'll drive you," the woman said. "Best not to risk the alternative."

When they arrived, Allie rushed to her room and found that her parents were no longer arguing. But now, a thick web of the Ghost of Christmas Lost's ice coated their hearts. Their exhaustion had lulled them to sleep in their chairs, which they had turned to face the body lying on the bed, the body that was breathing but effectively dead. Her mom whimpered in her sleep. Her dad wore the gaunt expression of one who would awake more tired than he had been before.

The woeful sight drew pangs of regret from Allie. She should have been here doing whatever she could in this incorporeal form to comfort her parents. She had centered her focus on fighting the ghost to the point that she'd lost focus of what mattered most. Then again, had she ever focused on what mattered most? No, she'd spent her whole life missing the point.

It all seemed trivial now—every fight she'd gotten into with her parents, all her parents' fights between each other, the time Allie spent complaining about them to Sadie, telling the dog how much she resented them, how they didn't love her. If they did, they wouldn't be angry with her so often.

Now, as Allie watched her parents mourning their daughter, she realized how wrong she had been. All the contention had been the ghost freezing their hearts and working to tear them apart. Allie had let him, and now she saw the truth too late.

Her gaze turned from her parents to her body, bruised and broken by the crash. This pulled her thoughts back to the moment it happened—the blinding snow, the truck in the wrong lane, her car spinning out of control and crashing into the snowbank, the bell...

It was in that moment Allie realized what the Ghost of Christmas Lost meant when he had spoken of a bell tolling thrice. She hadn't heard the bell at any of their destinations, but she had heard the bell after she crashed, the bell marking her end. For the others the ghost had touched, they still had time to change. Not for her. She was dead. Game over. No going back to fix old mistakes. She could only hope that after this final farewell, she could escape the worse fate that was overtaking her.

Allie wrapped her arms around both of her parents at once.

"I'm sorry," she said through tears. "I forgive you."

They stirred. Allie pulled away and watched in wonder as the ice shrouding their hearts melted. After failing in all her attempts at melting the ghost's ice, she couldn't understand how this was happening. She was even more baffled when her arms felt wet, and she looked down to find the ice melting.

Fully awake now, her parents fell into each other's arms.

"She's never going to wake up, is she?" her mom said.

Her dad considered his answer for a long while before speaking. "No, I don't think so."

Allie embraced them again. "It's okay. It wasn't your fault. Let me go."

She didn't say it to escape the Ghost of Christmas Lost's curse as she had first intended. Instead, she said it to free her parents from this torment. Losing her would be hard enough. Prolonging the inevitable would only make it hurt more.

"Let me go," she said again.

She didn't think they could hear her, but her words had at least some influence.

"It's time," her dad said.

Choked by tears, her mom nodded.

They called for a nurse and let him know they were ready. He left, giving them time to say their goodbyes. Both fell to their knees at their daughter's bedside.

"We love you, Allie," her mom said, stroking her brow.

Her dad couldn't form any words, so instead he kissed her hand and held onto it as though his life depended on it.

Allie tried to comfort them, but they were inconsolable.

The nurse returned with a doctor, who turned off the machines. Allie's body let out its last breath.

Allie faded, leaving this state of half-death and journeying to whatever came next.

"Goodbye," she said to her parents, tears running down her cheeks.

SHE AWOKE IN A FOREST. It was winter, but everything was warm. She lay there stunned for a time before getting up, a cascade of red velvet billowing around her as she did. Her clothes had changed. Instead of a bulky coat, long-sleeved t-shirt, and jeans, she wore a magnificent gown with golden embroidery and long, flowing sleeves. So this was death? A tranquil forest with a dress like those she had fantasized about sewing? She hadn't expected to be alone. Shouldn't someone have been there to give her The Afterlife 101?

Confused and disoriented, Allie wandered the forest, hoping to find someone. The forest was empty. Did that mean death was being alone forever? Was this the consequence of always pushing people away during her brief life? If that were so, she might as well make the best of it. For her first act of achieving this, she wanted to get a better look at her gown.

Allie found a frozen lake and admired her reflection in its mirror-like surface. The gown was stunning, but even more stunning was the crown of holly atop her curled locks. The dress looked like the one worn by the statue that had been in the Ghost of Christmas Lost's castle, which was looming in the distance. Since the castle was nearby, did that mean she hadn't left her world? And the crown...

Allie understood now. In the beginning, she had been fighting the Ghost of Christmas Lost with ice in her heart, the fruit of anger. That was why she hadn't been able to rid others of the ice. That was why melting the statue hadn't restored the Ghost of Christmas Spirit. Heat doesn't melt anger, and you can't fight anger with anger, only love. Love had thawed her and her parents, and now that she was free of her anger, she could thaw others.

How was she supposed to help anyone when she didn't know how to get to them? She was lost in a forest. She circled to get a better look at her surroundings, and something in the corner of her eye caught her attention—a streak of gold in the pond. She turned her head to get a better look.

She gasped. She had golden wings. They folded themselves against her back so tightly she hadn't seen them when examining her dress, but now she unfurled them. They spread out around her, a gleaming twelve-foot wingspan. The feathers were woven rays of sun, and heat radiated from them, not an unpleasant heat but a heat that thawed the snow around her.

She had escaped the ice of the Ghost of Christmas Lost, for now, she was warmth. She had escaped the darkness of the solstice, for now, she was light.

Allie marveled at her new form. It seemed impossible, but melting the ghost's ice had also seemed impossible, and she had done it. She would do it again, as many times as she could.

She jumped into the air and let her wings catch her. They flapped behind her, each stroke a testament of her newfound purpose.

She went about, soaring on her wings of light, undoing the work of the Ghost of Christmas Lost. The wife who planned to leave her husband returned home to find that he wanted to forgive her as much as she wanted to forgive him. The younger brother and sister went looking for their estranged brother, and the three reconciled one with another and celebrated with an early Christmas dinner. Allie didn't stop there. She revisited everyone the Ghost of Christmas Lost had frozen that day, turning Christmases lost into Christmases won.

When Allie was in the middle of thawing the neighbors who had disputed parking arrangements earlier that day, the Ghost of Christmas Lost intercepted her.

"How can this be? Once frozen, none can undo it!" he said.

"I can, for I am the Ghost of Christmas Spirit."

Allie returned his hard glare with a soft smile.

And so it began, a new age in which both Ghosts of Christmas strove to turn the hearts of men, one with the intent to destroy, the other to save. In the end, it was up to the people to decide if they would choose anger or love. Thus, Allie's work was never done. Some Christmases were lost, but most she won.

STRANGER COME KNOCKING

BY DAVID J. WEST

"It always is Christmas Eve, in a ghost story."
— Jerome K. Jerome

ANONYMOUS—DECEMBER 25TH, 1865

W hile the following poem is uncredited, it was likely based upon a rumored incident that happened to the Thomas Carlyle family in that same year. They were settlers in the inhospitable Moapa Valley, located at what is now the northernmost point of Lake Mead above Las Vegas. The city was drowned under those waters and most of the ghosts there have returned to the ether, but every now and again, something floats to the surface to give us pause and wonder.

I found a trunk, a collection of letters and diaries that relate some of the strange occurrences from that blasted place, and this one, I think, would especially be of interest to those reading this collection.

The aforementioned settlers were plagued by heat, beasts, and even unfortunate struggles with the natives, but no one expected something supernatural to add to their woes. Especially at Christmas time, when there should have been a reprieve from the usual troubles.

In any case, this brief poem was found in a trunk with a multitude of journals and letters. This was unique in and of itself, despite there being no clear author found amongst the cache. The handwriting was very discernable and had no apparent similarity to any other journal or letters contained therein.

The incident was alluded to in the diary of Martha Carlyle as happening to her grandmother's homesteading family and thus our assumption of same.

It was the coldest of remembered evenings and we were gathered about the fire, singing carols of pleasantries, Christmas and such, when a stranger come knocking upon our door but said he...nothing more.

I went and answered, saying 'I trust you have need of something friend, enter eat, drink, and be of good cheer'.

But of a man or woman or child there was none near...

Shutting the door, I was given pause and more on who could have been knocking there at our door. The children were hushed and all drew near as yet another knock came and this time to the rear...

Thinking they had passed by too quickly from the front to the back, I called out, 'You're welcome here Jack, come and join us and celebrate the New Year and Christmas time snack'.

But when I rose to the door, there again was no one more. Alone was the threshold and cold still moon waiting for someone to show their face soon...

Back to our song and verse and feast, when all of a sudden the knocking increased.

The call at first to join was unheeded, but the curiosity was yet unneeded for we felt a chill and a crawling as boot steps walked cross the floor, though no one was seen entering our rear door.

The tramp was weighty, and the heavy presence felt, by all in the home who therein truly dwelt.

'Twas asked, 'Who goes there, here in my house, your steps do frighten my children and spouse.'

Silence met us, for none answered my speech, and then when we smelt his sulfur and brimstone odor, then did we screech as it spoke, meeting our ear, saying and I quoth, "I am here."

Under the tree and through the cupboards did the children run and hide. With this now unwelcome guest I did in vain attempt to collide.

But of his material there was none, I crashed through him and 'twas no fun, to be cast off like a shoe and have the dinner table given me stars for a view.

The plates were smashed and Christmas hopes dashed as the dogs did bark and the flames went out—one and all to the last spark.

We were trapped in the gloom and crushing dark while he laughed at us as if on a lark.

The lights of Christmas were dimmed and gone as our hopes too were smashed and suddenly withdrawn. And I never thought I was a coward until that hour when I was trapped there within the Devil's power.

And then as all faith was lost and to the point of exhaust, did my little baby girl open her mouth and let loose all we had taught her in a whirl.

She said her prayer loud and true that we might come safely through, and to the Devil she said to leave and go, that we might never have to know him again, as above and so below.

The Devil did heed the spawn of my seed, as she called on the angels of Heaven and Jesus to save us from he who had so cruelly seized us.

Like a hurricane he did depart, and never did it swell so strong my heart, for that brave little girl with her gospel art. She showed us the way, brave and true and to utterly convey just what to do.

So if a stranger come knocking (and he will) careful who you invite without first talking, know their light, or you could be in for quite a terrible late Christmas fright.

LOVE ME, I PRAY

BY STACI OLSEN

Virgin snow muted sound as it fell from a looming gray sky, binding the wide fields in suffocating cerecloth, slowly burying the Corolla which butted up against a broken fence post on the edge of a two-lane highway.

Justin's frustration built to a level he could no longer contain, and he renewed their argument by snapping, "I'm freezing. We're going to die out here, Jessica."

"Well, whose fault is that?" she countered. "You were supposed to wake me up if you got tired!"

"I wanted to let you sleep! It was your idea to take this 'shortcut'." Justin air-quoted the word. "If we were on the freeway, this wouldn't have happened."

Jessica's arms tightened across her chest. "My parents are going to be sick worrying about us. This isn't how I wanted to spend Christmas Eve!"

The words rattled, shaking the foundations of their relationship like a California earthquake, making Justin wonder if he had miscalculated and his Christmas plans were premature. They had repeated the same squabble throughout the last two hours in various forms, growing more heated as the time passed and the snow fell and no other vehicles came along and they realized that they were seriously, dangerously stranded.

Justin's teeth clenched, his silence charged with rage.

As darkness descended, the sky cleared. Though snow stopped falling, it had piled so deep on the highway that only a plow could make it through, and there was no telling when the Department of Transportation would decide to clear this obscure road. No one was coming.

Jessica shivered in the passenger seat, despite the oily, old blanket under which they huddled together.

"We can't stay here," Justin finally admitted.

"Try the car again," commanded Jessica.

"It won't start."

"Just try it!"

He obliged, but the engine still made no sound, not even a click to indicate it was attempting to start. The smell of spilled engine fluids had faded since the accident.

Justin shoved the door open with a frustrated thump, scraping snow back, and stepped out of the car. This was not the first time he'd walked out of the ditch to the edge of the highway and gazed a long while in both directions. No telltale light on the horizon hinted of other travelers. His eyes lingered on a distant old house, stooped and leaning, merely a dark, squarish shape far across the white plain shining in the moonlight. Nothing else disturbed the barren landscape.

He trudged back down to the car in the ditch. The trunk revealed little that would help them: a toolkit, a small collection of wrapped gifts, and two suitcases containing their clothes for Christmas break with Jessica's family.

He slammed the trunk closed, then opened the passenger door.

"Come on, Jessica," he said. "We're going to that house over there."

"We shouldn't leave the car," she protested. "When you're

stranded, you're supposed to stay with the car so searchers can find you."

"I know!" Justin snapped. "But walking will warm you up and we'll be able to find something to burn."

"Fine!" she shouted and clambered out of the car.

Despite her grumbling, he pulled the blanket from her seat, wrapped it around her, and vigorously rubbed her arms to help her get warm. He filled his pockets with napkins and receipts gathered from the center console, grabbed the plastic bag of road trip snacks and drinks, and pocketed his cell phone. Together they scraped a large arrow across the highway pointing at the structure, wrote SOS in the snow on the back window of their car, and began to walk.

The rising moon leered down on them, casting cold, white light.

Justin went first, breaking trail through thigh deep snow. Jessica followed, stumbling occasionally, but she refused Justin's hand when he offered to support her, so he turned his back and marched along.

Creaking boards sagged under their feet and the awning over the door looked about to collapse when they finally stepped onto the porch and paused to stomp the snow off their shoes and brush it off their legs. The house almost seemed to stir, breathing a petulant sigh. They passed a doubtful glance to each other, and then Justin knocked open the age-weakened door with a bump from his shoulder.

A gust of wind swirled out and followed them in through the open door. Howling filled the air and subsided.

"Oh, my word," said Jessica.

"The chimney is probably full of holes," said Justin.

The door shut behind them with a resounding crack, plunging them into full darkness.

Jessica jumped, jostling Justin from behind and forcing him to take a blind step.

Justin fumbled at his pocket, retrieved his cell phone, and turned on the flashlight, revealing a small, windowless vestibule. On the left wall stood a dusty and tarnished grandfather clock, an accusing sentinel. Two doors offered options, one straight ahead and one to the right.

"I'm going to find a spot to build a fire," Justin said, stepping forward.

His girlfriend glanced uneasily around and then followed on his heels. She cringed closer to Justin, placing herself against his back.

"I don't think we should be here. Let's go back to the car." Jessica whispered as if someone might hear her. She rubbed her arms.

Justin shrugged her off with irritation, his ego still stinging from the embarrassment of falling asleep at the wheel. "We're not going back. We need to build a fire and get warm." He gestured at the decomposing clock. "No one has been here for ages, obviously."

The couple crossed the vestibule to the door straight ahead, which stood ajar. Justin peeked into the next room. A table stood surrounded by six stiff chairs, all pushed in but one. A china hutch and a sideboard lurked against the walls, dusty with disuse. The cell phone's light cast heavy shadows.

"Weird," he said. "There's still furniture." Though dusty, the condition of the furnishings belied the exterior state of the house.

Jessica shoved under his arm to see the room. "There's nowhere to build a fire in there."

Justin turned toward the closed door on the right, turned the stiff knob, and pushed. It opened with a reluctant screech, revealing an antique parlor stagnating in time. Before the front window and silhouetted by moonlight, the tall, skeletal twig of a dead plant stood in its strange, cast-iron pot. A pump organ hunched against one wall, a roll-top desk huddled against another, and a settee and two armchairs formed a semicircle before a fireplace in the corner, completing the furnishings. Cobwebs hung between the murky ceiling and the tallest furniture, thickened with grime and swaying every time they moved.

"Ok," said Jessica, entering the room behind him. She removed the blanket from her shoulders and dropped it on the settee. A cloud of dust erupted, making her sneeze. She wiped her mouth and said, "How are you going to build a fire, genius?"

Before Justin could retort, an exhalation shivered through the room, speaking desolation to him and making him feel as if he were invading. He hesitated.

Jessica whispered, "What was that?"

Unwilling to reveal his apprehension, Justin tightened his shoulders and moved toward the fireplace as if he'd heard nothing. "There's still wood in the log holder."

"We don't have matches," Jessica replied.

"I was a Scout for years. I'll figure something out."

In silence, Justin bent and placed logs in the firebox atop cold, gray dust, the remnants of ancient trees. He didn't have a clue how he would build a fire without matches, but he would never admit as much to Jessica. He took his time building a nest with the trash he'd scavenged from his wrecked car.

"I'm going to look for the kitchen. If all this stuff is still here, maybe there will be matches in there," Justin said once he'd completed the preparations for a fire. He left Jessica alone in the night-darkened parlor.

Jessica barely glanced in Justin's direction when he left the room, her anger with him still simmering, but as soon as he had gone, her eyes darted about. The house felt tainted to her, dirty and stifling. A cold twinge shot down her spine and spread around her neck like a tightening noose or a pair of cold, dead hands.

Attempting to distract herself, she moved about the room, examining antique vases and oil lamps, bending to look at a yellowed black and white photograph of a stern man in a dark suit, trying to distinguish the details of his features in a shaft of moonlight.

She turned on her own cell phone's flashlight, slid open the cover of the pump organ, and pressed a key, but it made no sound.

On the roll-top desk lay an old newspaper clipping under a dingy glass star. Jessica pushed the star aside to read:

SOCIETY JOURNAL
by Mrs. Mary Cosen
5 January 1870

The date gave her pause. The dilapidated exterior of the house seemed to match the time period, but the interior, though filthy, was in much better condition. Surely it couldn't have been abandoned for so long without maintenance.

A tremor ran through her muscles as she wondered yet again if she and Justin were truly alone. She continued reading, hoping to calm her nerves.

Edward Dulaine Tells Why He'll Never Marry Eleanor Wright

Disappointing those awaiting the announcement of their engagement, Mr. Dulaine and Miss Wright have unexpectedly ended their highly publicized relationship. "She isn't the woman I thought she was," Mr. Dulaine confessed to me. "I will not be so crass as to divulge the shocking evidence to you. However, I wish them—Miss Wright, I mean—the best and hope she will choose a life of penitence in the future." When I approached Miss Wright about these accusations, she rudely refused admittance to her home and called me a "gossip-mongering old hag"! Miss Wright has not been seen at a society event since the falling out, though it's unlikely she will be sent any invitations if the rumors are true.

With a bemused snort, Jessica lost interest and moved on until she stood before the plant, shining her light over it. The top almost brushed the ceiling, and a circle of debris covered the floor around it. She studied the twigs and detritus, noting a few small candles, bits of colored glass, browned pine needles, and long pieces of string and ribbon.

"It's a Christmas tree!" she said.

Sweeping her light around the room, she noted other indications of Christmas: two moldering stockings hanging from the mantle, a bundle of twigs dangling from the lintel, a pair of blue and white nutcracker soldiers guarding the windowsill with white teeth bared in rictus grins and wide eyes staring.

Floorboards creaked near the vestibule door, making Jessica believe that Justin had returned from the kitchen, but when she looked, he wasn't there. With a spasm of anxiety, she resumed her perusal of the parlor, trying to overpower her tendency toward fear of the dark.

After circling the room once, Jessica noticed an odd, bronze candlestick sitting atop the mantle. The base formed a circular container. She prised open the lid of the canister. The interior held matches, tinder, flint and steel, and a scorched rag.

Jessica considered calling Justin back, but decided it would be satisfying to rub his face in it if she started the fire herself. She attempted to use a couple of the matches, but their chemical tips had degraded too much over time.

Once again, the floor squeaked, drawing her attention to the doorway. "Justin?" she asked and received no reply.

With a shudder, she returned her attention to making the fire, anxious for the feeling of safety it would provide.

Though she had never used a flint and steel, she knew theoretically how they worked. Jessica removed them from the box, propped her cell phone on the hearthstones, and bent over Justin's pile of napkins and receipts. Her first attempts failed to create a spark, but soon she learned the knack of it. She blew gently on the glowing orange cinders that fell on the tinder and managed to coax a flame out of them. Soon the napkins and receipts burned brightly. She broke bits of bark and splinters off the wood pieces and added them to the pile, encouraging a stronger fire.

Assured the fire would continue burning, she replaced everything in the tinderbox and set it unobtrusively back in its place on the mantle, intending to bait Justin with her superiority.

ALONE IN THE KITCHEN, Justin opened canisters, drawers, and cupboards, searching for something to use to make fire. He took his time, needing a few minutes of separation from Jessica's accusatory body language and words. He picked up a small wooden box sitting askew on the table.

The weight of eyes on his back turned him toward the door to the dining room, but his cell phone flashlight didn't penetrate past the lintel and the doorway gaped black.

"You better not be trying to scare me, Jessica," he muttered, just loud enough that if she were there, she could have heard. There was no response.

A draft of icy air grazed the back of his neck, almost like the caress of fingers. Shivering, he rubbed his neck to dispel the feeling, then slid open the lid of the box, revealing six sections filled with unidentifiable powders and bits of leaves, but no matches. Frustrated, and a little unnerved, he set the box down, gave up his search, and returned to the parlor.

His jaw dropped when he discovered that she had started the fire without him. The first couple of logs were catching. "How the heck did you do that?"

Lifting her chin, Jessica gloated, "Scouts aren't the only ones who know how to start a fire without matches."

A sound, like a malicious chuckle, broke the silence.

"Someone is here!" Jessica exclaimed, grabbing Justin's arm and pinching it.

"No one has been here for a hundred years," he insisted, pulling free of her grasp. "I think it was an owl."

"Owls don't sound like that!"

"Yes, they do! The barred owl makes a sound like a laugh. Google it."

"No service," she shot back.

His girlfriend turned her back on him and held her hands close to the flames.

Justin joined her, nudging her over to make room, scowling and resentful. To conserve battery power, they turned off their flashlights and put away their cell phones, relying on the firelight to see.

They sat on the hearthstones, as close to the fire as they could get, with inches between them that felt like miles to Justin. Though side by side, loneliness permeated the air, the emptiness emanating from the house and being absorbed into the weave of his thoughts and the pumping of his warm, living blood.

An hour passed in silence as they warmed themselves. Justin foraged through the bag of snacks for something to eat and drink. He handed Jessica a package of potato chips and a soda. She ate them without a word.

Decades of rain had rusted the damper into place and no amount of Justin's meddling would move it. Because the chimney didn't vent very well, smoke slowly began to build up on the ceiling, swirling and ominous. Justin eyed it with trepidation.

"We may have to open the windows if it gets too smoky in here, and we're going to need more wood," Justin said. "This pile won't last through the night."

"You could burn the Christmas tree," Jessica suggested.

"What Christmas tree?"

"That one!" She pointed to the gaunt plant before the window as if it should have been obvious. "Just look at it. There are candles and glass ornaments and bits of garland all around it." She swatted the two socks hanging at their backs. "These are stockings. Those are nutcrackers. That bit of twigs over the door is mistletoe. There's even a star on the desk right there!"

Justin glanced around with new interest. "I think you're right."

"Yeah," she retorted. "And I was right about the shortcut too."

With a sigh, Justin stood and approached the Christmas tree. After a cursory inspection, he bent and grabbed one of the pins screwing it into the stand, but the cast iron shot a spark that jolted him.

"Ouch!" he yelped and jumped back, wringing his injured hand. He turned toward Jessica. "It shocked me! That wasn't static, but this house can't be wired for electri..."

His words trailed off as Jessica rose slowly to her feet, eyes widening, the color fading from her cheeks. She raised a shaking finger, pointing just over his right shoulder, and breathed, "J-Justin!"

Dread blossomed in Justin's core. He could feel a presence there, just behind him, sucking away the warmth he had gained before the fire. He turned, reluctant, unwilling to see what lurked there, knowing viscerally that Jessica wasn't fooling around.

An apparition stood near the tree, an old woman formed of black smoke, her eyes cavernous darkness where orbs should have been. Though her mouth didn't move, a voice crept through the parlor, the words incongruent with the fear they caused.

"We can't have Christmas until you put the star on the tree."

Justin tripped backwards to Jessica's side and clutched her about the waist.

The figure shifted toward them, neither by walking nor by floating, but it lurched from one spot to another, progressing without visible exertion as if he had blinked the moment it moved.

Justin shoved Jessica before him out of the parlor and into the vestibule. They turned toward the front door, but the figure was there, blocking their escape and getting closer. They ran, flying into the dining room, but it was there too, revealed in filtered moonlight.

A soulless cry rose up, converting the apparition's mouth to a pit into which he might fall. They fled up the stairs to the second level, with that horrid wail chasing them all the way, threatening to split their eardrums. They careened through a hallway, tripping and scrambling, and burst through the closest door, slamming it shut behind them.

They pressed their weight against the door, holding it closed against the terror following behind them.

The cry cut silent.

Jessica grabbed her phone from her coat pocket and fumbled to turn on the light. The beam wobbled in her shaking hands.

Breathing hard, they listened, trying to mute the volume of their own living.

A stair creaked. Heartbeats later, so did another, closer than the first. Two breaths, and a third creak sounded at the top.

Extended silence.

Justin almost believed they were safe.

Something banged against the door, rattling it in its frame.

Jessica shrieked and flinched away.

Without her additional weight against it, Justin couldn't keep the door closed. It opened a crack. Aghast, he snapped, "Help me!"

Jessica threw herself back beside Justin, forcing it closed. "Justin," she whispered, a plea he couldn't appease.

His girlfriend began to babble, and it took Justin a moment to recognize what she was saying, or rather, singing. The words were from a song she'd recently sung for a Christmas choir performance that he'd attended.

> *"Away in a manger, no crib for his bed,*
> *The little Lord Jesus laid down his sweet head."*

Justin attempted to join her, but a swallow jerked his Adam's apple before he managed to add his hoarse voice to hers. Through a constricted throat, he wheezed out the first and second verse and sang into the third with Jessica while the door rattled and cold emptiness emanated through the wood between them and the ghost.

> *"Be near me, Lord Jesus; I ask thee to stay*
> *Close by me forever, and love me, I pray.*
> *Bless all the dear children in thy tender care,*

And fit us for heaven to live with thee there."

The pressure on the other side of the door eased. Their fear-weakened voices warbled into silence. They waited long minutes, trembling, expecting further attack.

"I think it's gone," Justin murmured.

With a sob of relief, Jessica turned to place her back against the door.

She screamed and collapsed to the floor.

Justin whirled around to face the room and saw what lay upon the bed: a skeleton, propped against the pillows, coated with a layer of dust and mildew. A moonbeam lit it up like a spotlight. The bones wore a nightgown and cap and the right hand rested upon an open, blemished book lying on the sheets. Decomposition of the corpse had stained the sheets in a dark circle around the body and holes spotted the material where maggots had eaten the fabric soaked in fermenting body fluids. The room reeked like an ancient tomb.

Justin's hand shook as he reached to help Jessica back to her feet, his grip lacking its typical strength.

"It's *her*," Jessica whimpered. "*She's* haunting this house!"

"We have to get out of here!" Justin eased his shoulder away from the door, prepared to shove it closed again if it started to open. Nothing happened.

He crossed to the window, giving the bed and its horrid occupant a wide berth, and peered out toward the ground below and then across the fields, wishing to see headlights on the highway or even a pinprick of light from a distant house, something, *anything* that indicated the presence of another living human.

Darkness.

"We might be able to jump from here," he said. "The snow should be deep enough to cushion our landing."

But no matter how he tried, he couldn't get the window to even shift in its frame. He looked at the door that let into the hallway.

Jessica shook her head. "I don't want to go back out there," she stammered.

"Maybe I can find something to break the window," Justin muttered.

He moved to search the bedroom, but the corpse caught his attention once again and a morbid fascination drew Justin to the bedside. He stood over the remains, gazing into empty eyeholes, trying to imagine the face with flesh. A blanket covered the skeleton to its waist. Its torso leaned against rotted pillows and the headboard. Though the flesh was long gone, frazzled gray hair still peaked from beneath the cap.

"Justin, don't!" Jessica whispered.

Justin leaned over to look at the book, brushed away the dust, and noted the thin, cursive words, the incomplete sentence, and the increasing shakiness of the letters.

"She died while she was writing," he concluded, running an unsteady hand through his hair. He reached out and delicately slid the book from under the fragile hand. Tiny finger bones broke away and fell to the floor. Hidden by the dust and wrinkles of the sheets, a fountain pen dropped from the edge of the bed and stuck upright by its nib into the wooden floor near Justin's foot, like a knife. His heart lurched.

Emotion plunged over them, not fear or hate or sadness. A hollowness so consuming that it felt like drowning. Stifling loneliness. Despair so deep that Justin felt it as an ache in his stomach.

An invisible force collided with Justin full in the chest, knocking him back from the bedside and throwing him through the closed door and against the plaster wall in the hallway beyond. White dust exploded in a cloud around him and bits of broken plaster clattered to the floor.

"Justin!" Jessica scrambled from the room through the splintered door and froze when she saw Justin suspended against the wall.

He dropped to the floor, leaving a man-sized indentation in the plaster. The force pressed down on him, keeping him on his back, becoming heavier and heavier. Justin gasped and tried to pray, but he couldn't force words out of his mouth. Weight stopped them in his throat.

Jessica struggled to help Justin to his feet, but she behaved as if he weighed a thousand pounds.

"Justin! Justin! What's wrong? Get up!"

Justin couldn't obey her. The pressure on his chest made his eyes feel like they were bulging from their sockets.

Jessica swung at the air above him, but her fists met nothing.

"Get off him!" she shrieked.

Justin's lips and fingers went numb. His vision grayed.

"I'll burn it!" Jessica screamed. "I'll burn the Christmas tree!" She turned and started for the stairs, holding her cell phone ahead to light the way.

At Jessica's threat, the pressure on Justin eased for an instant, allowing him a single, short breath.

With enormous effort, Justin wailed a one-word prayer. "God!"

The weight on Justin vanished, and he took a great gasp of air. Jessica spun and returned to his side. She helped him sit up.

"Please, Justin," she pleaded, tears streaming down her pale cheeks. "Let's leave! Before that thing comes back!"

Justin nodded his agreement, dazed, still savoring the taste of air moving through his lungs. Jessica pulled his arm over her shoulders and helped him down the stairs. They passed through the rooms into the vestibule together and tried to exit through the front door. It wouldn't budge.

Jessica threw her weight against it and then Justin tried, but the door remained firmly shut. They ran into the parlor and attempted the windows, only to find those also sealed them in. Justin grabbed a poker from the fireplace and swung at the glass. The poker stopped short, as if caught in an invisible hand.

They tore through the house, trying every door and every relentless window, screaming and beating at the barriers. The house kept them imprisoned, stronger than its obvious age warranted. A melancholic sigh seemed to follow them from room to room.

In the kitchen, Justin banged against the door leading outside, slamming his shoulder into it. The door might as well have been made of steel.

Consumed with panic, he didn't notice the discoloration of the hardwood beneath the window where driving rains let in through the warped sill had soaked the floor. He gave up on the door and leaped for the window with Jessica on his heels. As his feet hit the weakened floorboards, they collapsed beneath his weight and he plunged into the cellar below.

Unable to stop herself, Jessica fell behind Justin, but his body broke her fall. Stunned, it took her a minute to roll off him.

"Justin," she beseeched, realizing he wasn't moving. "Justin?"

No response.

Fear for Justin's life and safety instantly sobered her terror of the ghost. She kept her head, found his wrist in the darkness, and placed her cheek almost against his lips. His breath stirred against her skin and his pulse beat against her fingers.

He twitched as she sat back, gasped, and then bellowed his pain into the darkness.

"Where are you hurt?" Jessica implored.

"My legs!" Justin groaned. "I think they're broken!"

Jessica had lost her cell phone in the fall and the flashlight had gone out. In the pitch black of the cellar, she probed his legs, finding by feel the tear in his jeans, the wetness of blood, and the jagged edge of bone through the skin of his right leg. His left shin bone was broken as well, out of alignment bad enough that she easily found the break, but his flesh was intact.

Moaning, Justin tried to sit up and then collapsed back to the dirt floor. "Phone, pocket, light," he choked.

Jessica pawed his coat until she found the pocket and retrieved the phone. She tapped the power button to wake it up and activated the flashlight.

Shining the light over her boyfriend, she gulped at the sight of his crooked legs and sprawled body. Broken shelving and a smashed wooden barrel littered the surrounding floor.

"I don't think you should move," she said. "Did you hit your head?"

Justin labored to speak. "I–I don't know."

Jessica prodded his head and found a growing goose-egg. "What are we going to do?" she cried.

Justin stuttered out words through his anguish. "I'll be fine. Just wait for help."

Jessica wasn't reassured. "What help? Even if someone finds our car and comes here, that thing won't let us out!"

Justin didn't answer.

Jessica sniffed, thought for a bit, then removed her coat and the shirt underneath.

"What are you doing?" Justin asked.

"First aid," she explained.

She put her coat back on and began tearing her shirt into strips. Using the cell phone flashlight to see, she applied pressure to Justin's leg until the bleeding slowed, then bandaged the wound. Next, Jessica searched through the debris until she found four pieces of wood from the shelf that were relatively intact. She also found her own phone, its screen shattered and unresponsive.

Feeling queasy, Jessica used the rest of her shirt to bind each leg between two pieces of wood.

Justin clenched his teeth and roared through them while she worked. He looked pasty in the phone's white light. His body shook from more than the cold.

"Justin," she said, trying to hide her terror. "I have to leave you here to get the blanket. You're going into shock."

Justin nodded, eyes closed.

Fighting the rattle in her legs, Jessica stood and shone the flashlight around until she located the stairs out of the cellar.

"I'll be back." She bent, brushed her lips across Justin's forehead, then headed to the stairs. They rasped as she put her foot on them but held her weight. Jessica half expected the door at the top to be stuck shut, like the ones letting outdoors, but it opened with a screech, allowing her out into the pantry.

JUSTIN WAITED, shivering and shaking. He couldn't see anything in the black of the cellar, but he heard the squeaks of the floorboards as Jessica moved around the house. He tried not to wonder if it *wasn't* Jessica causing the noise. He tried not to imagine something he couldn't see creeping closer and closer to him. Though they were already sightless in the dark, he squeezed his eyes shut and clamped his teeth against the urge to scream.

ON EDGE, Jessica passed through the kitchen, the dining room, the vestibule, and then into the parlor, expecting to be accosted by the ghost. She tried not to remember the horror film she'd seen in which a demonic baby doll scuttled out of the darkness at people like an upside-down, backwards crab. The house remained quiet, so she grabbed the blanket off the settee.

Passing back through the vestibule, the brush of fresh winter air caused Jessica to stop and turn towards the front door. It stood wide open, revealing their tracks through the moonlit snow, stars in the sky, and freedom. She stared, allured by safety from the spirit that terrorized them. But that would mean abandoning Justin. She couldn't do it. She turned her back on the temptation and rushed back to the cellar.

The front door banged shut behind her.

Justin was moaning when Jessica returned, in too much pain to speak. She tucked the blanket tight around him and then sat beside him, stroking his knuckles with her thumb.

She did not weep aloud, but tears fell down her cheeks as she contemplated their helplessness.

The house was silent above them as the minutes passed, but Jessica knew the ghost was still there, watching. She felt its awareness like the eyes of a predator on a rabbit.

The pressure only increased over time, and the chill in the cellar deepened. It ought to have been steady in the underground room, but Jessica began to shiver, and Justin's hand turned to ice in hers. She realized that the ghost's attack continued as the weight of over a century's worth of resentment and misery bled into them from the darkness, leeching away their warmth. To save the battery, she turned off the cell phone light. However, being blind to the threat proved too much. She turned it back on.

Justin's shaking turned to shuddering despite the blanket. His face felt cold yet sweaty. In his condition, Jessica knew he would not survive the temperature in the cellar.

She shook Justin's shoulder. "Babe, it's getting colder down here. You need to be by the fire, but I'm worried about moving you."

He stirred. "I think...my spine...is ok," said Justin. "Doesn't hurt... just my legs." He wiggled his fingers as evidence.

Jessica hesitated, but their situation was becoming more dire by the moment. "Can you help me get you onto my back?"

Justin gave a minuscule nod.

Sliding an arm under him, Jessica lifted him into a sitting position.

"Ah!" Justin gasped.

After a minute of maneuvering which caused Justin to claw at the dirt in agony, Jessica realized there was no way she could get him into a fireman's carry position. He was just too heavy.

"Drag me," Justin suggested.

Tucking the phone in her back pocket, she hooked her arms

under his, locked her hands together over his chest, and pulled. The motion jarred his legs, and he cried out. Inch by inch, they crept closer to the bottom of the stairs. Once there, Jessica discovered she couldn't lift him up the steps by herself.

Justin had to chair-lift himself up each step. Jessica helped as much as she could, but he often had to pause to let the pain subside somewhat and to catch his breath.

At the top, Justin announced, "I think I'm going to pass out."

His chin fell forward against his chest as Jessica dragged him the rest of the distance between the pantry and the parlor. The effort to move him caused her to suck in the smoky air in the parlor, and she coughed as she maneuvered Justin closer to the fireplace.

She wanted to lift him onto the settee, but lacked the strength, so she laid him out at the edge of the hearth, tucking the blanket around him. Shining the phone flashlight over him, she found his face an alarming shade of pallid green.

Hoping help had arrived, Jessica went to the parlor window and looked out toward the road, but could not distinguish it from the fields in the darkness and moonlight. No headlights shone, and their car in the ditch was not visible. She wished for a first aid kit with medicine and bandages, but didn't dare leave Justin alone in the haunted house.

She pondered other options. Remembering the old bottles she'd seen on the shelves, she took the cell phone and returned to the pantry to examine them more closely. Most of the contents were indistinguishable, home-bottled foods darkened with age, some burst from the pressure of their decaying contents. On the top shelf, she found an antique blue-glass bottle with a yellowed paper label printed with red letters, which read:

LAUDANUM

POISON

3 months, 1 drop

1 year, 4 drops

4 years, 6 drops

10 years, 14 drops

20 years, 25 drops

Adults, 30 drops

She hesitated. Jessica did not know much about laudanum other than it was once used to treat pain. Unsure how such a mixture decayed over the years, she feared it might actually poison him, but she was also desperate, so she grabbed the bottle.

On her way back through the dining room, she saw the book Justin had taken from under the corpse's hand. He must have dropped it while they were trying to escape. Nervous, she picked it up and hurried back toward the parlor and to what would feel like safety in the firelight.

Approaching the door to the vestibule, she slowed, sensing the menace now emanating from the room that hadn't been there when she'd passed through just minutes before. Wary, she stepped into the vestibule.

A shadowy figure blocked the doorway to the parlor, stopping Jessica short. It flickered like shadows beyond a fire. The roiling smoke of its form distorted the features of its grotesque face, making its mouth bend and writhe in a silent scream.

"Move!" Jessica commanded, anxiety for Justin making her bold.

The ghost maintained its place between Jessica and Justin.

"What do you want?" she begged, desperate.

Though the ghost's mouth continued to gape, a chasmic voice answered from all around, raising goosebumps on Jessica's skin, creeping like spiders into her ears.

"I want...*him*."

The front door opened, exposing freedom once again, and the ghost raised a long arm to point Jessica towards it.

Jessica's heartbeat slowed until each thud echoed in her ears. She understood that the door had not opened by chance that first time. The ghost wanted her to leave. Her, but not Justin.

Jessica's fingers tightened around the book. "No. Never."

Defiant, she hurled the book at the phantom. It passed through the ghost's chest, rupturing the form. Smoke drifted and Jessica dashed into the parlor before the ghost could reorganize and claimed her place beside her boyfriend.

Justin was still unconscious when she unscrewed the cap, wet the tip of her finger with the medicine, and swiped it inside his mouth. The third time she did it, he choked, gagged, and muttered, "Gross! You poisoning me?"

The words stabbed. She already felt the weight of guilt for making him take the shortcut that led to their current quandary. She blamed herself for the car accident, being trapped in the house, and Justin's injuries. At that moment, she saw no hope of a coming morning, no rescue. She only saw Justin dead on the floor and her propped against a chair beside him, mere bones, like the body upstairs and the Christmas tree before the window.

Hopeless, she said, "Shut up and take it. It's laudanum. They used to use it for pain. I don't know if it will still work, but it's all we've got." Though her words demanded compliance, her tone and her touch were gentle.

"It's so bitter." Tears of agony trickled out the corners of his scrunched-up eyes.

She frowned, stopped the bottleneck with her finger, tipped it, then swiped her finger in his mouth. "Four."

"How many?" he asked, gasping as the pain overcame him.

"Thirty."

"Oh, no."

Once all thirty drops of laudanum had been administered, Jessica took up the fireplace poker and rested it across her knees, knowing it was an ineffectual weapon, but feeling better to have it all the same. She put her back to the fire, with Justin behind her, and stared at the shadows in the room, tense and bracing herself for another encounter with the ghost. She knew it was still there, listening to every word they said. She could feel its attention like a hair inside her shirt, tickling her skin.

The floor creaked near the door to the vestibule and a shimmer of sound whispered from the chimes of the grandfather clock.

Jessica glared at the dark doorway, but nothing emerged.

Justin wished he had listened to Jessica when she told him to wake her up if he got tired while driving. He'd only meant to be sweet to her and instead he had crashed the car and gotten them into this predicament. He'd made a stupid mistake and wished with all his strength that he could undo it.

He drifted through pain, sometimes acutely aware, sometimes almost in a doze until his mind replayed the image of the ghost coming for them and then he'd startle alert. After several repetitions of this cycle, he noticed the book splayed open beneath the nearest armchair. In an attempt to distract himself from the pain and fear, he took up the book and began to read.

So, the interminable minutes passed.

"Is the laudanum working?" Jessica asked after a while, turning to check on Justin. "Your color is better."

Justin lowered the book to look at her. "I'm still in pain, but I also feel like I'm floating, and the pain just doesn't matter as much anymore."

He smiled drowsily and realized he was high, but at least he wasn't unconscious or shuddering and sweating from agony. "This book, though, Jessica. This book…"

"What is it?" she asked.

"It's Eleanor's journal. She was so, so *lonely.*"

"Eleanor? The body in the bed? The ghost?"

"Yes." He lifted the book and continued to read by firelight.

After an hour or so, the fire had almost burned out. Justin was squinting at the pages.

"We need more wood," said Jessica. She glanced around.

Justin cautioned her. "She won't let you burn the tree. *Edward* was supposed to put the star on top. She couldn't bear to take it down until it had its star."

"Who's Edward?"

"The man she loved, but he didn't love her." His voice floated, mirroring thoughts affected by the laudanum.

"Wait. All this haunting nonsense is because she's a jilted lover?"

"Don't judge, Jess. You've never been alone, not the way she was." Something compelled him toward compassion he wouldn't otherwise feel. Perhaps it was the laudanum. But he couldn't forget the way Eleanor's misery had spilled into him upstairs.

"Well, I've had it," snapped Jessica. "I'm not going to let her freeze us to death." But she didn't touch the tree. Instead, she scooped up a handful of the debris beneath it, the dried pine needles, the bits of candle. When the ghost didn't react, she picked out the little glass ornaments and a small box, laid them aside on the desk, and gathered the remaining detritus. Then she threw the mess of wax and needles onto the coals in the fireplace and flames burst alive, licking them up. Despite her impatient tone, Justin suspected that the ghost's loneliness had affected her too.

"That will burn too quickly. We need something more substantial," said Justin.

"If she won't let us touch the tree, do you think she'd let us burn the furniture?" asked Jessica.

After musing a moment, Justin said, "Go down to the cellar and get the pieces of wood from the broken stuff. She shouldn't be mad about that."

"I don't want to go back down there. We shouldn't be separated."

"I'd go with you, but I can't walk!" He hadn't meant to jab a sore spot, but his girlfriend winced.

"Fine," she grumped.

JESSICA SURGED to her feet and marched out of the parlor. Encountering the darkness in the vestibule, she turned on the phone flashlight, then proceeded through the rooms to the pantry and crept down the stairs into the cellar.

The debris from their fall lay scattered on the dirt floor. After shining the light around the cellar to check for anything ominous, Jessica propped the phone on an intact shelf, pointing toward the space, and began collecting wood.

She had an armful when the cell phone light behind her suddenly winked out. Jessica gasped and spun towards the phone, dropping the wood. She found it easily enough because of the red LED light glowing in its upper left-hand corner. Her rattling hands missed the power button and she dropped the phone.

Crouching, she felt for the phone where she'd heard it fall, but it wasn't there. Trying to smother the panic rising from her center, she swept her hands in growing circles until her fingers brushed against it. She snatched it, punched the power button to wake it, and tried to turn the flashlight back on. Instead, it displayed the message "flashlight disabled due to low battery".

After a moment, she collected her wits and began to gather up the wood a second time, using the light from the phone's screen, her movements perfunctory with irritation. She hated feeling exposed to a creature against which she couldn't fight.

A scuffling noise in the corner made her turn with a jerk. Holding her breath, she peered toward the darkened edge of the cellar, but she couldn't discern anything. She took a step back toward the stairs and then another, holding her pile of wood between herself and the possible threat.

"Leave me alone!" Jessica shouted at the room.

MEANWHILE, Justin lay before the fire, his attention focused on the book. After Jessica had been gone for a time, he felt someone lay next to him. Such was the effect of the laudanum that he didn't identify it as odd. He assumed it was Jessica and marveled that such a short time away from the fire had allowed her body to grow so cold. Then he heard her yell in the cellar.

With a jolt of horror, Justin turned to the person at his side. His eyes widened to see that hideous face so close to his, the blank eyes, the gaping mouth, the void within her.

"Love me, I pray," she sighed.

She kissed him with withered lips, a kiss devoid of love, a desperate kiss, a kiss cold from an empty bed and an empty life and an empty grave. For a moment, her image flickered to how she had appeared in youth, lovely and provocative, but her kiss tasted of mold, dust, and decay. Justin jerked back and screamed.

WHEN JUSTIN STARTED SCREAMING, Jessica realized that her imagination had been feeding her own fears while the ghost preyed upon her vulnerable boyfriend. She ran, leaping up the stairs, careering through the rooms, and burst into the parlor.

Justin was up on his elbows, panting, his eyes shut, his teeth gritted.

"What is it?" she cried. "What happened?"

JUSTIN REACHED FOR HER. "JESSICA! JESS!"

Jessica dropped the wood and held him. "What happened?"

"Sh-she..." He shuddered in revulsion, clinging to his girlfriend, desperate to remove the feeling that tainted his mouth. He wiped his coat sleeve across his mouth, swallowed convulsively, trying to calm himself. "She kissed me."

"What?!"

"Jess, I *felt* her loneliness. It was awful, like a black hole of misery! I can't get it out of my head."

Jessica snarled, "If that witch were alive, I would *kill* her!"

Ironically, those words made Justin chuckle. He leaned his head on Jessica's, savoring the warmth of her in his arms, relishing her life. "I know you would, but you're too late." Introspection obligated him to add, "Don't be too mad at her."

"Why not? She's evil."

"Maybe not. She's doing bad things, but I think she's just trying to end the loneliness." He paused, thinking, then continued. "She expected that Edward would propose to her on Christmas day and she got him a pocket watch with her portrait inside, as a gift. Instead, he told her on Christmas Eve that he loved the girl from the next farm over. Eleanor realized he'd been pursuing her inheritance and using the other girl as his mistress. It broke her, Jessica."

"You read about it?"

"Yes. It's in her journal."

"And she left the tree untouched all these years," Jessica murmured. Then she stiffened in his arms. "It sounds like a stupid reason to stick around after she died. Why the haunting?"

"She's still lonely."

"She's not going to find love now."

"No," Justin agreed.

"So, what? Did she kill herself after they broke up?" Jessica sounded disdainful of such weak feminine behavior.

"No, she didn't. She lived her whole life in this house, suffering with isolation. She had no friends, no family. Society labeled her unchaste and rejected her, and she rejected society. She talked to people on occasion, grocery clerks and bankers and the like, but never had a close relationship with any of them. Listen to her words." He picked up the book and read:

"Loneliness coats this house like dust, dimming the brightness of my life and emotions. Everything is a reminder to me that I am alone:

*the one china plate I use of the set, my narrow, celibate bed in the
largest bedchamber, the audible ticking of the grandfather clock. I
have no one to turn to in the dark, no hand to hold in mine, no peace
in the presence of a friend..."*

He continued. "She watched from her parlor window as he
married and later divorced the girl next door and tore down the house
near hers that had never been a home to him. He never stepped over
Eleanor's threshold again. No one did. She was left alone in her
house, alone in the fields that stretched on and on."

Jessica stared at Justin, his face lit by fire and moonlight. His
words were almost poetic, probably a side effect of the laudanum, and
they affected her more than she liked to acknowledge. She didn't
want to empathize with such a vicious creature as Eleanor's lonely
ghost. She didn't want to investigate the dark place inside herself that
bore potential to make her what Eleanor had been.

"He probably loved the other girl because *she's* a neurotic,
obsessive, hideous witch!" Jessica didn't care if she angered the
ghost.

"Maybe so. Eleanor couldn't understand Edward's choice. She
was talented, educated, wealthy. She decided it must be because she
wasn't as pretty as the other girl, so she destroyed every image of
herself in the house."

"Every image?" Jessica asked. She pulled away from Justin, went
to the Christmas tree, and picked up the small package off the desk.
Old paper crumbled beneath her fingers.

Justin warned, "She'll attack us again!"

The smoke swirled above them and the Christmas tree rustled as
if something had brushed against it. For a heartbeat, the scent of
fresh-cut pine drifted through the room.

But an insatiable curiosity drove Jessica, the same that had driven

Justin to retrieve the book from the corpse's hand. She broke the brittle string.

A wordless, sobbing shriek pierced their ears. The ghost appeared in the smoke, stuttering toward Jessica, black mouth and dark eyes widening until they almost consumed her face.

Jessica screamed and ran from the parlor, past the clock in the vestibule, and into the dining room.

She stopped there, turning and turning, but finding nowhere to go that wasn't where the ghost could follow. The ghost's keening grew louder and sharper as it followed her, the noise excruciating.

Jessica dropped the box, spilling the pocket watch. She clamped her hands over her ears.

Eleanor loomed before Jessica, mouth and eyes opened too wide for a physical being, exposing the emptiness within her.

Unable to hear her own voice, Jessica sobbed, "Stop it! Stop it! Stop it!"

At the moment Jessica believed she might die from the cacophony, an impact broke the windows and shattered the china in its hutch. A maelstrom formed in the room, with the ghost of Eleanor at its center, lifting the shining bits of glass and china and flinging them like leaves in a hurricane.

IN THE PARLOR, the detonation drove Justin to flip onto his stomach and drag himself after his girlfriend, exerting great, agonizing effort. He wouldn't leave her to face that creature alone. He called her name repeatedly as he moved by inches toward the door.

JESSICA DOVE under the table and huddled there in a ball to avoid the cutting glass fragments.

When she peaked between her arms, a glimmer on the floor caught her attention. The pocket watch.

Snatching it up, she pressed the pin to pop it open, and studied the portrait within while the shards continued to spin about the room. Jessica turned the image toward the window to better catch the light. She saw brunette hair swept up on an elegant head, dark brows, a straight, fine nose, and full lips.

"You were beautiful," Jessica murmured to the air, voice full of compassion.

The glass fell abruptly, a tinkling rain pattering against the table over Jessica's head and onto the wooden floor.

After a long hesitation, Jessica gingerly unfolded and looked for the ghost. Seeing nothing, she crawled out from under the table.

"Jessica!" Justin called. "Jessica!" His voice strained with pain.

She rushed to him.

Justin had reached the vestibule and was half-way to the dining room door. Moisture beaded around his lips and eyes from the exertion.

"I'm all right!" she assured him and helped him roll over, then dragged him back near the fire.

"You're bleeding," he said, concern drawing his brows together as he examined her.

Jessica discovered that her face and hands bore dozens of cuts from the glass. Her coat and jeans were slashed and snagged, with spots of blood where bits of glass had passed through the fabric and cut her. Some of the wounds were deep, so Justin removed his coat and shirt. He handed the shirt to Jessica and then put his coat back on. Jessica tore his shirt into strips, picked out the glass shards embedded in her skin, and bound the worst injuries tightly to stop the bleeding.

With a sigh, she sat by her boyfriend and leaned her head against an armchair. "What are we going to do, Justin?"

"I don't know."

Miserable silence saturated the room.

Jessica loved the man beside her. He awoke in her the power to be herself without shame. What could she be without him? Everything she wanted to be, she knew. Not having him would not limit her in the least. But *with* him, she could be so much more. Yet over the last few hours, she'd tormented him with his mistake, throwing it at him at every opportunity, angry long after anger was warranted. Her shoulders sagged as she contemplated her own disappointing behavior. Justin deserved better.

After all, it was her idea to take the shortcut.

She leaned close to him, lifted his hand, and kissed his knuckles. "Justin, I'm so sorry. You were right. We should have taken the freeway. I'm sorry for being so mean to you about it."

"Mm," Justin groaned.

"What?"

"My fault," he said. "I should have let you drive when I got tired. I'm sorry." Justin's voice faded as he fell asleep under the effects of the laudanum and trauma.

Jessica's eyes felt raw with the lack of sleep and her chin kept falling to her chest, but she was too jittery to sleep. When her head dropped, she jerked it back up again.

On perhaps the third or fourth repetition of this, the ghost was there.

Jessica scooped up the poker and surged to her feet, blocking the apparition's path to Justin.

"Leave. Us. *Alone!*" she snarled.

Eleanor flickered, mouth yawning, eyes bottomless. She stared at Jessica, at Justin.

Her voice came, grating at Jessica's ears. "You... Not angry... Anymore."

Prepared for battle, the innocuous words flustered Jessica. The poker dropped a degree. "What?"

"...With him."

Jessica's eyes darted a glance at Justin, still sleeping, his face relaxed and so pale. Worry for him swelled through her. "No," she breathed.

"Why?" The word drew out long and sighing as Eleanor jittered.

"I forgave him."

"And he...you," whispered the ghost.

"Yes."

Again a question, "How?"

Jessica wrung the poker in her hands, remembered to hold it high like a bat. "We chose to forget."

"Chose," repeated Eleanor.

"You know, like Santa Claus," Jessica prattled. "He says he won't bring presents to naughty children on Christmas, but then he always does."

Eleanor contemplated long. "Like...the *little Lord*."

The ghost's words were so quiet Jessica couldn't be sure she heard them at all. She remained silent.

Time crept along and the poker grew heavy in Jessica's hands as the ghost hung before her and fixed her under its unwavering, disconcerting gaze.

Then it said, "I...too ..am sorry." The words seemed to encompass more than all she had done to Justin and Jessica.

Jessica watched the ghost fade and as she faded, she transformed, morphing from hideous apparition to a vestige of the young woman she must have been when she took up her burdensome grudge.

After a stretched-out moment, Jessica realized that the ambiance of the house had converted from malice to mourning. The ghost wept somewhere in a distant corner of the house.

As the minutes lengthened and they remained unmolested, Jessica resumed her seat near Justin, laying the poker next to her within easy reach. She breathed easier without Eleanor's heavy presence threatening them. Lacking fear to power her, she could no longer withstand the exhaustion and eventually fell asleep too.

WHEN JUSTIN WOKE, the night was not so dark through the windows. Christmas morning had arrived. He turned toward Jessica and found her watching him, expression solemn, eyes sleepy as if she had just awakened.

Anxious to take advantage of a lucid moment, unsure if he would get another one, Justin reached into the pocket of his bloody, torn jeans and pulled out a black velvet box. He opened it with some fumbling, lifted it towards Jessica, and said, "This isn't how I wanted this to be, but I better not postpone any longer because I just don't know if we'll ever get out of here. Jessica, I love you so much. You make me feel capable of being everything I ever wanted to be and more that I never dreamed of. I want to be with you all my life. Will you marry me?"

Jessica received the shining diamond with shock, admiring the way it sparkled in the firelight. Justin lacked the strength and finesse to perform the customary dressing with the ring, so she slipped it on her own left hand.

"I will!" she exclaimed, crying with joy.

Her happy face was the brightest light in the room. She kissed Justin to seal the agreement, a quick peck so she wouldn't hurt him, but when she pulled away, he cupped the nape of her neck and drew her back to kiss her more passionately, relishing the pressure of her lips against his and the taste of her, erasing the lingering stigma from the ghost. This kiss savored of Jessica's luscious, living energy.

When they finally parted Jessica was breathless, leaning over Justin with her hands bracing against the floor on either side of his chest, her hair a silky screen around their faces. She bore a sweet smile on her lips.

"You can keep that ring forever if you tell me one thing," Justin murmured.

"What?"

"How did you start the fire?"

"Oh, that's something you're never going to find out."

"Give me the ring back."

"No," laughed Jessica, and she kissed him again.

"Hello, in the house!" the voice, a *human* voice, cut the quiet of the breaking dawn.

Jessica gasped and then screamed, "Help! Help us!"

She leaped to her feet and ran to the door, expecting that it wouldn't open, but it yielded easily to her hand on the knob. She dove into the arms of a befuddled man, hugging him tightly.

"What in the blazes?" he asked. "You look like you went through the windshield! Are you all right?"

"I'm ok," she gasped. "But my boyfriend, my fiancée, he broke both his legs! We need an ambulance."

"I'll go radio for one," the man said. He turned back toward an orange snowplow parked on the highway far away.

"Thank you! Please don't leave us!"

"I'll come back and stay until it gets here," he assured her.

Jessica ran back into the house, making sure to leave the door open.

She knelt by her fiancée and grabbed his hands. "Help is here. A snowplow came, and the driver is calling an ambulance for you. We are saved!"

"Thank God!" Justin breathed, and tears of relief fell from the corners of his eyes.

At long last, the driver returned, bringing them another blanket and a thermos of hot chocolate, which they gratefully shared.

During the lengthy wait for the ambulance, Justin and Jessica sang all the Christmas carols they could think of, but they kept returning to "Away in a Manger" until the snowplow driver, who sang with them, shrugged his heavy shoulders and sighed each time before picking up the lyrics.

As the emergency responders finally carried Justin from the

home on a stretcher, with Jessica walking beside him, they heard a faint sigh.

"Is someone else inside?" an EMT asked.

"No. That's just wind through holes in the chimney," said Jessica, and Justin squeezed her hand as they shared a grim smile.

Morning sun had altered the far-flung snow from cerecloth into wedding raiment, which sparkled like diamonds and dazzled her eyes which had become accustomed to darkness.

"Wait!" Justin gasped when they reached the bottom of the steps. He grabbed Jessica's hand. "Put the star on the Christmas tree. It shouldn't spend another Christmas without it."

She studied his eyes and then nodded. She rushed back into the home, through the vestibule, to the parlor. The glass star lay on the rolltop desk. She picked it up, dusted it until it shone, then reached on her tiptoes to set it atop the tree.

"Merry Christmas, Eleanor," she whispered. Then she returned to Justin's side. Behind her, light flared through the house. Perhaps it was the dawn sun shining through the windows as it rose. Perhaps it was something a little bit more.

The EMTs appeared oblivious, but Jessica heard a gentle, sad voice singing the old Christmas hymn as they walked away.

> *"Be near me, Lord Jesus; I ask thee to stay*
> *Close by me forever, and love me, I pray.*
> *...and love me, I pray..."*

'TWAS THE FIGHT BEFORE CHRISTMAS

BY JAMES T. LAMBERT

The fat man grunted as he lifted the fallen rail and put it back on the snow-covered fence. He pulled a clean white handkerchief from the pocket of his red trousers and wiped his bearded face. Even in the chill air and with snow all around, hard work made him sweat.

He looked down the length of the split-rail fence and smiled. All fixed. Time to take a break. The busy time of the year was coming fast, and he wanted to be well-rested. People depended on him.

His gaze followed the fence-line, looking for any damage he might have missed, and he noticed something. Not the fence, something outside the fence at the edge of the trees. Not visible at first, but now it stood out, plain as day.

Who would have built a snowman right at the edge of the woods? He shook his head. Nice work, though. Classic. Three nice, round balls of snow, big one at the bottom, smaller one above that, smallest on top. Oh. And another one stood a little farther down. And another.

He rubbed his eyes. Had he really not seen them until now? He turned the other way and looked down the fence. Several more had appeared there as silently as the first few.

He looked back and forth as more gathered, backing away from the fence, trying to keep them all in view. But as he turned his head they vanished without him ever seeing them move. In the end, only the first one remained. In the blink of an eye it disappeared too.

All gone.

He shivered despite his layers of insulation.

Time to make a call.

CHARLIE HAMBLIN STALKED the corridors of the Prometheus Project's underground headquarters like an intemperate specter, concrete walls and floors echoing her steps. *If one more person wishes me...*

"Merry Christmas!"

She whirled around, ready to rend the flesh from her holiday well-wisher, but she froze at the horrible sight before her. Actual multi-colored, blinking lights hung down Matt's chest, tinsel from his shoulders, and topped off with an Elf hat. An actual, real-life fluorescent green one. A long moment passed. She lowered her head and covered her eyes against his Yuletide magnificence.

He's a Christmas fanatic. Great. And I've got to put up with him for three more days before leave. The Marshals, like other federal employees, could take two weeks off for the holidays if they'd been wise enough to save up enough leave. And damned if she'd let him put her in a bad mood before going home. Unless he crossed the line. If he wanted to go and...

"Do you sing?" His face glowed with radioactive holiday cheer.

"Can I sing? Yes. Will I sing? No. Sing Christmas carols? Hell, no."

"Really? I can teach you the words."

His honest happiness blunted her desire to gut him and use his entrails as a garland to decorate a tree in the traditional style. Of course, he knew all the words. To all the songs. Every. Single. One.

"No thanks, Matt. Not a big caroler. Hit me up in a few months for Groundhog's Day."

"There're no songs for Groundhog's Day."

Exactly.

"Heading home for the holidays? Dreaming of a wet Seattle Christmas?"

Matt nodded cheerfully. "Yeah, visiting the family. We'll go up into the mountains and do some sledding, big dinner, secret Santa, the whole thing. It'll be great!"

"I'm glad." *I'm glad we won't be stuck here where I have to put up with it.* Her own family had adjusted to her anti-Christmas sentiments, even if they didn't understand them. The years growing up in the shadow of her three older brothers set the foundation, but the real reason felt more selfish. Her parents acknowledged her tomboy nature and thought they could simply get the same sort of gifts for all four kids. And her brothers, as older brothers do, decided all the toys were common property. She didn't get a gift of her own, other than clothing, until she was a teenager and totally soured on the magic of Christmas. She'd sent letters every year for her dream gift. It never arrived. But Matt obviously loved everything about the holiday.

"Sounds like you'll have fun." She turned to hide in her office for the next 72 hours.

"Can you help me with the tree? And the lights?"

"Sorry, Matt. Real busy. Can't spare a minute."

Both of their HOUND devices howled, as if listening for their cue. It still amazed her something as small as the original iPod could make so much noise. Maybe the incomprehensible acronym, which she never remembered, explained it. She sighed and checked the message on the tiny screen. Liefsson's office. Now. So much for hiding.

SHE CONVINCED Matt to ditch the Christmas tree disguise before they met with The Angry German. Who knew what caustic remarks he'd use to express his displeasure with holiday levity? She braced herself for their usual verbal sparring match. Liefsson earned his *nom de guerre* with epic dressing-downs blasting from his huge frame. Charlie prided herself for standing up to it and giving as good as she got when arguing about the insane missions he sent them on, but there was no reason to give him any extra ammunition by showing up in costume. They'd already taken on Jersey Devils and the Thunderbird, what could possibly top that?

She knocked three times and entered as they'd been instructed on their first day at the facility. She'd heard they'd inherited the custom from the military, but Liefsson made it his own. She'd had enough shouted lectures on decorum and procedure to want to move to the next topic of argument.

Behind the desk should sit their saturnine master, Herr Professor Erik Liefsson, The Angry German, a giant Norseman covered in faded tattoos featuring Viking runes and symbols with fiery red hair and a beard. But some imposter had taken his seat. Some resemblance remained, but Charlie could tell in an instant he was a fake.

He smiled.

Liefsson still strained his dark blue suit, looking more like a wrestler than a professor of history or a practiced administrator. But he leaned back in his leather desk chair, fingers laced together casually, displaying the tattoos across his knuckles and radiating an unfamiliar cheer.

"Come in, come in! So sorry to interrupt your holiday planning," the imposter called jovially, further ruining the impersonation.

She entered with care and perched on the edge of the hard, high-backed chair, ready to flee. It *couldn't* be Liefsson. Or maybe it was some trick to get them off guard. Her mind spun insidious training scenarios as Matt took his seat beside her with no visible sign of worry.

"I hate to do this to you right before leave, but a situation came to our attention in Maine, south of the Canadian border. A reindeer farm has come under threat by some animated snowmen."

Charlie launched to her feet and planted her hands on the desk in front of the imposter. "That's it! Who the hell are you, and what have you done with Liefsson?"

He leaned back and steepled his fingers as his smile faded. "You have a problem, Marshal Hamblin?"

As the unnatural smile faded, so did her certainty this was all some kind of trick. But she couldn't back down now. "Yeah, you, the smile, it's..." She stopped and realized she couldn't accuse him of being too nice about interrupting their Christmas furlough. "It's called leave. And it starts in three days. This is no time for a trip to the Frozen North."

"Ah, I understand," he said as the terrifying smile returned. "I too have plans for the holidays and will regret any time I miss with my granddaughters. They so enjoy my Christmas stories."

Screw your Christmas stories! Reindeer farm? Animated snowmen? "This sounds more like a holiday prank than a real mission." *Wait a minute, granddaughters? He has granddaughters? And he's going to read them Christmas stories? Krampus, anyone?*

"I assure you the source is unimpeachable. Utterly reliable. Marshals will investigate. *You* will investigate." His smile disappeared for a moment, replaced with his typical volcanic glower. "Understood?"

She flopped down in the chair. She'd given up challenging that tone. Two months of guard duty taught her the futility of going head-to-head with the operational leader of the project. Who knew what these snowmen were, really? She'd believe them when she saw them, and maybe not then. She looked at Matt who shrugged. "Yeah, understood. We stop snowmen from eating the reindeer. Check."

NEXT STOP: Wonderland, the realm of Hannah "Wonders" Wonderly, resident scientific genius and supplier of their equipment. The gorgeous blonde beamed a ten-thousand watt smile she usually reserved for some new scientific principle or its application to their next mission.

"Happy Hanukkah! I hear you are headed north and facing snowmen. I have just the thing!"

Hanukkah? Jewish? I had no idea...

"Flamethrowers, of course. Lightweight with extra fuel canisters and an extending nozzle for more accuracy. It also keeps your hands from getting too hot. And you might remember the thermite claymore grenades I issued you on a previous mission." She hefted a clanking bag and let it drop. Charlie winced. "And a brand-new invention. I was inspired." She scattered a few of the new items on the table.

Charlie picked one up. A cube of dark brown wood with a pyramid shape at one end and a dowel sticking out the other. Strange symbols decorated the sides of the central square.

"Twist the stick, give them some spin as you throw them. When they land they'll whirl and explode, spraying flaming shrapnel. I call them Dreidel grenades."

Charlie's fingers went numb and the device slipped from her hand. She scrambled to catch it before it hit the table. "Grenades? Couldn't you have led with that?"

"Sorry. I've also packed several boxes of ammunition with thermite, or other flammable loads. Shotgun, pistol, rifle. And incendiary rounds for the rocket launchers."

Matt grinned. "It must be Christmas!"

Wonderly frowned her sweet frown at him. "Must it? I'm afraid I don't celebrate."

Charlie waved frantically. "Just an expression. About delightful gifts. Like these. Thank you, Wonders. We'd better get going if we want to get back for leave."

"Oh, yes. We've arranged for a helicopter to take you to the site after your plane lands. You should arrive this afternoon and be back just as fast tomorrow. Or whenever you finish the case."

MATT AND CHARLIE reviewed the mission briefing and inventoried equipment on the flight, so there was no way to avoid the idle chit-chat she dreaded on the helicopter's intercom.

"So what's with you and Christmas, Charlie?"

"So what's with you and that big nose, Matt?"

"Come on, you can tell me."

She probably could, too. And it might be nice. *Except it sounds so damn stupid I didn't get the toy I wanted when I was a kid. Great reason to be pissed off every December.* "But then I'd have to kill you. It's in the contract, didn't you read it?"

Matt shrugged, his impenetrable Christmas cheer unruffled. "Whatever you say. What do you think of the weapon mix?" His face glowed like he had a mound of the biggest, most elaborately wrapped presents under his tree. Getting him to sleep on Christmas Eve must have driven his parents nuts.

Heavy on the flammables, she thought, but a glance outside at the ground whipping by revealed a heavy blanket of snow. Hopefully there would be no major forest fires this time. A wide swath of snow, packed down by the passage of many animals, crossed beneath their flight path. Some herd migration, she supposed.

They discussed armaments and tactics until the pilot interrupted and gestured to their left, pointing out a rough, circular clearing containing a few buildings and surrounded by rail fencing smashed to splinters. Some of the larger buildings still stood, but several smaller sheds were smashed flat. A huge number of animal tracks were nearly obscured by some sort of crisscrossing trails that looked like they'd been made by a child's disc sled. Hundreds of these strange paths wandered through the clearing and led off into the surrounding woods.

"Where do you want to land?" asked Bill, their pilot, swinging the helicopter around in a descending circle. "Not too close to the trees or buildings is all I ask."

"That end." Charlie pointed over his shoulder. "In the clear, but near those buildings and close enough we can take a look at what happened to the fence."

"Sounds good. You going to be long? I could use a chance to stretch my legs, if you know what I mean." He gestured to a huge, insulated mug for coffee mounted in a gimballed cup holder.

Charlie snorted. "Yeah, go take a piss, we'll be at least fifteen minutes, probably longer."

He sighed in relief and brought the copter down in a fast but gentle landing, right where Charlie had indicated. He unbuckled and trotted out beyond the tree line before either of the marshals even opened the door.

"When you gotta go..." Charlie muttered.

She and Matt carried a miniature flame thrower each, along with a shotgun, service pistol, and a duffel full of the various devices Wonderly issued them. Most of the claymores and the rocket launchers they left stowed. Their bulky, clanking gear boosted her confidence. Something had bulldozed the place, so better well-armed than sorry.

A quick inspection of the smashed fence turned up no new information. One split-rail fence, smashed to kindling. Whatever left the sled tracks was the obvious culprit. The same was true of the flattened outbuildings. Sturdier buildings survived the attack with light damage. It appeared they'd been mostly ignored.

What they didn't see was a bit of good news, bad news. No bodies, human or animal. But no survivors hiding out to give them an eyewitness description, either. The facility was abandoned, probably at speed. Indications remained of people dropping what they were doing—a cracked coffee mug in a wide, still-damp stain—and making their exit. Missing were clues to what was to blame for the mass exodus. Snowmen? She snorted. Not likely Frosty could trash a place like this.

Not far from the surviving buildings, the sled marks seemed to congregate and lead off into the woods. The narrow strips between the furrowed tracks were churned and trampled. Someone—most likely the occupants—retreated this way, pursued by the sled-foots.

Charlie looked back and saw the pilot leaving the cover of the nearby trees at a relaxed saunter, which also gave her a perfect view of the blossom of fire erupting from the side of the helicopter. The sound of the blast hit them a second later, and all three dove for cover as the fire ate its way into the craft. Whether it reached the thermite packed claymore mines, the rocket launcher, or the craft's fuel tanks first, the tower of flame and the ear-rending blast left little to investigate.

Both veterans of firefights, Charlie and Matt scanned the area for hostile forces. Indistinct movement in the shadows of the trees to their right seemed to be the source of the attack. A fusillade of spears flew from the shadows and pierced the ground around them.

Charlie drew her Glock and returned fire, unsure of her targets, but hoping to suppress their attack. Matt went all in. A gout of flame reached for the trees, and he played it over a short arc, creating a temporary wall of fire. No more spears.

They crouched and ran for better cover. Matt sought protection behind a tree, Charlie grabbed one of the spears as she passed. Once behind cover of a surviving building, she examined the weapon.

An icicle? A damned icicle? *Of course they throw icicles.* A quick glance caught a last flicker of movement withdrawing deeper into the trees. They'd pulled back rather than take on the flamethrower. Wise move.

The pilot stumbled through the snow and slid down beside her. She eased her finger off the trigger before she nearly put two rounds through his head. Obviously he had no ground combat experience.

"What was that? They killed my bird! Crap, am I gonna have to pay for that?"

She shook her head. He wouldn't be much use. "Hey, head for the big building, lock the doors and look for a telephone, radio, anything. If you don't find one, find somewhere to hole up, maybe the basement. That," she tilted her head at the flaming debris and the column of smoke reaching for the sky, "makes us easy to find when our people come looking for us. Stay calm and wait for rescue." *Or death.* He had enough on his mind, so she kept the thought to herself.

He nodded and stumbled toward the front door. She caught Matt's eye and signaled she was coming over. Seconds later she sheltered behind a tree a few feet from him.

"Okay, Bill's taken care of. The bad guys are gone. So is our transport and extra heavy weapons. I do *not* want to walk home from here." Charlie scanned the surrounding forest as she detailed their situation.

"What, it's a winter wonderland. It's perfect to walk in." Matt grinned but kept watch, covering his arc of the circle. "I think the mission calls for pursuit. We need to track down these clowns and find out who's naughty and nice."

"You realize I'm armed, Matt? Got a gun right here. One more Christmas crack..."

"And I'll get a lump of coal in my stocking. Sorry, can't help it."

He didn't look sorry. Yet.

THEY TRIED to approach the flaming wreck, but the heat drove them back. A few scraps of metal, one with a hole the same size as one of the icicle spears, lay scattered around it.

"And the quarterback is toast," Matt muttered. "Well, there goes our ride. Think we can keep up with them on foot?"

Charlie wondered the same thing as she stared into the blaze. She kicked at the snow. As long as they wanted to follow right behind whatever made those sled-tracks, they'd have hard packed snow to walk on. If they wanted a more indirect approach, they'd sink in to their knees without snowshoes. "Maybe."

"Then we should get moving before they get any farther ahead." He tugged at his coat and pulled the hood tighter around his face. "And it will keep us from freezing."

"Yeah."

The two of them turned and trudged through the snow, following the wide trail left by attackers, in pursuit of their prey. She'd been optimistic about the snow. They broke through the crust every half-dozen steps. Still, even slow progress counted.

A movement in the trees to one side caught her eye. She examined it without turning her head. If it were unfriendly, she'd rather it not know she'd spotted it.

"Matt, do you see it?"

"Yeah, just spotted it. Doesn't look much like the ones we saw earlier. Darker, bulkier."

"Take it down anyway?"

"It's not doing anything."

She snorted. "You want to wait for it to put one of those icicles through your nice, new coat?"

He grunted and adjusted the hang of the flamethrower and shotgun.

A second form separated from the first. "Matt, they're coming this way." Her fingers twitched, longing for the comfortable feel of a pistol grip.

But they weren't attacking. Weren't charging. Just getting closer. Damn it, they were going to have to wait for them to shoot first. Blazing away at unknown figures in the woods remained, as Herr Professor had reminded them, *verboten*.

Matt stopped walking. She took a few more steps to make them two distinct targets before she stopped and turned. Now she could hear the crunch of the snow and a loud click-click-click as their visitors approached.

The first thing they saw were antlers.

Big, pointy antlers. Attached to a large head. And that connected to a massive, hairy body.

"Matt, it's a reindeer. It's a reindeer, Matt. A reindeer." She couldn't stop repeating the obvious. It was a reindeer. Big as life and twice as hairy.

And she was wrong. They were two reindeer, a matched set who continued their sedate stroll toward them. The clicking came from their legs, probably their knees. They clicked with every step. She leaned back as one head and antlers invaded her personal space but didn't retreat. It took a long, close look at her, then turned its head. But it didn't move away, it stood with its head turned like it was showing her something. A strap of leather ringed its neck, with a small brass plate and etched letters. "Blixem," she muttered under her breath. She turned her head to see Matt with a grin so big it reached past his ears.

"Charlie, it's got a collar!" Matt practically danced with excitement. "A collar! And a brass nameplate." He leaned close, seeming oblivious to the wicked points only inches away. "Dunder?"

"Dunder and Blixem? Somebody forgot how to spell."

"Wait a minute!" Matt's eyes glowed with pure Christmas geek. "The names Donner and Blitzen came later. German rather than the original Dutch. But both of them mean the same things." He grinned. "Thunder and Lightning. Gives a bit of a different meaning to 'arose such a clatter,' doesn't it?"

It took a moment, but the full horror of the moment crashed in on her. "Matt, these things move a lot faster in the snow than we can. We have to ride them, don't we? Crap."

Matt's shout of joy dumped snow from overloaded branches for a hundred yards.

Turns out, climbing aboard a reindeer was not for the faint of heart.

She reached out for a handful of fur to pull herself up, but Blixem half snorted, half squealed, and whipped his sharp antlers around in a pointed warning. "Right, gentle on the fur. Got it." She grabbed for an antler instead and he yanked her off her feet and dumped her in a snowbank. "And don't touch the antlers. Picky reindeer."

A clumsy run, a staggered jump, and she slid down the huge beast's side to land on her rump. The snow made a lousy surface for floor exercises. A standing jump got her arms up over the animal's back, but without something to push against with her feet, she slid off the hairy body. The huge antlered head swung around and looked at her laying on her back under the reindeer. "Don't you say a word, Blixem."

"What's keeping you?" shouted Matt. He straddled the other one, looking down at her. *It's his long legs. He didn't have as far to climb.*

She rolled over and got to her knees, leaned against the animal's muscular leg and climbed to her feet. The creature's shoulders topped her head by a few inches. She put her hands on her hips and cocked her head at it, considering the problem with the last of her patience. A gentle tap on the neck got it to turn its head and stare at her with dark brown eyes. Maybe a little laughter lurked in the depths of those eyes, but she ignored it.

She waved it down closer and stretched up on tiptoe to whisper in its ear. "Cut a girl a break?" The ear flicked and with a clicking of knee joints it kneeled down beside her, allowing an easy vault to put her astride it. Its knees clicked again as it rose. She met Matt's incredulous stare calmly and brushed some snow from her hair. "I'm all set. You?"

But once mounted, how did they control the damn things?

Apparently with psychic power. In practiced unison the reindeer turned to follow the path, first at a walk, advancing to a bone-jarring trot, then whatever silly name they called the next faster run. *Impressively smooth once they got up to speed.* Charlie held her weapon bag tucked between her body and the beast's neck, and her arms wrapped around both. The snow-covered ground sped by in a blur. *And they hardly kick up any snow.*

The thought took some time to seep through the walls of common sense. She resisted it with all her will, but eventually it made its way to the center of her consciousness and waved frantically. *We're flying. On reindeer. We're flying on reindeer. Flying reindeer.*

Matt whooped beside her. She turned to look. She'd never seen him this happy. Any more joy and he'd burst a blood vessel in his pleasure center.

"Charlie! Charlie, we're flying! It's the reindeer, they really are—"

She cut him off. "No! Don't you dare say it. I will shoot you right out of the sky with a rocket launcher if you do. And bury you with a stake of holly through your heart."

The ecstasy drained from his face, replaced by a mix of fascination and purpose. "Targets in sight. I'll be damned."

She craned her neck to see around Blixem's head. Movement all across the path, white on white. She stared, picking out edges and forms. Each of the creatures left the distinctive dished trail behind it, removing any doubt about their targets.

"Snowmen... Really, truly, Frosty snowmen," murmured Charlie. They followed the classic design, three balls of snow stacked, largest on the bottom, clearly the source of the dished tracks. Thin branch-like arms jutted from the middle ball. An orange nose and black eyes appeared as some turned their heads to the side. Each gaping mouth filled with icicle teeth. Most carried a few icicle spears. They made good time sliding across the surface of the snow.

Lifting her gaze to the horizon, she could make out a dark mass of movement. The herd from the farm. It was hard to judge who was winning the race, but animals needed to stop and rest. Who knew what kind of supernatural stamina sinister snowmen possessed?

"Should we try and drive them off?" asked Matt, the peacemaker.

"They killed our chopper. Rules of engagement say we melt the damn things."

"Snowmen roasting as we open fire?" Matt's grin should have been illegal.

"Break right, I'll go left. We'll strafe them."

"Roger Iceman, I'm going in." Matt said and his ride banked away.

"First Christmas jokes, and now cheesy eighties movie quotes," Charlie said, and pressed gently on the side on her mount's neck, and it peeled off in the opposite direction. "And *I'm* obviously Maverick!" Her surge of cheer at her control disappeared when Blixem's head turned and he gave her a look that convinced her he was the pilot and she the passenger.

And gunner. She freed the flamethrower, extended the nozzle as far as it would go and pointed it out at an angle to avoid lighting her ride's fur on fire. Blixem made a tight turn and dropped low, skimming over the treetops as they approached the mass of marching snowmen. He dropped even lower as they crossed the tree line and she sprayed the front rank with liquid fire.

"Ho, ho, ho! Now I've got a flamethrower!" *Ha! I can mangle eighties Christmas movie quotes too!* She laughed maniacally as the creatures became pillars of flame. The weapon sputtered as the fuel ran out, but she'd crossed most of the group by then and reloaded as her ride climbed and turned for another pass.

Another parallel line of burning figures stood where Matt had made his run. It might take some time, but they could turn the whole army into a big pond and be back to base in plenty of time for their leave. That is if they could get another helicopter to come pick them up. She felt in her ammunition bag and counted the remaining fuel cartridges for the flamethrower. It might be enough.

Except the burning figures still advanced, and the undamaged ones hurled icicles at them. Blixem jinked and climbed higher, out of range. She and Matt watched from Reindeer-back as the flames burned themselves out. She couldn't tell which had been inhuman torches and which hadn't. They continued their advance.

"Plan B?" asked Matt.

"Plan B."

THE REINDEER LANDED them well ahead of the line of advancing snowmen. Charlie and Matt pooled their goodie bags, laid out two rows of claymores, and set up firing positions for the three rocket launchers. Dozens of Dreidel grenades lay lined up for a bombing run. This was as ready as they could get.

And as futile. The first line of thermite claymores sent fiery death scything through the lines of snowmen, but the melted holes iced over immediately and they continued their advance. The rockets smashed the three they hit, and a half-dozen surrounding each target, leaving only hundreds more. The Dreidel grenades fell like misguided Hanukkah presents, but only the ones landing directly on a snowman drilled down into its head and scattered the pieces in a muffled blast. The rest spun merrily and scattered flaming shrapnel but did little damage.

The reindeer cruised back and forth over the horde, and Charlie could make out the herd more clearly now. The ice creatures gained on them. They'd exhausted their most powerful weapons without slowing the pursuit at all.

"Time to pull a rabbit out of the hat, Matt."

"You mean a present out of the stocking."

"I'm pretty sure this ammo works on you, want to find out?"

"Sorry. I got nothing." Matt patted Dunder's neck. "Even with air superiority we're not carrying the day."

Charlie nodded. In spite of their advanced weapons, they couldn't make a dent in the pack of pursuing predators. Their opponents were made of snow, had no legs, and threw icicle spears for weapons. Yet they'd blown up their helicopter, and would soon overtake the fleeing herd.

Not a holly, jolly Christmas. Not this year.

Her mind drifted into the sea of remembered Christmas carols, songs, and stories. She tried to concentrate, to come up with a new plan, but fatigue and defeat made it impossible. "The moon on the breast of the new-fallen snow," she muttered. Even years after the last time she'd heard it, she could probably recite the entire poem. She bet most people could. "On Comet, on Cupid." Blixem tossed his head again, making the nameplate flash in the waning sunlight.

Blixem. Silly name. Blitzen wasn't much better, but...

Her mind ground to a stop, emergency lights flashing in the back of her brain as she struggled to recognize what drew her attention.

"Matt?" She called out carefully, as if afraid to frighten the idea away.

"Yeah? What's the matter, Charlie, you okay?"

"Matt, what's Blixem mean again?"

"It's Dutch for lightning. Dunder means thunder. Dunder and Blixem, thunder and lightning. Like the German version—"

"Matt! Thunder and lightning? With six other named Reindeer, why do you think we got these two?"

Matt's mouth worked without making a sound. A rude snort from the Reindeer sounded suspiciously like "It took you long enough!"

Charlie leaned forward and whispered in Blixem's ear. "Really?"

He tossed his head.

"Okay, let's light them up like a Christmas Tree!"

Blixem spiraled toward the ground. Charlie clamped down hard with arms and legs as they plunged.

A flick of the antlers, a crackle of static electricity jumping from one point to the other, then a bolt of lightning flashed across her vision and stabbed down to dozens of points on the ground. Each snowman touched flared and steam rose off them while a wound melted into their body. The injured snowmen stopped, slumped.

A rumble followed by a thump pulled her gaze from her targets as

Dunder and Matt rose from their attack. A divot in the snow, clear of all snowmen, pinpointed the ground zero of their strike. Balls of snow formed a rough circle around this epicenter, the remains of the broken snow bodies.

Blixem flew her close beside Dunder. "This may take a while, but we can beat them this way," said Matt, shouting over the wind whipping past. "Once we break them…" His voice trailed off and she followed his stare down to the victims of their last attack.

Her targets slid forward, their wounds icing over to leave ragged scars. Moments later they marched on, perhaps stiffer, but still ready to fight. Matt's adversaries reassembled their tumbled forms, pulling themselves along with tree branch arms to gather heads and bodies. They could slow them down, but not stop them, not defeat them.

Charlie shivered, not from cold, but the fear of what failure would mean. Belief in Christmas, in flying reindeer, in wished-for presents, all died at the age of eight. Now she confronted the reality of it and would see all of it die, for everyone. Her hands fisted in the thick reindeer fur, but Blixem didn't flinch this time. He must have felt this as keenly as she did. Failure.

She'd never gotten what she wished for in her childhood. No reason to believe she'd get it now, either. Still… *I wish…* The reindeer's antlers glowed with sparks crackling along them and jumping from point to point. Blixem turned his head and flicked his ear at her. Maybe ear flicks meant approval.

"Hit them again!" He angled down toward the mass of marching snowmen and lightning leaped from his antlers, skewering white bodies. A few collapsed, their forms turning from hard-packed snow to running water. The rest slowed, stopped, repaired, and then marched on. *Not enough. I didn't give him enough power.*

But what power? Wishing? *When you wish upon a star…* No, Christmas. Christmas meant something else.

Do you believe in Santa?

The question prodded her from her childhood. Parents and grandparents asking, their eyes full of hope her innocence still survived. Younger kids asking at school, honestly questioning the truth of what they heard. Older kids taunting, mockery and anger at their own gullibility driving them to sour the enjoyment of others.

But the question remained. Do you believe?

Do I believe?

She considered a life of struggle, disappointment, and obstacles. Heart-wrenching tragedy. Hard-fought battles. Bittersweet victories. Did she believe in gifts, presents, rewards for being nice and not naughty? How could she?

But... She'd given over her life to protecting the innocent, enforcing the law, making things right. Devotion and generosity. Even love. She believed in those. The true spirit of Christmas resided in those.

Yes, Charlotte, there is a Santa Claus.

She leaned down against Blixem's warm, furry neck, wrapping her arms around it, closing her eyes, and pressing her face into the fur. "I *do* believe," she whispered. Static electricity crackled along her arms and in her hair. A bright glow penetrated her eyelids, getting brighter as her hair stood on end. She opened her eyes and smiled down at the naughty snowmen.

"You better watch out!" she caroled. Her arm stretched out and pointed to a knot of snowmen. Blixem dove toward where she pointed, streamers of power trailing behind his antlers. He dipped his head, and lightning arced down to pierce dozens of them. Each snowman touched by that lance of power burst into pieces before flashing into steam. Fragments shredded the ones beside them and even those fifty feet away tumbled to the ground.

She laughed hysterically and shouted at Matt. "You have to believe!" Blixem turned to make another run. They strafed a regimented line of the monsters before rising. Matt and Dunder plunged down a hundred yards away.

A rumble shook her very bones before a clap of thunder hit her so hard her vision dimmed. When her sight cleared, Dunder and Matt rose above what looked like a bomb crater. No snowmen remained in the center, though a few individual balls rolled away from the edges.

"I think we just saved Christmas," said Charlie.

I⊤ ᴛᴏᴏᴋ over an hour to rout the remnants of the snowman army. The scattered remains of the horde fled into the trees before the reindeer flew them back to the ranch. They landed outside the fence and out of sight of the buildings, and hiked the rest of the way. Upon their arrival, another helicopter settled to the ground, rotors still turning as half a dozen armed men spread out to guard it.

Charlie and Matt waved and approached carefully. Their flight home awaited, courtesy of their pilot's successful call for rescue. They invoked operational security to avoid answering uncomfortable questions and stared vacantly as the copter bore them back to the airport. A quick nap on the flight back to base gave her the stamina to face The Angry German, or his jolly Christmas Doppelganger.

To her surprise, a brief statement of success satisfied him.

"Take some notes while it's fresh in your minds, leave the official report until after the break. We'll investigate who sent the snowmen, and why, after the holidays. Which will be much happier now that... the owner of the ranch and the reindeer are safe and back to work. *Sehr gut*, marshals."

Charlie stumbled back to her room, and Matt followed. His concern irritated her, but telling him to mind his own business would take all her energy.

Her undecorated, Christmas-free zone calmed her somewhat, until she spotted the presents.

"Matt, what did I tell you about getting me a gift?"

"What? They're not from me."

"Then who?" She stalked the presents like bait concealing some sinister trap. Simple wrapping paper covered one box the size of an extra-large briefcase and one quite a bit smaller. A folded tag hung from the larger one.

"You going to open them?"

She put her hands on her hips and cocked her head, regarding them warily. She pulled the tag off and unfolded it.

Thank you for your assistance, Charlotte. You've been a very good girl. This time, the gift is just for you. A stylized S. C. signature at the bottom glittered in the light. She shifted her hand and the C changed to an N, then back again. She strained her eyes trying to see both letters at once before setting down the tag.

She reached out and pulled the larger box toward her and carefully tore the paper to unwrap it.

Matt loomed overhead, crowding her.

"Back off! It's my present, not yours!"

He held up his hands and backed away, but with a knowing grin on his face. She'd wipe it away later, but for now, the mystery of the presents needed to be solved.

With a flick of her wrist, she uncovered the box inside. And stopped dead. "No. No, it can't be. Not possible."

Matt looked back and forth between the box and Charlie. "Crystal Castle Playset? Who would get you a doll house?"

Like a sleepwalker she reached for the other present. "No one could know. No one at all. So it couldn't be..." She pulled it close and shredded the wrapping paper, sending scraps flying around the room.

"What is it, Charlie? The doll that goes with the castle? A Disney Princess?"

"It is! It really is!" She hugged the box to her chest. "He really brought it." She tried to shoot Matt a dirty look but couldn't pull it off. "It's not a Disney Princess you dope. It's She-Ra! Princess of Power!"

She smiled so wide the top of her head should have fallen off. "And she's all mine!"

A CUP OF KINDNESS

BY MISHA BURNETT

Karin had broken up with him a week before Christmas.

At that moment, full of sick anger and pain, he had thrown the bracelet he had bought for her—which had cost him more than he could comfortably afford—at her before he had stormed out.

Later he regretted that. He could have returned it. Later still he accused her, in his mind, of timing the breakup with the expectation that he would make such a grand—and expensive—gesture.

He wouldn't ask for it back. He knew it, and he knew that she knew it. By the time the wounds she'd made in his soul had scabbed over enough to brave that conversation she would have sold it, he was sure. It was gone, gone like everything else he had given her, the money, the gifts, the last year of his life.

All gone.

And yet Christmas, truth to tell, hadn't been *that* bad. He'd driven up to see his parents and their response to Karin's conspicuous absence had been gentle sympathy and—he suspected—a bit of relief. They'd never liked her much.

His kid sister had been too focused on her pregnancy to comment on Karin's absence or even notice it. She had her new husband in tow, a burly former football player turned boat salesman, and every topic of conversation had to be turned to how it would affect the baby, as if anyone could forget that she held in her belly the winning ticket in the first grandchild sweepstakes.

The day had been surprisingly relaxing. The boat salesman—not a bad guy, all things considered—had talked football with father, and kid sister had talked prenatal vitamins with mother. He ate too much and let the familiar surroundings lull him back in time to a place where Karin had never existed.

So that was Christmas, and he got through it okay, just fine, no problem.

But now it was New Year's Eve.

He had made reservations for the *best* party, the one that all Karin's friends would be attending. More money he'd never get back. Of course he wouldnt go there. Even if Karin weren't there, all her friends would be—rich kids comparing vacation tans and graduation present BMWs. But she *would* be there, he was sure, wearing that electric blue dress that clung to her body like a coat of enamel and made her look too perfect to be real. She would be there, dancing with the boys and chatting up her next sucker.

He hadn't made any plans, thinking, *hey, I'm twenty-six, that's practically thirty years old. I don't have to prove I'm old enough to drink anymore. I'm a grownup, I can stay home and go to bed early. I've seen clocks hit midnight before, it's no big deal.*

And that worked up until 8pm on the 31st of December. Then, sitting alone in his apartment—it had always been *his* place, never *their* place, they had talked about moving in together, but had never been able to find a place that she could accept and he could afford— he knew that if he didn't get out of there, something bad was going to happen.

Not front page of the newspaper bad, just painfully humiliating bad, involving calling Karin and leaving messages either begging her to take him back or screaming at her that she was a horrible bitch, or most likely both.

It was his fear that he was turning into *that* guy—worse, his horror at the thought that Karin had *turned him into that guy*—that forced him out into the brutal cold in search of escape.

He could have gone looking for people he knew, but he frankly wasn't up to explaining that *no, Karin isn't with me, and yes, we broke up, and no, I didn't break up with her, she broke up with me, and yes, you were right all along, the bitch was poison...*

Nope, not going to go there. He lived in a major metropolitan area, home to millions of people, and it was the busiest party night of the year, so surely there would be some place he could go that would be full of lights and music and friendly people and booze...

You'd think so, anyway.

Mile after mile of packed parking lots guarded by men in layers of coats and cardboard signs. Parking $5. Parking $10. Others where the men had fled inside, leaving bigger signs saying LOT FULL.

And the bars with lines outside, people shivering in the cold.

He ended up in an American Legion hall, lured in by the promise of NO COVER and "CHAMPANE" TOAST.

He parked in the lot—three pickup trucks and two motorcycles that must belong to yetis, since surely nothing human could be riding a bike in this weather—and went inside. The front hall was wide and empty. He shook the salt off his shoes. Snow had been threatened all week, but never materialized. It was too cold for snow.

A broad curving staircase took up most of the entrance. He went around it and saw a pair of double doors with plastic sheeting taped over them and a hand lettered sign that said, "Closed for renovation."

Up the stairs, then.

At the top of the staircase was a big open space that looked kind of like a high school gym. A half dozen folding tables ringed by folding chairs had been set up randomly in the space, each with a cluster of balloons. Against one wall was a raised stage area, empty. Music played through the space, that Madonna song that was everywhere. Thankfully at low volume.

A big man in biker leathers sat on a folding chair at the doorway to the big open area, reading a battered paperback book. The biker glanced up with a face that was massively scarred by an old burn. An equally scarred hand waved towards the open area and without speaking, the ravaged face bent back to the book.

At first the big space looked empty. It wasn't, not quite, there was a bar in one corner of the room with some figures clustered around it.

He walked over, feeling awkward and out of his element. The girl at the end of the bar was slim and blonde and looked too young to be in a bar. He hoped the plastic cup in front of her just held soda. Her hair was so pale that it was almost white and hung straight as a ruler around her face.

Next to her was a woman of maybe thirty, her hair the same white blonde color as the girl's, but wild and curly. She was voluptuously curved and packed into jeans and a T-shirt just a little too tight to contain her body's generous curves.

Past her was an old woman, stooped and wrinkled, her hair in a bone-white braid down her back. She was knitting, something long and tangled, made of bright red yarn that sparkled like it was sprinkled with glitter.

"Hi," he said. Nervously he added, "This isn't a private party, is it?"

The old woman cackled at that. "Hardly," she said.

"Open to everyone," the woman in the middle said, her voice low and with a seductive edge to it.

The girl just ducked her head, a shy smile on her face.

"So...how do I get a drink?"

The girl gestured at the bar. "Help yourself."

Sitting on the bar were several bottles of booze and soda and a bucket of ice.

Moving cautiously, in case the offer had been a joke, he mixed a drink—plastic cup, a couple of ice cubes, a splash of some obscure store-brand whiskey, and the rest from a bottle marked simply, Cola.

"Thanks," he said. He looked around for a jar for tips or donations, didn't see one.

As if reading his mind, the woman in the middle said, "Your money's no good here. Drink up."

He raised the cup to his lips and took a sip. Not bad. He suddenly realized that all three women were watching him intently, identical smiles on their faces. They looked like they were waiting for him to notice the plastic bug frozen in one of the ice cubes or something.

He finished his swallow and smiled back, a little uncertainly. "Thanks," he repeated.

"We dance at midnight," the girl said brightly.

"Sounds like fun."

A laugh from the woman in the middle, deep and erotic. "Oh... you have no idea."

At that, the old woman cackled again. "Perhaps you'll dance with me," she said.

He took another sip of the drink, feeling even more uncomfortable. "Sure," he said. "I'm not much of a dancer, though."

"You will be," the old woman said, suddenly looking very serious. "When the time comes. You were born to dance with me...but not now. Not this year."

"I'll just, uh..." He waved at one of the empty tables.

Smiling and nodding, he took his cup to the table and had a seat, making a show of looking around the nearly empty ballroom. An effort had been made to decorate it, paper streamers and balloons were taped to the walls. A banner read, "Happy New Year," all the vowels wearing top hats.

Better than drinking alone in his apartment? It was a tough call. But maybe more people would show up—people who weren't quite so...odd. It was still early.

He sipped his drink and it was suddenly empty, just amber ice cubes. Just as suddenly he realized that he didn't want another bad enough to brave the trio at the bar. He shook an ice cube into his mouth to chew on, and—

Someone was sitting across from him at the table.

It was that quick. Nobody there, a glance at the bar, and then somebody was. An older man, a buzz-cut of gray hair, unhealthy looking, too thin.

He sputtered, started to say something.

"Shut up," the old man said. "I haven't got much time."

What the hell? Was the American Legion hosting a New Year's Eve party for some mental institution?

"Ya gotta leave Karin alone," the old man said.

"*What?*"

"Leave her alone. Don't call her, don't go by her place, do everything you can to avoid crossing paths with her—*ever*. You got that?"

"Who are you?"

"Who the hell do you think I am? Listen to me—I just *died*. Went code blue and flat-lined. In about five minutes some prison doctor is going to be cracking open my ribs to fondle my heart. I'm staring down the barrel of eternity here and I went all in to come back and talk to you, so you better listen up."

"Uh..."

The face across the table from him was disturbingly familiar. Older, yes, much older. Maybe sixty? The skin was a sickly jaundiced color, dry patches around the mouth cracked and raw. He was in a gray uniform of some kind that hung on him like a sack.

"You can't let her screw up your life, boy," the old man went on, his voice quivering with intensity. "This is the time, right now, when you can change things. You can avoid making my mistake."

"Which was...?" He took a long drink from the plastic cup, not even registering that it had been empty a moment ago.

"*Karin!*" the old man shouted. "She was my mistake. Walk away, man, just walk away. You see her coming, you cross the street to get away from her. I..." his voice broke. "I didn't do that. But you gotta. Promise me, man."

"Wait...prison?"

"You picked up on that, huh?" A wry grin that showed gums

devoid of any teeth. "Yeah, prison. It all started with her. Violating a restraining order, yeah, I'll cop to that. But the rest of it was bullshit. The assault was just her word against mine, and the judge was golf buddies with Karin's dad. Didn't even look at the evidence."

The old man looked away, sighed. "Then...more shit inside. Stupid shit. I figured I could make some money, you know, for when I got out. Only I never got out." The eyes tracked back to his face, the stare piercing. "I *died* in there. Just now. Or...maybe thirty years from now. Depends on where you're sitting, I guess."

"Thirty years?" It seemed like all he could do was repeat random words from the old man's ravings.

"Thirty years. Life, as it turned out."

He took another long drink, the plastic cup full again, and looked at the old man across the table from him. That gray outfit could be a prison uniform, he supposed. "So...I'm supposed to believe that you're me? My...*ghost*? From thirty years in the future?"

"Yeah, you wanna put it like that," a dry chuckle. "*Ghost*. Yeah, I guess that's the word. Don't got a bed sheet—they don't give us sheets in max."

"Because of Karin?"

"Because *I wouldn't stay away* from Karin," another sigh, this one like air escaping a slashed tire. "You know, I can't even remember her face now. But when I was your age—hell, when I was *you*—I kept after her. I got stupid. And she screwed me. She screwed me good."

"So...what, you're from the year 2020?"

"Not quite. 2019. Missed 2020 by a couple hours. But, yeah, that's when I died."

"What's it like?"

A bark of bitter laughter. "Not that great a view from the exercise yard, you know?" A sigh. "Hell, the world was supposed to end a couple of times, but it didn't. Right at the turn of the century there was a big computer glitch that was supposed to shut down civilization. Then some Arab assholes flew a couple of planes into the twin towers in New York. Bunch of wars. Lots of new computer stuff, video games and shit, but we're not living on Mars or anything. When you're inside, man, nothing really changes."

"But..."

"You want me to tell you what stocks to buy, boy? I got one thing to say, man. *One thing.* You got that? Stay away from Karin—stay right the hell away from her. The rest of the shit, you can figure that out for yourself."

The old woman from the bar touched the old man on the shoulder and said, "It's time."

Without a backward glance the old man got up from the table and took her in his arms and there was music playing, an old, old song...

> *"For auld lang syne, my dearest,*
> *for auld lang syne,*
> *we'll drink a cup of kindness yet,*
> *for auld lang syne."*

They danced slow, the old woman's long braid swaying gently down her back, and she was in a gown that brushed the floor and shimmered like water in sunlight, and then a bell was ringing, a church bell, the sound deep and somehow heavy, the weight of the world tolling, *one* and *two* and *three* and somewhere far beyond the ringing of that great bell there were shouts and car horns honking.

His eyes snapped open. He'd fallen asleep on his couch, a half-full bottle of whiskey on the floor beside him, the TV chattering something over a video of balloons sailing fuzzily into the night, and outside his neighbors were whooping and hollering.

Midnight. January 1ˢᵗ, 1990. A new decade. A new start.

He got up and stretched, picked up the bottle and carried it into the kitchen, put it firmly away in the cupboard above the stove. Outside the commotion was dying down, the drunks running out of steam and the realization settling in that it was too damned cold to be outside yelling like a lunatic.

In the kitchen he took down his old calendar and put up the new one—helpfully provided by the gas company. In the kitchen drawer, he found a thick marker and wrote across the map of January in big letters.

RESOLVED: Never see Karin again.

And he never did.

ECHOES AT MIDNIGHT

BY AMY BEATTY

When I met William Bradshaw, he was sitting on a bench down by River Street drinking coffee from a battered tin cup. It was New Year's Eve, and in his dark trousers, rumpled gray vest, and partly unbuttoned white dress shirt with the sleeves rolled up, he looked as if he'd just come from a party. I was wandering along the red brick plaza that edged the Savannah River, watching the boats carve their slow way through the swaths of moonlight that reflected off the water. I should probably have been watching where I was going instead, because I nearly tripped over William's long legs, which sprawled out in front of him.

"Oh!" I gasped as I pulled up short. "I'm so sorry, I didn't see you there."

A lazy grin spread over his face. "That's all right. Most people don't," he said. "But I'm glad you did. It's been a while since a pretty woman noticed me." His voice was rich and gentle, with the honeyed, drawn-out vowels of a true Southerner. He glanced around and straightened, his grin shifting into a slightly troubled frown. "You're not alone?"

I felt my back stiffen. I was a big girl; I could take care of myself. Still... I moved back a step and folded my arms across my chest, shrugging nonchalantly. 'My friends are up at Wet Willie's." I waved a vague hand toward the bar at the edge of the plaza. "I came out for some air." It was almost the truth.

He relaxed a bit. "I'm sorry. Only—they say it isn't always safe here at night for a woman alone."

I shrugged. "They say a lot of things."

"Very true." He leaned back against the wooden slats of the bench, and the grin returned. He had the sort of mouth that looked as if it grinned a lot, but there was something sad, and a bit tired, behind his eyes. Nostalgic. He was a good-looking guy, a little over average height with muscles that looked as if they knew about hard work. It was difficult to tell how old he was, but I thought maybe a few years older than me—safely past twenty, but not yet settled into thirty. His grin turned impish. "They say, for example," he drawled, "that Savannah is the most haunted city in the South."

I laughed. "Do they? Well, that I can almost believe."

"So can I," he said, "with wraiths like you haunting the waterfront." A soft breeze off the water ruffled the pale folds of my dress, and my cheeks warmed as I tugged my sweater closer.

He slid over on the bench, making room for me, should I decide to use it. "I'm William," he said. "William Bradshaw." He waited, smiling, for me to make up my mind.

Well, I thought, *why not?* It was that kind of night. I slid onto the bench. "Rachel Moorland," I said.

"Rachel Moorland," he mused, turning my name over on his tongue in that way only a Southerner can really pull off. I'd never actually liked my name, but he made it sound sexy. "Well, I'm very pleased to meet you, Rachel Moorland." He paused for a moment, and the mischievous humor returned to his smile. "You don't quite talk like a Yankee," he said.

I laughed. "Colorado. I'm an art student. You?"

He looked out over the river. "Oh, I was raised a few miles outside Savannah. My father grew cotton." He shrugged.

"Cotton," I repeated, raising an eyebrow. "And what do you do?"

"Well," he said slowly, "naturally, my father wanted me to follow in his footsteps. But I had ideas of my own, so I ran off and joined the army."

The army. I wondered if he'd seen combat; that would explain the sad eyes. "So you're stationed at Hunter?" I asked, referring to the airfield the army maintains in Savannah. But then I realized his tousle of wavy hair was much too long to meet army regulations.

"Oh, it's been a while since I was a soldier," he said softly. He drew a long breath and raised his tin cup halfway to his mouth, then stopped abruptly. "Where are my manners?" He shook his head. "Would you like some coffee, Rachel? I have another cup." He reached down to tug a small basket I hadn't noticed out from under the bench.

Sure, I thought. *Because it's really smart for a girl to take coffee from a complete stranger in the middle of the night on River Street.* "No thanks," I said. "I'm fine."

He shrugged and leaned back, stretching his legs out in front of him again. "Well, you let me know if you change your mind."

We sat for a while in companionable silence, watching the water slide by. After a while, I said, "So...the most haunted city in the South?"

He looked at me sideways, raising one eyebrow. "That's what they say. Lots of pirates. Wailing women waiting for their men to come back from the sea. Dead soldiers from the War Between the States."

I smiled back. "Maybe the dead soldiers are keeping the lonely women company."

"Oh, assuredly," he laughed. "And keeping them safe from the pirates, too."

After another brief silence, he said, "They say..." and waited for me to look at him again so he could wink at me before he went on, "they say that New Year's Eve is the best time to see ghosts."

"Oh, do they?" I laughed.

"They do indeed," he continued with mock solemnity. "Before the clock strikes twelve on New Year's Eve, just as the old year is dying, and before the new year fully asserts itself, time wears thin and the edges blur. All the years that came before blend together, and sometimes the things that *were* get mixed up with the things that *are* in unexpected ways. Like an echo."

His eyes held mine, and a shiver wriggled up my spine that had nothing to do with the chill in the humid winter air.

"You're cold." He frowned. "Maybe you'd better go back inside."

I laughed. "I'm fine. It gets a lot colder than this in Colorado." I eyed his thin shirt. "But aren't you cold?

"I don't really get cold." He shrugged and looked back up at the bright lights of the bar. "Your friends will be wondering where you are."

My laugh came out bitter, and he raised his eyebrows at me. I hesitated. Then I told him. "There's no one waiting for me." I looked out over the water. "I came with this guy I met in my art history class. Kyle. I don't know him very well, but he's cute, and when he asked me out, I figured why not? Every girl should have someone to kiss at midnight on New Year's Eve, right?" I slouched down on the bench, hugging my arms around my shoulders. "Turns out when he drinks he gets a bit...handsy. So I left."

"Are you all right?" William's gentle voice sounded genuinely concerned.

I lifted one shoulder and let it fall. I didn't look at him. "I can take care of myself."

He didn't say anything. After a few minutes something dawned on me, and I sat up straighter. "But you brought two cups. Are you waiting for someone? I can go away if..." My voice trailed off as I turned and saw his face. The tired sadness had emerged from behind his eyes and now lay across his face, tightening his jaw and furrowing his brow.

He dumped the remains of his coffee in the planter next to the bench and leaned down to tuck his tin cup into the basket. "I have been waiting," he said softly. "Every New Year's Eve since..." He straightened and looked out over the river again. I followed his gaze and found that the moon had passed behind a cloud, and the water through which the passing boats drifted had gone black as ink. I looked back at his profile. He sighed. "She never comes." Then he turned to meet my eyes and smiled gently. "I suppose we all have our ghosts."

I smiled back a little wryly. "I suppose we do."

He drew a deep breath, as if to clear his head, then stood and held out a hand to me. "May I walk with you, Miss Rachel?" he asked. He laid his other hand over his heart. "If I promise not to...get handsy? I'd like to know you're safe before I go."

I hesitated only half a heartbeat before I put my hand in his and let him help me up off the bench. He tucked my hand into the crook of his elbow so he could use both of his hands to settle a strap on his picnic basket over one shoulder. We talked quietly as we walked east beside the river. About my home in Colorado. About a swimming hole he and his brother played in growing up. The plaza narrowed to a walkway that passed between the river and a parking lot, and he shifted closer to me to allow a rowdy cluster of college students to pass. "Ten minutes 'til midnight!" one of them shouted, and we grinned and waved. When they had gone, William didn't widen the space between us again. Neither did I.

We followed the walkway around the end of the parking lot. As we emerged onto River Street, another group of students surged past on the opposite sidewalk. I tensed as I recognized one of them.

Kyle punched one of his buddies in the arm, and bellowed something unintelligible, and the whole group stopped to watch as he stumbled across the cobbles to where I stood. "There you are!" he slurred. "We wonnered where you got off to. C'mon, we're leaving." He grasped my arm just above my elbow and pulled.

I yanked my arm free of his fingers and said firmly, "Leave me alone, Kyle. I already told you I'm done."

"Aw, don' be like that," Kyle wheedled, grabbing my arm again, more firmly this time. "C'mon, Rachel."

"I believe the lady said no," William put in quietly.

Kyle looked over at William as if only just noticing he was there. The two men sized each other up. For a moment, I thought Kyle was going to start something, but when he looked back at me, he only said, "You don' waste time." He went back to his friends, and the whole pack moved up the street.

I looked up to find William's serious eyes fixed on me. "Are you all right?" he asked.

"Sure," I said. "I have a nice soldier to keep me company and protect me from pirates." I snuggled closer to him.

His eyes searched my face one more time before the slow grin spread across his mouth and he draped his arm around my shoulders. He smelled of coffee and the river. I wrapped my arm around his waist, and he gave my shoulders a gentle squeeze.

"Hey," I said, "can we go to the echo square?"

He frowned, puzzled. "Echo square?"

I think my mouth popped open a little. "You don't know about it?" I asked. "I thought you were from here."

He smiled sheepishly. "River Street has changed some since I was a child," he said. "Why don't you show me."

So I tugged him back off the cobbled street and down a short red brick walkway into an open space. The shrub-filled planters that occupied the corners of the square were curved on their inner edges to create an open circle. Dark stone was laid among the red bricks to form a border around the edge of the circle, and a bold X right across the center. I led William to the square of dark stone that lay at the center of the X and showed him the finer X scribed across it.

"Now," I said, parking him in the center of that X and taking a step back, "say something."

He looked puzzled. "What should I—" he broke off, and his face lit up. "Hello? But that's wonderful!" he exclaimed, laughing. "How does it work?"

I grinned with him. "I'm not really sure," I said. "Something to do with an acoustic effect created by the shape of the planters and... well... I don't really know. All I know is if you stand on the X and talk, your voice echoes back to you, and it sounds like you're speaking in surround sound."

"Can you hear it?" he asked, and laughed again at the odd echo of his own voice.

"Not from here," I explained. "You can only hear it if you're standing on the X."

"Well then," William grinned. "Maybe you'd better come stand on the X." He reached for my hand and drew me in so the two of us stood pressed close together in the middle of the X. When I looked up into his face, his eyes had gone solemn again, and something about the way he was looking at me made my heart start pounding wildly.

"Rachel," he said softly, and both of us grinned when the echo magnified the word. But then he went serious again. He brought one hand up to brush my cheek as his eyes searched my face.

Across the historic district, the cathedral bell began to ring. "Happy New Year," I whispered into the echo. The bell rang again, reverberating in the still darkness.

"Rachel," William murmured again. The bell rang. "I know we just met," I caught my breath, and this time when the bell rang, my heart sang with it. "I don't want you to think I'm..." his eyes flicked toward the street where we'd seen Kyle. The bell rang. "But I... well..." he hesitated until the song of the bell nudged him along. "You said every girl should have someone to kiss at midnight, and..." he left the unspoken question hanging in the air until the bell rang.

I laughed and cupped his face with my hands. "Yes," I said, drawing his face down to mine. The bell sang out as our lips met.

His kiss started out hesitant, but deepened and intensified as the night folded in around us, and the song of the bell stretched out, elongating, one peal blending into the next, into the next, wrapping itself around the hollow, echoing circle where we stood. He tasted of rich, warm coffee. He tasted of loneliness, and of darkness, and of time; of year piling upon year, upon year, gathering and condensing into a single, breathless, echoing moment.

The final peal of the midnight bell still hung in the air when we parted, and for a long heartbeat we only looked at each other. This time, when that lazy grin spread across William's face, his eyes held a quiet triumph. "Thank you, Rachel," he whispered, and this time my name sounded like a prayer.

"Rachel?" a shriller voice echoed from the street. "Is that you?"

I glanced away from William for only a moment—for a breath—to see who was calling me. Shawntel, a girl from my dorm.

When I turned back, William Bradshaw was gone. I stood alone in a tiny, echoing space beside a river that ran, like time, from darkness into darkness beyond darkness.

ABOUT THE CONTRIBUTORS

By day, **Jay Barnson** programs VR simulations. By night he writes about imaginary worlds. He is the author of the Blood Creek series, also published by Immortal Works, and plenty of short stories. You can find out what he's been up to lately at https://www.amazon.com/-/e/B00TQOCLKI.

Julie Barnson is a storyteller of the oral tradition specializing in ghost stories. She is heavily involved in the storytelling community, and currently serves on the executive board of the Story Crossroads Storytelling Festival, and the board of the West Jordan Utah Literary Arts Society as the storytelling representative. Come to her if you would like to hear tales of things that go bump in the night.

Amy Beatty was raised in the wilds of Yellowstone Park, where she walked to school through herds of elk and buffalo. She attended college in Savannah, Georgia and stayed for nearly a decade afterward, first because she fell in love with the Spanish moss and cobblestone streets, and later because she fell in love. Her husband proposed on a beach outside Savannah, and one of their favorite spots was the Echo Square on River Street. They now live in the mountains of Utah. Amy is the author of The Vanir Dragon Series and the Viper Series.

L'ren Beck has been writing for ten years, and persistence has paid off with her first published work appearing in this anthology. Through her writing, she has become a student at the University of Google, where she has studied a vast variety of subjects, including Ancient Egyptian, intermediate physics, and a few topics that may have resulted in the FBI flagging her as a potential danger. (They were important research projects!) L'ren is a citizen of Earth who lives near the salty lake to the south of Potato Land, but she feels more at home in fantasy worlds.

Misha Burnett has little formal education, but has been writing poetry and fiction for around forty years. During this time he has supported himself and his family with a variety of jobs, including locksmith, cab driver, and building maintenance.

Blog: https://mishaburnett.wordpress.com/

Amazon page: https://www.amazon.com/Misha-Burnett/e/B008MQ8W4K/

Jodi Lynn Chase has been making up stories since elementary school. She started devouring every book she could get her hands on at an early age. By the time she was in 5th grade, she had read most everything the local bookmobile had to offer. Science Fiction and Fantasy were her favorites, but anything with an interesting story would do. Nothing has changed since her youth. Reading and writing are a passion. A Utah native, she still lives there with her husband, Jeff, two dogs, and an ever-expanding library. Shh, don't tell Jeff.

Robin Cranney was born in New England, where she endured her share of boogie-man experiences while living in her family's haunted ancestral home. Though she currently resides in Germany with her husband, children, and cat, Nero, Cranney's childhood spawned a love for spooky tales. When she isn't plotting her next thriller, Cranney pursues more placid activities such as horse jumping, hiking, and mountain biking.

Allan Evans has written professionally in advertising and marketing for over a decade. He is the author of two Immortal Works novels, Abnormally Abbey and Killer Blonde (coming in February 2021). A youth soccer coach, Allan can usually be found on a field somewhere teaching kids about soccer and life. He lives in White Bear Lake, Minnesota. For more information, visit evanswriter.com.

James T. Lambert is an Idaho writer publishing his first novel in 2020. He writes various flavors of speculative fiction: SF, Urban Fantasy, and Steampunk. He's got a five of eight score for NaNoWriMo, attends various conventions, and hangs out in critique groups. He collaborates with Troy Lambert and Danielle Parker on a shared universe called Monster Marshals where each writer has two Marshals working for Project Prometheus. This is one of those stories.

Mark Minson enjoys playing games with his wife and five kids. He loves to sing and can often be found whistling as he walks. An avid shoe-wearer, you might run into him strolling down memory lane—either his or somebody else's. He brings humor to life through his many accents and movie quotes. He found his magic long ago, in a high school far, far away and now happily shares it with you. May you find your magic and share it with others.

John M. Olsen edits and writes speculative fiction across multiple genres. He loves stories about ordinary people stepping up to do extraordinary things, and he hopes to entertain and inspire others with his award-winning stories. He loves to create and fix things, whether editing, writing, or working in his secret lair equipped with dangerous power tools. In all cases, he applies engineering principles and processes to the task at hand, often in unpredictable ways.

He lives in Utah with his lovely wife and a variable number of mostly grown children and a constantly changing subset of extended family.

Staci Olsen lives in Utah with her husband, four sons, one daughter, a dog, and two cats in a townhouse that is much too small. She grew up in Alaska in a 16x20 foot cabin with ten other people (give or take a few), so she is used to small houses. She bathed in a wheel barrow, was hunted by wolves, and survived earthquakes and volcanic eruptions. She is the author of *Defender of Dragons* and her hobbies include salsa dancing, hiking, and escape rooms. Visit her website staciolsen.com and follow her on Facebook, Instagram, and Twitter.

Sarah E. Seeley is a fantasy and horror author, and an affiliate member of the Horror Writers Association. She has a Master of Science in Palaeoanthropology and Palaeolithic Archaeology from the University College London, and enjoys studying dead things to figure out what makes life on Earth so amazing. She explores the bright side of being human by writing dark fiction. You can learn more about Sarah on her author blog at www.Slithers-OfThought.com.

Lauren Stokeld is a medieval researcher based in York, UK. Although she has been writing for as long as she can remember, this is her first foray into the world of publication. When not writing speculative fiction and studying ancient languages, Lauren likes to read, bake, do historical martial arts, and drink heretically milky tea.

Scott William Taylor lives at the base of a mountain in Utah, on the same street where he grew up. Though now, instead of hiking the mountain daily, he spends his time writing, blogging, taking pictures, being a husband, and father to four children. Scott's debut novel Chaser, a middle grade sci-fi story, was released in 2018 by Immortal Works. He is also an award-winning screenwriter with his short film, Wrinkles.

Donea Lee Weaver is a perpetual daydreamer who has been creating and telling stories since her elementary school days. When she's not writing about the things she loves you can probably find her planning her next vacation, playing games with the girls, reading, taking the scenic route, or cuddling on the couch with her daughter and her dog, binge-watching a favorite show. She was born and raised in Utah and earned a BA in English from Weber State University. You can find additional stories by Donea Lee on Amazon, and can also connect with her on Twitter and Instagram: @donealee

David J. West writes dark fantasy and weird westerns because the voices in his head won't quiet until someone else can hear them. He is a great fan of sword & sorcery, ghosts and lost ruins, so of course he lives in Utah with his wife and children.

This has been an
Immortal Production